THE CHRONICLES OF OPHELIA WINTERS

THE LEGACY OF THE GORGON

BOOK 2

By

Rick Pridmore

MAPLE
PUBLISHERS

THE CHRONICLES OF OPHELIA WINTERS: THE LEGACY OF THE GORGON_BOOK 2

Author: Rick Pridmore

Copyright © 2025 Rick Pridmore

The right of Rick Pridmore to be identified as author of this work has been asserted by the author in accordance with section 77 and 78 of the Copyright, Designs and Patents Act 1988.

First Published in 2025

ISBN 978-1-83538-854-9 (Paperback)
    978-1-83538-855-6 (E-Book)

Book Cover and Layout by:
    White Magic Studios
    www.whitemagicstudios.co.uk

Published by:
    Maple Publishers
    Fairbourne Drive, Atterbury,
    Milton Keynes,
    MK10 9RG, UK
    www.maplepublishers.com

CONTENTS

PROLOGUE

York City Centre

Sunday 3rd May 11.45pm

Present Day.

The woman in the emerald-green-hood walked slowly down the old cobblestones of a well-preserved mediaeval street, following a small group of unsuspecting young ladies that had recently vacated a nearby tavern.

She was cloaked from head to toe in a flowing long coat of the same shade, and her stride remained consistent, as she got closer to the jovial group.

On either side of her were crooked and lean timber-framed buildings. The 14th century upper floors jutted out over the lower levels, creating eerie shadows down below on the narrow street. The rows of closed boutiques, bakeries, and historical shops didn't distract the woman from tracking her quarry.

It was mid-Spring, and a relatively quiet and warm night in this area of the city centre, except for the five women a few metres ahead. All of them, in their twenties, were merry and laughing, and it was evident a couple of them were slightly more intoxicated than the others, as two of the girls struggled to keep their footing on the uneven street, in their high heels.

The mysterious woman noticed the group turn into a side street that forked off, and the road widened out to reveal another row of shops, and a traditional pub called The Saxon Inn. She slowed her pace down, and discreetly peered around the corner of a building, as the girls began to walk past the pub.

The pub had just closed, and the cobbled side street was only lit by a few lamps. One of the tall lamp posts had a CCTV camera mounted on top that faced the front doors of the inn. The door supervisors had already departed once everyone had left the premises.

This was convenient for the four drunken young men who were grouped together on the side pavement of the pub. Two were sitting on top of one of the pub's benches, whilst their companions stood in the middle of the narrow road. All of them were boisterous, swearing and smoking, and holding bottles of various alcoholic beverages.

For such a beautiful place, their presence seemed to mark a stain, with their bawdy and anti-social behaviour. The sickening stench of weed filled the air. However, this didn't seem to affect the girls who approached them. The moment they were in proximity to the gang of boys, they were met with wolf whistles and jeering.

"Hey girls, fancy a beer, the night's still young?" said one guy loudly. He was clearly the most confident one in the group. His friends smirked and laughed along, hoping to score with these lovely ladies. His friend also then made his way closer to the girls, and tried to impress them with his so-called manly swagger, blowing putrid smoke near the face of one of them.

"No, we're just heading home," replied one of the young women politely, trying to steady herself on the cobbled stones.

"Naw, don't be boring, love. My mates and I will give you a good time, you only live once!" the man said. His friends on the benches were still laughing and goading.

One of the women in the group appeared from behind the rest of the group, and faced the intimidating gang leader.

"I said, we're going home, so why don't you back off and carry on sucking on those disgusting sticks, Zack?" the blonde young woman said confidently.

"Hey love, I can give you something to…" one of Zack's friends started to say until Zack raised his hand, which quickly silenced him.

Zack immediately recognised the blonde beauty. He looked embarrassed, and gritted his teeth.

"Oh, shit, sorry, I didn't see you there, Madison, erm, are you okay?" Zack tried to compose himself.

From a short distance away, still observing from the shadows, the hidden woman peered through her hood, and saw the street light irradiate the face of the person that she was following. She was definitely the one she was looking for.

Madison Trent. The thief that had bereft the woman of her sacred gorgoneion stone tablet a couple of weeks ago, on Kataramai Island.

Remaining at her partially concealed vantage point, the woman continued to spy on the two groups, listening in on their brief exchange. Madison had a confident pose, with her hands on her hips, and looking sternly up at the gang leader. She was fearless.

"It's alright lads, stop screwing around, she's from my kick-boxing gym," Zack shouted to his companions. They sniggered among themselves, probably hoping to see their leader get a good kicking.

"Right, do you want me to kick your arse again, in front of your little friends. No semi-contact sparring, no pads or ref this time?" Madison asked, raising her eyebrows.

"I'm only messing around, Mads," he chuckled, blowing out smoke, this time over his shoulder to ensure none of it even came close to Madison's face.

"Just get out of our way, Zack!" Madison warned.

"Jesus, chill out babes," Zack said.

"Seriously, you call me 'babes' again, you'll be wearing your bollox as a bowtie!"

All his friends laughed out aloud, and Zack raised his palms submissively.

"Okay, okay. Just having a laugh, I'll see you later." He shuffled back passively, and Madison grinned. She then proceeded to continue down the street that led to a small market plaza, and the nearest taxi rank.

The lads re-grouped on the road, pushing, jostling and joking with Zack, who was left humiliated. He downed another bottle, infuriated on the inside.

The cloaked woman then emerged from the shadows and headed towards the Saxon Inn.

The gang were still pushing and shoving each other in their drunken stupor, until one of them collided with the woman who tried to attempt to weave through them. The guy that had stumbled into her, spilt his bottled beer, and looked back at the woman in the hood.

"Whoa!" he shouted, as he nearly lost his balance. The woman, however, remained unaffected, and maintained her footing, but he had stopped her in her tracks. She lowered her head, the large baggy hood concealing her face, except for her diamond-shaped jawline and plump rosy lips.

The gang sneered and cheered, as the beverage spilt over her draping emerald coat.

"Well, what do we have here? Little green riding hood, eh!" the taller man shouted. Zack joined him, trying to bring some dignity and pride back to his already humiliated life. The woman did not speak. Instead, she just saw this gang as a hindrance, and tried to manoeuvre past the yobs, but Zack prevented her access, trying to recover his manhood in front of his mates.

"Where are you going, the party's right here?" Zack said, and the two guys from the bench started to make their way over. Zack and his friend continued to harass her in their intoxicated and intimidating manner.

They could ascertain that this woman was slender and looked enticing as she held her ground. Her lips remained closed, but they appeared to be developing into a subtle smile from within the dark hood. She peered over the hulking shoulder of Zack and noticed Madison and her small group of friends at the end of the street, completely oblivious to what was occurring behind them. They turned into the market square, out of sight.

The woman tried to push forward again, more hastily this time, but Zack placed his hand on the woman's shoulder, preventing her again from advancing. She was now facing the four thugs that had formed a human barricade in front of her.

She had no time for this, and no man would stand in her path.

Immediately, the woman whacked Zack across the face with the back of her hand, like she was swatting a fly. The gang leader was sent flying off his feet, six feet across the road, smashing into the lamppost with a bone-crunching thud. He slumped down, and lay across the cobblestones, lifeless.

The rest of his gang were absolutely stunned by this extraordinary feat of strength, from this slight woman. But it didn't deter the taller man, who suddenly grabbed her by the lapels of her coat. The woman, without hesitation, grabbed both his wrists, and twisted them, causing him to cry in pain. He was then thrown through the windowpane of the Saxon Inn. Glass, debris and framework came raining down on the thug, lacerating his face and body. He stayed prostrate where he had landed.

The third offender then pulled out a switchblade, and wielded it threateningly in front of the woman, shouting profanities. The fourth crept close behind her. She retreated a few steps, until they were all opposite the front doors of the pub. She was mindful of the deadly-looking blade. Even though she was powerful, she was just as susceptible to mortal injury as her attackers. The two thugs closed in on her.

But their prey became the predator.

The woman looked up, revealing more of her face from the armed thug's point of view. Simultaneously, her coat parted open and her right hand produced something unusual from the jade-green sash around her waist.

Before he could process what was happening, the thug completely froze in fear, as he held his switchblade in front of him. Barely a second later, his entire body completely turned to pure stone, leaving him standing there in mid-pose brandishing the blade, like a sculptured street statue.

Witnessing this shocking and unbelievable supernatural occurrence, the fourth thug screamed, as he saw the stone form of what was his gangmate. He started to back off, but the empowered woman whirled around to face him. Her face still partially concealed by her hood.

But what he saw was enough to raise his hands in front of his face, recoiling back in horror. He heard her hiss from inside her hood, as she sharply lashed out her right hand.

The last thing he saw was the woman, holding and extending out, an intricate two-foot ancient sceptre, with a glowing stone mounted on its ornate crown, which was adorned with bronze crossing serpents. Her action was followed by an instant blinding flash of light, as the sceptre struck him.

The miscreant was suddenly transformed into a petrified state of stonework. There were now two upright statues in the middle of the narrow street, looking like freshly constructed human monuments.

The whole incident took mere seconds, and the woman concealed the lethal magical object back in her coat, whilst looking around at the damage and carnage she had created. Zack was crumpled against the lamppost, and his taller friend was covered in glass inside the inn. They were both exanimated, but she had no time to check if they were truly dead or not.

She left the scene hurriedly, as she heard human voices emanating nearby, behind her. The brief altercation and noise from the incident had alerted others. The woman reached the top of the road, and went into the market square, where she managed to get a glimpse of Madison and her friends piling into a local taxi. It was the last taxi on the rank.

The vehicle drove off, around the other side of the market square, and disappeared into town. The woman had lost her quarry. For the time being. She would have to try another tact.

She had left the most incredible, yet deadly work of art next to the inn. More importantly, there were two bloodied and battered bodies, that were presumably dead. This was now a crime scene and inevitably would soon be crawling with police. She had to escape now.

Within a few hours, two totally strange and unexpected statues would greet the eyes of the early morning risers.

But not as deadly, as what had greeted the eyes of the souls trapped within the statues.

The mystifying woman slipped back into the shadows and vanished into the night.

14

PART ONE

CHAPTER 1

KATARAMAI ISLAND

1,700 miles away, the 'cursed' island in the Cyclades was a bustle of activity.

The entire island was under quarantine by the Greek government, after the bloody battle that occurred there two weeks ago, between a deadly cult and a secret squad of mercenaries.

The Greek authorities granted special permission to a certain corporation to fund and assist in the salvage and recovery operation that was currently taking place.

Situated on the high cliffs, the plateau of the former stronghold, the amphitheatre, and the whole area surrounding the collapsed ruins of the Athenian temple, were occupied by a wide range of large excavator vehicles, cranes, bulldozers, dump trucks, and dozens of Greek workers in construction site uniforms and personal protection equipment.

It was a hot morning, and the Mediterranean sun seared down from the clear blue skies onto the mountaintop grounds. Plumes of dust filled the vicinity as a result of the continuous labour from the plant machinery.

Amongst the workers were several men and women sifting through parts of the terrain, like archaeologists, removing various objects and items that were half buried in the sand or rocky outcrops. Watching the whole procession was an American man in his early forties. He was wearing a wide-rimmed khaki Boonie hat, fastened at the sides, a loose half-buttoned blue shirt and beige cargo bottoms.

Through his sunglasses, he observed with great interest a couple of his blue-uniformed colleagues, who had just recovered another crimson-coloured object from the sand. He stood next to his black and silver truck. It had an insignia printed on its side with the words of his corporation emblazoned underneath.

Legionshield Defence Industries.

Vincent Keyes was the CEO of Legionshield, an international defence contractor that specialises in the development and manufacture of state-of-the-art and sophisticated armaments. The corporation was reputed to be shady by various governments due to their connections to the criminal underworld and various factions around the globe, but they were a successful business nonetheless, and had produced an incredible array of hardware and advanced equipment for a vast range of clients. Some include legitimate agencies, militaries, mercenary groups, and the highest bidders on the black market as well. Legionshield, were also looking for more innovative ideas for their developmental weapons and defence programme.

Keyes was parked next to a black Wrangler jeep, with a logo that displayed 'The Black Knight Syndicate'. The Syndicate was also one of Legionshield's clients, and they frequently undertook jobs for them, as long as they were provided with excellent equipment and resources from the defence contractor.

The director of the Black Knight Syndicate, and former MI6 officer, Miles Matheson, stepped outside the vehicle and joined his American associate. Sweating profusely, he wiped his bald head with his tattooed forearm. He started to regret wearing his black polo-neck t-shirt and black cargo bottoms, as the heat was unbearable. He didn't even want to return here, either. It only seemed like yesterday when he was here, in the middle of one of the most intense battles that he had ever experienced.

Matheson glanced around at the dusty area, which was laden with massive boulders, and newly dug sites in the ground. A distant contrast to what he saw a short while back.

Where an ancient temple once stood, there was now a pile of rubble on the plateau. A huge excavator was shifting tonnes of rubble at what was the southern end of the temple. Other plant diggers, dump trucks, and backhoe vehicles were at the same location, removing piles of stone debris.

Matheson also reflected on the scene of the last desperate battle that had occurred a fortnight ago. Bodies of crimson-clad cultists, and a few of his own mercenaries, were killed during the final conflict and had been found in the debris.

During the aftermath, the Greek government quickly initiated a clean-up operation and removed all the bodies that were affiliated with the Order of the Crimson Claw. The few survivors of the cult were taken into custody and incarcerated for life. Matheson took his own casualties back to the UK.

As the Black Knight Syndicate were directly responsible for the destruction of the Order, aided by the support and resources from Legionshield, both companies were given special access by the Greeks to assist at the site. In addition to that, they were well paid off by Keyes, and were assured a lucrative deal in the future, by supplying the Greek armed forces, and law enforcement, with any new advanced military grade equipment.

Meanwhile, Matheson saw Keyes stride over to two of the defence contractor's crew, who had recovered a crimson gauntlet. Matheson followed behind. The crewwoman wiped sand off the contraption she found, and it was a gauntlet. It looked mediaeval in design but, under closer inspection, the sleeve armour was bulkier and had futuristic attachments inside.

"Is that one of them?" Keyes asked, as he turned to Matheson.

"Yes, be careful with it," Matheson replied, remembering the lethal qualities of these specialised crimson gauntlets.

Keyes examined it, and handled the gauntlet meticulously with caution, whilst surveying every inch of his new find.

"I can understand why they referred to themselves as the Crimson Claw," Keyes said, admiring the gauntlet. The piece itself was battle damaged and inside the housing was a broken panel that revealed mechanical dials and springs. Also, there were a cluster of firing darts on a mini-belt feed.

"I'm sure your engineers could create these, blindfolded, Vincent," Matheson said. "Wouldn't you say, primitive in comparison to what you usually manufacture?" he added, as Keyes was still inspecting the interiors of the gauntlet, as if he was verifying something.

"We're in the days of ballistics, drones, energy weapons, and computerised weapon technology, but I'm sure there is still a place in modern day warfare for these nasty little toys," he uttered, with a grin.

"They did their fair share of damage, against us, and the police back in the UK," Matheson reflected once again.

"Well, close-quarters armaments are always something we can improve on. We are just looking for something a bit more inspirational. More unique for our weapons development programme." Keyes took one of the metal briefcases from his colleague and placed the gauntlet inside. "Take this, and anything else like it to my truck."

"Yes Mr Keyes," the engineer replied, and obediently made his way to Keye's vehicle.

At that moment, Keyes' two-way radio handset crackled, and it was the voice of the Greek foreman, speaking from where the temple once stood.

"Mr Keyes, are you receiving?" the foreman said. The noise of the hydraulic machinery and diggers, nearly drowning out the sound of his excitable voice.

"Go ahead," the American responded.

"We've found something!"

Matheson and Keyes exchanged looks.

Immediately, they ran across the plateau and headed towards the debris field of the fallen temple.

CHAPTER 2

AN INSPIRATION

The powerful excavators had removed endless piles of colossal boulders from the south site of the temple.

It had taken days for the mechanical behemoths to lift the huge rocks and dig deep underneath them. Until the crew discovered what used to be a long underground passageway beneath the foundations of where the temple had collapsed.

It was only now that the foreman cleared the remaining stacks of rubble away, revealing the former tunnel.

It had previously collapsed in on itself and was buried underneath its own ceiling. At the end of the open-aired tunnel, were splintered shards of wood that was once an old door, and a few stone steps were also uncovered from the rubble that led to it.

Yiannis, the foreman, signalled to the two foreign men that had just reached the dig area.

Matheson looked down and paused when he glanced at what was protruding out from underneath the rocky surface. His jaw dropped. He didn't really want to see this again, but he knew deep down, that this was the true reason, Keyes was there, overseeing the operation.

A shiny metallic prong jutted out from the ground. The moment the sun cast its rays down on it, the metal shone with a gleaming brilliance. The rest of the object was mostly buried underneath some smaller stones, but not too heavy or cumbersome to remove by shovel.

"Down there, Mr Keyes, silver or steel, perhaps?" Yiannis shouted in his broken English.

"Good, Yiannis, grab those shovels!" Keyes ordered, and the foreman grabbed a couple of entrenching tools from his vehicle.

"Vincent, wait." Matheson interrupted. He really started to regret coming on this expedition, but he had no choice. He felt he was indebted to the powerful businessman, even if he was rumoured to be corrupt.

Keyes spun around as he and Yiannis made their way over to the object.

"Problem?"

"Maybe you should just…"

"What?"

"Leave it, some things should be best left alone." Matheson warned him. He recalled the destruction that the object had inflicted during the battle. He personally was at the brunt of its power, and it had nearly killed him.

"Typical limey. Always overcautious. I don't need to remind you why we're here. You are my security here. You stick to what you're doing. What I do is my business."

Impetuously, the CEO removed his sunglasses, as he bee-lined onto the prong. He took a shovel, and assisted by Yiannis, they carefully removed excess stones and sand from the rest of the object. Mathesonwatched anxiously.

The ancient bident laid there in the sand, fully exposed. Its sharp twin prongs glistened in the morning sun. Its shaft was scathed and dented from the immense rock fall that had previously buried it. The unusual blades were scored with rock damage, and there were a few chipped and jagged sections on the blade of the spear that had broken off during the collapse of the tunnel, but most of it was miraculously intact.

"Is this it?" Keyes looked up at Matheson, who reluctantly nodded. Keyes then motioned to Yiannis, who marvelled at its intricate design. "Go ahead."

Yiannis understood, and nervously stretched out his hand to pick up the bident from its resting place. His eyes seemed fixated on the Bident of Hades.

It was in the same place where Ophelia Winters had recently discarded it, during her frantic escape from the temple, before it collapsed around her.

Yiannis picked up the bident. He stared at the legendary weapon, transfixed. His hands on a piece of true mythological history. There was no adverse reaction, and nothing disturbingly horrible happened to the foreman. There was also no supernatural effect that came from the spear, either. Matheson breathed out a sigh of relief.

Keyes smirked and laughed at himself. He then snatched the bident from Yiannis' grasp and claimed his prize.

"You see Miles, you're too superstitious. This is an unusual metal."

"I saw what it could do," Matheson said, "but luckily, it's nothing more than an old, useless, battered spear now. You need the grimoire to invoke its true powers."

"Is it here, too?"

"I destroyed it."

"Ah, right. I recall you mentioning it. There could be scraps of it left somewhere."

"Unlikely. The thing was vaporised by the business end of my RPG."

"So, the curse is on you then, as legend says, to the one who destroyed the grimoire?" Keyes laughed mockingly, trying to wind up his British associate.

"I've been living a bloody curse all my life, so one more is not going to make much difference. Besides let the powers of darkness curse the RPG. That's what destroyed it," Matheson responded cynically.

"Good point," Keyes walked over to him, holding the bident. This was the closest he had been to the relic, which nearly blasted him into the next world. He was still wary of it.

"So why don't you return the damn thing where you found it, or donate it to Dr Winters, who will keep it preserved and safe?" Matheson advised.

"You must be joking, right?"

"Does it look like I'm joking," Matheson's face was serious.

"I don't know. You Brits are hard to read."

"With or without the grimoire, this thing is dangerous."

"That is the business we're in Miles. You're an operator. My corporation is the machine that provides for agencies like you. Listen, we're looking for new innovations and opportunities. This is just a mere example of the range of possibilities that we are presented with."

"Vincent, I had to believe it for myself. It is hard to deny, but dark magic is real. I experienced things which I could never explain. Resurrection of a seven-hundred-year-old warlock, a mythological weapon of intense power. Magical potions. God knows what else is out there. I don't want you dabbling in forces you cannot even comprehend, or control!"

"I think you're missing my point, Miles, imagine what we can create by reverse-engineering such magnificent and divine devices like this?" Keyes said.

"You really shouldn't," Matheson replied.

"With the study and replication of unique lustrous materials, we could develop powerful defences that can protect and counter against other unearthly weapons," Keyes explained enthusiastically, trying to convince Matheson.

"Yes, I know you are a major defence contractor, but I am also aware of your other, more unscrupulous clients around the world that you do business with. What if things like this end up in their hands?"

Keyes raised his hands, cutting Matheson off.

"And if it wasn't for Legionshield, not so long ago, supplying your Black Knight Syndicate all the necessary equipment, transport, and resources, and all at a moment's notice, your operation would have failed. Every single member of your expedition would have perished, along with the others that didn't make it."

Matheson tightened his lips. He knew the executive was right, but he didn't want to admit it openly. A moment later, Keyes gestured to Yiannis, who stepped forward.

"Yiannis, take this to the truck before the old hag notices, we're done here." He then glanced at his subdued associate. "Unless we find the remains of a very old sorcerer, and a certain phial of everlasting life under all that?" Keyes scooped up the few broken metal shards from the sand and placed them in the pockets of his cargo bottoms.

He turned his gaze over to the mountain of boulders piled high in the centre section of the temple site. Matheson shook his head and placed his hands on his hips. It was a long time since he was essentially put back in his box and treated like a subordinate.

Matheson didn't directly work for Legionshield, but they had financed, supported and equipped his mercenary organisation, since he launched it twelve years ago.

"Ophelia killed the sorcerer and destroyed the elixir. There is nothing to unearth in the temple, you have my word," Matheson replied sternly.

"Well, this Ophelia sounds like a force to be reckoned with. Maybe our scientists should reverse-engineer her." He laughed heartily at his own joke. Matheson remained grim.

A moment later, a sharp shrill voice resonated from the edge of the temple dig site.

"Mr Vincent Keyes. Wait there a second please, sir. You too Yiannis!"

It was the hag that he wasn't overly keen on.

Valentina was the chief official sent in by the Greek archaeological institute to fully supervise the salvage operation. She hurriedly approached Keyes, as he started to walk away from the site. He was headed towards his waiting vehicle, accompanied by Matheson.

"Mr Keyes, please wait. This wasn't a part of our agreement. I forbid you take that artefact. It belongs to the Greek Institution in Athens."

Keyes sighed with frustration, as he looked over at the short, skinny, middle-aged woman dressed in her field attire. Her long silver hair blew in the wind, as she raced to keep up with him. Yiannis followed her.

"Listen Valentina, I have already arranged this with your consulate, and your board of directors. I have exclusive rights to anything we salvage from this expedition, in the interest of science and technology. Are you forgetting that we liberated this godforsaken island, and quelled a very dangerous terrorist organisation that was operating in *your* waters?" Keyes responded angrily. He clearly had a commanding presence, and appeared to be in full control, in front of her workers, as he increased his stride towards the truck.

"Mr Keyes. I understand and appreciate that. I am not contesting what you have done here. But from my understanding, you are permitted to remove anything from this island that was connected to the incident."

"Thank you."

"However, I cannot allow you to take what is considered a truly significant archaeological relic, which is a unique part of our national heritage. A historical representation of Ancient Greece. It must remain with us. The law, and the agreement specifically states, that anything which is recovered here, that has a national archaeological importance, is accredited to us, and must remain in Greece. I am sorry."

Mathson could feel the emotion of this poor woman and knew that her pleas were falling on deaf ears, as Keyes didn't slow down his pace, neither did he look bothered.

"This is a very important piece of evidence that caused numerous deaths during the incident, and I am removing it for research purposes, once I have completed my research, I will have it returned to you. That is all I will say on the subject," Keyes said as he reached his vehicle, and placed the bident inside, with a few other security cases.

"No, no, no. Please, Mr Keyes," she protested. His arrogance infuriated her.

Matheson got into the driver's seat of his Wrangler and started the engine. Keyes did likewise and slammed his door shut before Valentina could burn his ear any further.

She stood there with Yiannis, helpless and powerless to do anything.

"Yiannis, continue the excellent work, start on Lot 4, and if you find anything, consult my crew here. I need to head back to my UK office," Keyes instructed.

"Yes, Mr Keyes, have a safe trip." Yiannis obeyed politely, much to the disdain of the annoyed official standing next to him.

Keyes gunned the engine and drove off through the huge bullet-ridden gates, followed by Matheson's Wrangler. They had a waiting vessel that was anchored on the far side of the island, which would take them to the mainland.

Meanwhile, Valentina tossed her hands in the air, the moment they drove away. The dust from the vehicles engulfed the defeated woman.

"Bloody yank!" she shouted and shielded her face from the billowing sand and dust left in their wake.

CHAPTER 3

CRIME SCENE

8.10am Saxon Inn. York.

"Why do I get the weird ones?" DS Nicole Mervier said, exasperatingly.

The detective was standing in the middle of the cobblestone street, facing the two human statues that had attracted a small crowd of people. They were taking photos on their mobile phones from behind the extended police cordon tape that surrounded the cramped area.

She was accompanied by her colleague, DC Jake Branning, a newly appointed officer of the local special crime unit. He was making notes and directing uniformed officers to hold back the inquisitive members of the public. The place was filled with CSIs, a few police vehicles, an ambulance, and a coroner's van.

Mervier remained dumbfounded and assessed the statues. Perfect sculptures that remained surprisingly upright, considering that they had no bases. Their stone feet seemed to have fused or cemented onto the stone cobbles.

What was more perplexing, is that their clothes were heavily incrusted in solidified sand molecules, and not rock-hard stonework. However, the sections of the statue that represented the actual body parts of the figure were solid stone.

"That's odd," she said, and Branning walked up next to her with his notepad.

"Tell me what's not odd here," he answered, as two medical technicians, carrying stretchers with body bags on top of each one, approached the coroner's van. "Guys, just hang on a sec," Branning instructed. The technicians placed the body bags into the vehicle. CSIs continued taking pictures of the small area, and the smashed windows of the pub.

Mervier approached the statue that was brandishing a small knife. She analysed it closely, and noticed that the stainless-steel blade looked real, as it glistened in the sun.

"Have you guys already dusted for prints?" she looked over at one of the forensic officers.

"Yes, ma'am. But I advise you not to touch them. The sculpture is very fragile with no base. We're waiting for a vehicle to collect them."

"What is it, Nicole?" Branning asked.

"The knife."

"What about it?"

"It's real, it looks like the handle has been fused into the statue, rather than inserted in its hand," she explained, completely befuddled. She then proceeded to carefully place the tip of her forefinger on the tapered point of the four-inch blade and pressed it lightly. A miniscule puncture mark appeared on the padding of her finger, drawing a small drop of blood.

"Be careful," Branning said.

"That's real, alright," Mervier confirmed. She noticed, when she removed her finger from the blade, that the statue rocked slightly, verifying its instability.

"So, let's get this straight. Someone, or some people, came here, just after 'kicking out' time, was transported, then randomly placed two life-size statues of a couple of scumbags outside The

Saxon, and to add to the mix, we found two dead young males. One crumpled against the post, with a smashed skull, spine and ribs. The other, just as worse for wear, sprawled out inside the pub, most likely thrown through the window." Branning frowned at his notes.

"Appears so."

"Weird or what?" Branning studied the statues. "I should have stayed as a beat cop."

"You know what's weirder?" Mervier said, as she studied the statue.

"What's that?"

"I think I recognise the face on the statue," she spoke softly, still astonished at the detail and expression on the statue's face, its eyes totally in awe, jaw gaping wide open, revealing crooked teeth, and a hint of a subtle scar that looked like it had been carved onto the cheek.

"Who do you think it's supposed to be?" Branning enquired.

"Well, whoever sculptured it, has got a good eye for detail, or personally knows the kid who the statue is supposed to look like," Mervier said.

"Go on."

"This is a very close likeness to Chris Buckley."

"Name rings a bell. You know him well?"

"Oh yes. A local prolific offender. He's got a previous record as long as your arm, shoplifting, burglary, GBH, ABH, drugs, you name it," Mervier revealed.

"Why would someone make a statue of a known undesirable and present it here for the world to see? Some kind of prank? And the other?"

Mervier stepped towards the second statue. The figure appeared to be shielding his face with his arms. The statue was leaning back. Mervier was concerned if it were to be slightly knocked, the whole thing would topple over, due to its posture. She looked at its face.

"Not sure about this one, but it wouldn't surprise me if they were both connected."

Branning then quickly paced over to the back of the coroner's van, and the technicians parted either side to allow him through. Mervier followed him. Branning then unzipped one of the bags, revealing the battered face of Zack. The back of his skull was caved in. Mervier had seen so much death already this month, the corpse did not shock her, although Branning winced at first glance.

"Zack Coleman," she informed her colleague. The second bag was unzipped, and she nodded.

"John Staples," Mervier added. Branning then zipped the bags back up, and the technicians then climbed into the van, and slowly eased out of the street. The van headed towards the marketplace area, whilst the crowd gave way on either side.

"Officers, get these people back," Mervier ordered, as she turned to a group of uniformed police officers in high-vis tactical vests. They immediately assisted their colleagues on crowd control duties, as more civilians were seen congregating in the area.

"All part of the same gang, I suspect the other standing effigy is as well," the detective clarified to her colleague, who shook his head in bewilderment.

"Two murders, two statues, what is this?" Branning asked, "Some kind of sick, twisted statement?"

"We don't know what *this* is, yet. In the meantime, I'll put a press release out soon, gang related. Believe me, these boys have many drug rivals and enemies. I'm sure the press and public will buy it."

"Could be a drug or gang related. Vigilantism, either way, two less chavs in the city," Branning quipped.

"Jake, please," Mervier gave him a laser look, "Anyway, we can't speculate. I need you to visit Chris Buckley's address and bring him in for questioning. I think he may find it interesting that he has a statue erected in his honour, outside their drinking hole."

"Of course, do you want me to find out who the other fella is?"

"Yes please."

Mervier then looked upwards, and noticed the CCTV above her, tilting down at the activity below.

"I'm going to see what the CCTV can tell us. I'll see you back at the station."

Branning, after finishing scribbling in his notes, nodded to her, and quickly made his way to his Cavalier. Simultaneously, news vans from the local press began to show up.

Mervier took one last look at the two chilling statues. She squinted her eyes. They were incredibly life-like, and she had a hundred questions were still going around in her head, like a roulette wheel. She still couldn't fathom the complexity of the sculptures, with the non-human parts that weren't solid stone. The statues were disturbing, as well as being urban masterpieces.

She needed answers. This was another bizarre case for her.

A case that she couldn't afford to be left unsolved, this time.

⚬⚬⚬

CHAPTER 4

AN ILLUSION?

CTV Operations Centre York

DS Nicole Mervier had signed in at the reception and was escorted to the CCTV control room by a guard from the city council's private security firm.

Once she was admitted through the door by the security officer, she flashed her warrant card at the controller, as he rose from his desk.

"Good morning, DS Mervier, North Yorkshire constabulary."

"Morning, I'm Ray," the slightly overweight CCTV controller replied. His white short- sleeved shirt showed the company's crest on its chest, which was very crumpled and creased. The back of his shirt was hanging off of his waistline, and the top buttons undone. The man looked unkempt and looked tired. He also stunk of tobacco.

Mervier had been here a few times in her career, and each time, the main operations centre always impressed her, as the oval control room had banks of flatscreen monitors that were lined up across the wall. The main control desk had two stations, each with a trio of smaller monitors, a computer, and a digital CCTV control system.

Filing cabinets and office equipment surrounded the control desk, which was situated in the middle, facing the wall of screens. Each screen displayed many different locations of York's city centre, car parks, bus stops, taxi-ranks, and main roads, as well as various images of the cathedral, landmarks, and many historical sites. It looked like the bridge of a starship, from a science fiction film.

"Are you the day shift?" she asked, noting his scruffy appearance.

"No, I'm coming off a night shift, my daytime relief guys should be here in half an hour, I was kind of expecting you, but not so soon," Ray answered. This explained his dishevelled appearance.

"Right, you covered the shift on your own?" Mervier enquired.

"We usually have two on the night shifts, Monday to Thursday. One controller is here, and a security guard in reception."

"Okay. Well, you clearly know why I'm here. Did you see anything last night, outside the Saxon Inn?"

Ray ensured that his colleague, who escorted the detective into the operations room, had shut the door and left the area. Ray coughed and then took a seat in front of the control console. He glanced at the clock. It was 8.30am. He sighed, and pressed a few buttons on the control pad, to access the playback function.

"I wasn't monitoring that actual screen at the time, I'm afraid. At that time of night, I mainly focus on the taxi ranks, and the bigger clubs in the city centre during last knockings," Ray said, a little embarrassed. "But I can bring up the footage for you. Camera 32 is pre-set to monitor outside the Saxon. But only static. Like I said, I wasn't viewing it at the time of the altercation."

"When were you actually aware of this, Ray?" she asked, a little annoyed.

"I'll be honest, not at the time. I…er, was watching a group of lads, leaving the Starlight Club that were scrapping with a couple of doormen. When it had diffused, I went out for a fag, about midnight, and came back, then went to the toilet…"

"So, you didn't notice anything unusual on camera 32?" she interrupted, exhaling a sigh of frustration.

"Most of the screens are over there," he said, pointing to the twenty screens across the wall. "I usually observe the monitor here at my workstation, which, like I said, are the taxi ranks and the clubs." He started to get disgruntled, as if she had made him her new suspect.

"This was called in to us, around half past midnight. Weren't you alerted?"

"Not until your colleagues showed up at the Saxon. I noticed some police activity, just thought it was another scrap, so I kept monitoring. I didn't know what had happened. So I went on playback, just to see what had occurred, and well…see for yourself. Unbelievable. I don't know what to make of it."

Mervier had seen a lot of strange and unimaginable things recently, but nothing prepared her for what she was about to review.

Ray operated the system, and started the footage, the moment when a small group of women came into the static camera view. And then, Mervier looked in disbelief, as she observed the three males that she had already identified, joined by the fourth approach the girls, outside the inn.

"That's them. All of them," she squinted her eyes, as she looked into the monitor.

The footage continued, as she then recognised Madison Trent, debating with Zack, holding a confident posture.

"Madison Trent don't tell me you were responsible for this," she whispered to herself.

"Who's Madison Trent?" The controller asked, frowning.

"She works at St George's Museum. She's also a pretty good kickboxer."

"Well, keep watching, whoever this Madison is, had nothing to do with what's about to happen."

Ray's response was confirmed when Madison and her friends left the boys a few seconds later, and headed further up the street, disappearing out of the camera's range. Only a moment had passed, until another woman entered the area, wearing a long green coat, with a hood. No facial images were seen from the camera's point of view, due to its fixed position. Mervier leaned closer to the screen, making Ray tilt back in his chair, so she could get a better view.

The detective's face displayed a look of complete disbelief and awe, when she observed snippets of the altercation from the angle the camera was facing.

For a few seconds, the woman appeared to be harassed. A moment later, a quick lighting fast whip of her arm sent Zack hurtling off-screen. Another partial image showed John Staples flying through the window of the inn.

"Ooh!" Ray reacted when he saw the image again, for the second time.

Mervier continued watching and noticed that the two other offenders forced the woman back, more into the camera's view. It was at this point, that her surprised expression changed to that of complete astonishment. She thought she had seen everything because of what she had witnessed with the bident, a couple of weeks ago – until now.

Chris Buckley had been at The Saxon all along. After he pulled out his knife on the mysterious woman, she seemed to raise her head towards him and brought out something from within her flowing coat.

A second later, Buckley froze, and instantly, turned into the very statue the detective was studying earlier.

"Jesus Christ!" was all she could murmur.

"I know, right? Neat trick," Ray said. "Watch this."

It was only a moment later, that Mervier saw the last thug meet his terrible fate. The woman swivelled around. But this time, the footage showed that she was holding a very elaborate implement. An exotic-looking, 2ft handheld staff, with an ornate crown at its apex, and a smaller amulet on its aft.

The mystical tool seemed to have struck the bare, muscular arms of her final victim, who had attempted to raise them defensively. Like his friend, he was converted into a stone figurine.

Mervier gasped again and remained awe-struck. The woman appeared to quickly assess her handiwork and then headed out of the camera's line of sight, towards the same direction where Madison's group departed.

"Where did she go?" Mervier asked immediately.

Ray switched cameras, to try and get some continuity, but no surveillance cameras showed any traces of the woman's direction of travel, or any evidence of where she went.

"I did try to track her earlier, when I played back. All the other cameras that are in good proximity couldn't pick her up, anywhere. I even tried cars parked in the nearby vicinity. Nothing. It's like she did a disappearing act. The whole incident looked like an illusion. Who is she?" Ray said, trying to make some sense of what magical trick he saw.

"I don't know, what I do know, is that this is no illusion," Mervier said, still staring at the screen, where the two sculptures remained. "Ray, can you play back again? I need to see what she was holding."

"Sure."

The controller quickly brought the image up again, and this time in slow-motion. Mervier leaned forward, but couldn't see the face of the hooded woman, who had moved so sharply, and had effortlessly despatched four vicious criminals.

"Pause," Mervier said. "Zoom in."

Ray obediently followed her instructions, and the crisp image of the ethereal sceptre was enlarged. It looked truly amazing, and the shaft itself had a serpentine design.

"What the hell is that?" Ray asked.

"Can you send me a copy of that, to this number?" she said, handing him her card.

"Yeah, no problem."

Ray tapped the necessary controls on his console, as he uploaded the image. Her mobile pinged. A full-colour close-up screenshot of the picture appeared on her mobile. She also told him to send a few more pictures of the woman, from different angles, which he did without question.

"I need a copy of the entire footage, too," she said, with a sense of urgency.

"Sure, just one second." Ray operated the keyboard, waited a few moments for the footage to download onto a saved document, and then sent the digital file to her number. Her mobile pinged again.

Mervier then turned to Ray.

"Listen Ray. I going to make myself abundantly clear. Do not share any of these images with anyone else. That includes the press and social media. Keep this strictly confidential between you and me. Until I find out what is going on. Is that understood?"

"Of course. What about my boss, and the company?"

"They'll understand. This is a police investigation. Your firm is bound under data protection laws. If this should leak to the public, I know who is responsible. I am the leading officer of this case. If you find anything else, contact me immediately," Mervier advised.

"I will, detective."

"Thanks." Mervier acknowledged and headed to the door. As she exited into the council building's corridor, she closed the door behind her.

The determined detective hurriedly made her way down towards the reception of the civic premises, and her mobile buzzed in her leather jacket pocket. She answered. It was Branning.

"Yeah. Hi, Jake."

"Okay, you're not going to like this," he said. "Buckley is not at his home address, his parents said he went out with Zach and the others last night. Never came back."

"Yes, I know. Buckley is down in the middle of the street, encased in stone, along with the other chap." She couldn't believe she said that sentence.

"What?" Branning's tone was mystified.

"This is going to be hard for you to understand. I'm barely coming to terms with it, myself. I feel this is happening all over again."

"What are you talking about, Nicole?"

"Look, I'll explain later. I've got a few connections. I need to make a few calls. In the meantime, I need you to search for someone. I'm sending over to you an image of a woman. Not a great description, but it's all we've got to go on at the moment. Check out all taxi firms, train stations, and B&Bs in the nearby area to the crime scene." Mervier quickly sent Branning a text message with an attached file.

"Okay received. I may need to pull in some more help on this."

"Do whatever you can. I will help you. There's a lot of ground to cover. I've got CCTV checking on areas too. I intend to solve this one."

"What did you see?" Branning asked. She could hear him getting into his car.

"All I can say is that we've got four dead lads on our hands, and one extremely dangerous suspect, we need to catch her as soon as possible, whoever she is," she replied, trying to keep her voice down, as she approached the guard, sitting behind the reception desk.

Mervier, propping up her phone on her shoulder, signed herself out, and dashed out of the council premises.

Recent memories flooded back into her head, from what had happened at the museum, a short time ago. What she saw on their cameras, and the other strange weapon that decimated the police. This was all too familiar. But she had a lot of canvassing to do first.

Time was of the essence.

The detective needed expert help.

CHAPTER 5

"THE FLAG STILL FLIES"

Two Days Later. St George's Museum North Yorkshire 10.00am

Ophelia Winters was standing in deep thought whilst she observed the hectic work taking place at her beloved museum.

Or what was left of it.

The whole place was a bustling construction site. Surrounding the perimeter, the entire site was interlocked with Heras fencing that rose 1.8 metres high. Some of the steel mesh had fabric covers that displayed the company name of the local contractors.

St George's had commenced rebuilding the moment she had returned from the Cyclades islands. Scaffolding had been assembled all the way across the façade, and roof of the front building, where the majority of the heavy damage was. This was the area where the police helicopter had crashed into the museum, caused by the cursed bident, and the evil warlock that wielded it. Isaac Kane.

Reflecting back, she was glad that she had abandoned the magical bident in the ancient temple, now buried under tonnes of rubble. She was equally satisfied that Kane had met his comeuppance, by the very thing that had partially destroyed her museum and slain all those poor police officers.

Her eyes welled up from behind her glasses, as she surveyed the surrounding area. Her devoted Doberman, Anubis was sitting beside her on his leash. The dog was watching all the workmen, and diggers on the grounds, continuing their work.

The construction firm were making efficient progress, and most of the rubble and steel girders from the building were removed from the car park and entrance steps, as well as the wreckage of the helicopter. But she pondered, knowing that every piece of debris that were scattered around was a dark reminder of the devastating assault at the museum, caused by the wretched Order of the Crimson Claw.

It was all over now. The Order had been destroyed, and she emerged victorious -but at a tragic cost.

A red mini pulled up at the temporary security barrier behind her, distracting her from her deep ruminations. The barrier was the only source of access control to the site and was controlled by three of her loyal uniformed security guards. Next to it was a large welfare cabin, from where one of the guards came out, and greeted the young blond woman in her gleaming new vehicle.

"Hi, Miss Trent," the veteran guard smiled.

"Thanks, Sebastian," she replied. He admitted her through, and Madison drove her car right up to the nearest bay and parked. She spotted Ophelia and they exchanged waves.

Madison embraced Ophelia lovingly, as the young protégé noticed the curator discreetly wipe a tear that had trickled down her cheek.

"Hey Mads," Ophelia said, feeling her warmth and compassion.

"Hey you. At least the flag still flies," Madison reassured, trying to take away the sting from the images that Ophelia was staring at.

"Yes." She glanced up at the tower, which had remained unscathed. The flag of St George flapped vigorously in the wind. Defiant and strong. This brought a comforting smile to Ophelia's sullen face. "Be like the flag," Madison added, rubbing Ophelia's arms.

"I will. It just pains me to see all the hard work and endeavour we put in to build this. Reduced to nearly a ruin," Ophelia said with a heavy heart.

"It's just stone and mortar. She will be rebuilt, Ophelia. Stronger and more resilient than before. The museum is always here, you know that," Madison said, placing her hand above her heart.

"I guess."

"And that heart beats strong, nothing will break it." Madison winked.

"It's been close to, anyway, what brings you here?" Ophelia asked, trying to snap out of her morose state.

"I thought you would be here. You need to get out, have a holiday. See some sights. It's going to be a few months before all this will be finished."

"I'm not in a slump."

"Really?"

"Just taking a break. Besides, I may be needed here," Ophelia said.

"Why don't we visit Reg, in Sheringham? I'm sure he'd like the company. I mean, you've not mentioned anything else about the *next adventure*. The trip that you were eager for us to take, a couple of weeks ago, remember?"

"I was considering seeing Reg, but he's still recuperating. You know what he's like. He doesn't want any fuss."

"Okay, and the trip, any more thoughts?" Madison said enthusiastically.

"It's definitely intriguing. It's just knowing where to start properly. Anyway, as soon as the construction began here, I was pre-occupied with all the admin, contractors, finances and everything. I still am. It's kind of taking priority for the time being Mads. I'm sorry."

Madison shrugged her shoulders and nodded. Typical Ophelia. Again, always work and no play. Speaking of that, she had just survived the most dangerous expedition that she had undertaken in her life and suffered terrible losses in the process. She needed time.

"The more reason that you should take a proper break, leave this in the capable hands of the guys here, they've got it in hand," Madison insisted. The student became the mentor.

"I'll think about it," Ophelia said as she turned around, and carried on walking a very chilled out Anubis. Madison walked beside her, and they approached the security welfare unit. "Besides, another reason I'm here is to pick up any correspondence sent directly to the museum, as my personal address is not listed, and I don't want all and sundry to know where I live."

"Can't the security guys deliver anything to you?"

Sebastian overheard that, and the ex-marine chuckled as he stuck his head out of the window.

"Hey, do you mind, Miss Trent, we're not postmen, unless you really need us to do that, Dr Winters?" Sebastian raised his eyebrows. She appeared a little embarrassed and sniggered.

Ophelia smiled for once and made her way round to the cabin entrance.

"Relax, Sebastian. It's all good. What have you got?"

She entered the pleasant welfare cabin, and saw another guard sitting at the rear table, drinking his coffee. Sebastian moved over from the camera console that was on the front desk and collected a small pile of mail.

"Nothing much, a few addressed to Professor Shaw, two for you, and…oh, this is for you as well. It was received earlier this morning, by special delivery." Sebastian handed Ophelia an A4 size brown envelope, with all the registered stamps, and delivery stickers on it. Very well sealed. "I signed for it."

"That's okay." Ophelia took the envelope. It was very light and barely seemed to contain anything at all.

Madison looked over Ophelia's shoulder eagerly, as she looked down at the beautifully handwritten address of the museum, and Ophelia's full title and name above it.

Ophelia, quite intrigued, carefully ripped open the top of the envelope, and removed the only content.

It looked like a single A5-sized folded up pamphlet. She checked the bottom of the envelope, and nothing else was inside.

Ophelia unfolded the pamphlet, and her eyes widened slightly with interest.

CHAPTER 6

THE INVITATION

The pamphlet was glossy, and showed various photo stills of archaic objects, ancient symbols from a range of cultures, and a passport-sized picture of an attractive woman showing her face and shoulders.

She looked like she was in her late forties, wearing her hair in a sophisticated black bun. She was wearing tinted reading glasses and sporting a lovely welcoming smile. Sparkling jewellery draped down her neck, and tear-shaped green earrings hung down from her ears. She looked quite glamorous.

In the centre of the pamphlet was a printed message in a small stylish font.

"What is it?" asked Madison, quite tantalised.

Ophelia started to read it aloud.

"Dear Dr Ophelia Winters. You are cordially invited as one of my special guests, to attend an exclusive and extravagant gala, on Friday 8th May 8.00pm, at my residence, Castle Ravenscliff, in Somerset. (Directions are on the reverse side). The gala is a fundraising event, and a celebratory gathering for selected distinguished men and women with 'unique interests' within our profession. A beautiful banquet, and overnight accommodation in the castle are also included. It would be an honour to receive you. Due to restricted numbers, you are permitted to bring 2 guests. PS: You will be enlightened of what we can share with you. Yours sincerely. Countess E. Dumas."

"Wow," Madison responded, "A Countess. This could be something you need right now. It sounds intriguing."

Ophelia continued to read the large font below the message. The pamphlet highlighted a list of historical cultures that the countess was a foremost historian and expert in. These ranged from ancient Greek mythology, Roman, Celtic, French renaissance, and English mediaeval literature.

She was drawn to the Greek mythology section. In addition to that, she studied the four corners of the pamphlet, and they all had the same symbol, which seemed like some form of logo. It was a gorgon's head. Just like the stone tablet she had at home. She had seen similar symbols in many forms of literature and in museum archives during her travels.

Ophelia had little memory of how she acquired the tablet. During the collapse of the chamber on the island, she was suffering from severe mercury poisoning. Madison was also hazy, during the temple escape, as she was coming out of her drug-addled state, but did recall taking something similar to the symbol prior to the chamber crashing down. The mysterious maidens that were momentarily there, must have perished underneath all the rubble, after Madison and Ophelia escaped.

But the sight of the symbol did make her pause for thought.

"Fascinating, her crest or logo here, looks very familiar," Ophelia showed Madison.

"All too familiar. Who is this lady?"

"I don't know, she must be very reputed in the fields that she claims to be an expert in. I've never heard of her, to be honest with you, Mads. Do you recognise her?"

"No, I can't say that I do. But she must have some noble lineage." She looked at the photograph at the bottom of the pamphlet. "Countess Dumas. Sounds French. I wonder what the E stands for."

Madison then shuffled inside her white summer jacket and took out her mobile phone. Straight onto Google. Scrolling through the search engine, she managed to find the brief information on the countess, as well as half a dozen pictures of her, which matched the one that featured on the flyer. She then read what was presented to her from the search engine. She bullet-pointed the essentials.

"She's legit. 49 years of age. She is of Greek and French descent. Married an English earl of the territory. A Count Richard E. Davenport. She was married for twenty years, until he died alone in a tragic sailing accident, in 2020. Inherited his entire estate. No kids. Never remarried. She is also a leading mythologist, folklorist, and has had an established career in rare antiquities, as well as having profound knowledge in ancient history. Since her husband's death, she has lived pretty much in isolation at Ravenscliff." Madison completed reading the bio.

Ophelia then turned to the other side of the prestigious-looking leaflet. There was a small selection of photo stills. Ancient Grecian relics, that consisted of a 3,500-years old Corinthian helmet of a hoplite warrior, a xiphos short sword, old painted pottery, a sceptre, and a wooden aspis shield.

"These pieces look like they're thousands of years old. Amazing, why have I not heard of this woman before?" Ophelia said. She could sense Madison's excitement.

"Two guests?" she replied, raising her eyebrows.

Ophelia smiled until her eyes darted back to one of the photographs.

"Well, I'll be damned."

"What is it?"

"I think I've seen this before."

"You're pretty consistent in doing that," Madison remarked wittily.

Ophelia pointed to the wondrous-looking sceptre, with an incredibly ornate crown that contained an emerald stone. Its shaft had engraved snakes that coiled to the crown, in a very elegant style.

"This sceptre that is featured here, the markings and the crown. I need to check on something at home."

"You've seen the artefact?"

"Not the actual thing. I have only heard legends and stories about something similar, just like the Bident of Hades. An object of such reverence and power, surely, this cannot be the same one," Ophelia explained.

"Maybe an old replication. You know yourself, there are hundreds of old sceptres and staves that are out there. Each, a great historical piece, but nothing more. You've got that look again. I'm sure the real one is nothing more than a myth."

"Have you heard yourself, Madison? We said the same thing about the bident, and the elixir. They were pretty real, alright."

Madison sighed and then looked at the photo again.

"Well, whatever, we should at least look into this, and find out more about this mysterious Countess, it's only a couple of days away," Madison encouraged.

"Pretty short notice."

Ophelia couldn't deny that she was exceptionally captivated by the contents featured in the pamphlet. This Countess may also be able to shed some light and knowledge on some of her own queries and theories, the curator thought.

Albeit, she was cautious too, based on her previous encounters.

Madison was right, a small break away at a remote castle in the west counties may be what she needed right now, and also it might give her some insight in what she possibly had in her possession at home.

"This is probably the 'proper start' you've been looking for even if it's just to get answers," Madison was persistent. She really wanted to get Ophelia re-motivated.

Ophelia relented and smiled. She couldn't deprive Madison an opportunity to delve deeper into the esoteric knowledge of the subject that she had passionately invested herself in, ever since the young archaeologist joined Ophelia's team.

"Who am I to argue with a promising young mythologist like you? If we do this, we take precautions," Ophelia advised. Her feelings towards her were still maternal, even though they were close friends and colleagues.

"Yes!" Madison said, and fist punched the air in glee, like an excited teenager.

CHAPTER 7

LEGIONSHIELD

Outskirts of Hexham.

Northumberland.

The dark blue helicopter, bearing the insignia of, Legionshield Defence Industries, flew over the main complex of a 400-acre facility. It descended towards the flat roof of a six-storey rectangular building that was covered with reflective reinforced glass windows and steel beams that were intersected between the levels.

The vast facility was situated in a remote rural valley that consisted of small woodlands and sloping hills. The closest town was the Northumbrian market town of Hexham, which was a few miles away.

Three people emerged from the oval operations centre, which was adjacent to the helipad, as soon as the helicopter finally landed on its circular bay.

The first one that appeared from the annex centre was a heavily built, brutish-looking man, wearing a tight-fitting shirt which emphasized his rippling muscles. Hugo, the head of security. He looked intense and foreboding. He was joined by another male, but he was much slighter in build compared to his hulking counterpart. Dr Theo Delanski was wearing a very stylish blue lab coat. He was head of special projects.

Following the men out was a lady wearing a smart white business trouser suit, with the LDI logo emblazoned on her left breast pocket. Vanessa Woodbridge. Vincent Keyes' dedicated personal assistant, and also a member of the special projects team.

CEO Vincent Keyes, climbed out from the rear of the company chopper, accompanied by Miles Matheson. Keyes' slick fair hair blew in the wind, created by the rapidly decreasing whir of the helicopter's rotor blades. Keyes was in a smart grey suit and had just returned to his UK field office. He was carrying a long silver metal case, as Matheson had two smaller similar versions in each hand.

"Good afternoon, Mr Keyes, I hope you had a pleasant trip," greeted his American PA loudly.

"Thank you, Vanessa," Keyes answered, and then quickly handed the large case to Delanski.

"Welcome back, Mr Keyes," said the head scientist.

"Dr Delanski, get these to the lab, have them meticulously analysed," he commanded.

"Yes sir, we'll get to work on them right away," he motioned over at the door of the annex, and two more company operatives rushed out, and collected the case on his behalf.

"This too," Matheson handed one of the smaller cases to the operatives. The syndicate boss kept hold of the other metallic case.

Once all the brief pleasantries were done, Keyes never broke stride, and headed straight for the annex room, followed by the others. They filed into the spacious elevator and descended into the bowels of the impressive-looking building.

The group came out of the lift and stepped onto the grey carpeted corridors of sublevel 2. Special Projects Division. They proceeded down the corridor, passing several laboratories and testing areas, until they arrived at a large oval window on the right.

"Mr Keyes, we have made some excellent progress with the MX2 Air Reapers," Vanessa reported eagerly.

The group peered through the 3-inch plexiglass oval window, and inside was a huge square room, the size of half a football pitch. The testing chamber was sparse, and had modernised mannequins, which looked like androids, dressed in khaki combat attire, dotted around the granite floor. Grey armoured walls surrounded the room.

Keyes observed with a keen eye two human operatives wearing urban black and blue fatigues, and futuristic grey exoskeleton armour, being assisted by four scientists. They were attaching hi-tech jetpacks onto the backs of the two operatives. The packs themselves looked awesome with their quad mini-rocket launchers and scaled-down chain guns. It also had a mounted dorsal laser cannon on top of the jetpack.

Within seconds, the two air reapers soared into the air inside the chamber, and the jetpacks' thrusters emitted bluish gases, as the pilots ascended until they were at eye level from their spectators, on the other side of the observation window. The four scientists quickly, scampered from the floor, and out of the chamber, as the reapers performed a few skilful manoeuvres in the air.

The pilots, with great aerial control, banked and proceeded to open fire, using the controls on their hand grips. The jetpack's on-board ordnance accurately launched its mini-ballistic rockets, which decimated half of the mannequin targets into smithereens. The rapid fire from the chain guns on either side of the pack shredded the others to pieces.

Only one target was left, and it was a robotic animatronic. It suddenly came to life and ran across the floor. A small weapon appeared from its forearm, and a laser beam shot towards one of the reapers. The reapers' next exercise was to weave and dodge the incoming non-lethal lasers, which they did with superb control.

Then, one of the pilots banked low and returned fire, but this time from the jetpack's dorsal laser cannon. The lethal beam struck the robot, and metal fragments were blasted across the chamber. The robot collapsed into a smouldering wreck. Its avatar controller was one of the scientists, wearing an animatronic exosuit. He had been inside the protected lab on the other side of the test chamber, controlling the animated robot. The scientist felt the system shut down on his body, with a dying electronic groan.

Vincent Keyes looked particularly impressed with this demonstration.

"That's very good. We could barely hear the packs."

"We've improved on its stealth technology since the last test. You could fly this thing, in a mild breeze, and not realise it's there," Vanessa replied.

"Well done," Keyes, acknowledged her. "Shame about the combat-bot. That prototype cost us two million dollars."

He knew deep down, success came at a certain cost, and he smiled as the air reapers came to a controlled landing on the ground amidst the debris from all the robotic targets.

"This is good work," Keyes summarised.

The group then proceeded down to the last window, which was the final test chamber. It was a narrow room that resembled a firing range. Glancing through, he saw several operatives in various positions at the rear wall, aiming highly advanced energy rifles down the chamber where further targets were erected.

Streams of red laser bolts were seen being fired from the unique weapons, disintegrating their targets, eighty metres away.

At that moment, Vanessa's earpiece glowed, and she tapped a switch on it.

"Yes?"

"Miss Woodbridge, we have someone here to see Mr Keyes." It was the voice of a female receptionist from the lobby.

Keyes, turned towards his assistant, with a look of annoyance.

"He's very busy at the moment," Vanessa replied.

"It's the police. The officer said, it's very important," was the receptionist's response.

Vanessa looked up at her boss, for some reaction. Keyes sighed, but he didn't have a clue what this was about. He had been under scrutiny from the authorities a few times, for suspicious activities or suspected illegal deals in his weapons development programme, but no evidence ever came to light. He also ensured that he contributed to the police and law enforcement agencies with very lucrative business deals.

"Fine, I'll be in my office," Keyes said, with a tone of irritation.

"Okay, you can send her up to the executive suite," Vanessa instructed the receptionist.

"Thank you." The receptionist said politely and hung up the line.

Keyes, feeling inconvenienced, made his way to the lift.

CHAPTER 8

THE OPPORTUNITY

It had taken just over two hours for Mervier to drive from York to the outskirts of Hexham. Once she had parked at the facility, she entered the spacious and polished ground floor of the building, and introduced herself to the receptionist, who, after a brief exchange with Vanessa, signalled over to a nearby security guard.

Mervier had mentioned that she didn't need a security escort, but the guard insisted, indicating that he could only access her into the highly secured areas with his digital ID card. It was standard protocol for a sensitive site like this.

The detective was shadowed by the guard, as they walked down the plush corridor of the sixth-floor executive wing of the complex. They reached a pair of double metal doors. The sign on the door read: 'Vincent Keyes. CEO.' The dutiful guard knocked on the doors, and was welcomed by Matheson, who opened them.

"Detective Sergeant Nicole Mervier from the North Yorkshire police," the guard announced to Matheson.

"Thank you," Mervier nodded to the security officer, and he remained standing outside the door in the corridor, as Mervier entered the large, exquisite office.

Matheson closed the doors behind her and stood next to the huge windows across the walls that overlooked the car park and fields. It had an incredible view of the picturesque landscape outside. The office was fit for a king, and boasted a uniquely shaped table at the end, where Vincent Keyes rose from his leather swivel throne.

"Detective, this is an unexpected pleasure. I am Vincent Keyes. CEO of this facility." He extended his hand, and she shook it, offering a mild smile. He could tell that she had more pressing thoughts in her head.

"Thank you for taking the time to see me. I won't take too much of it, Mr Keyes." Mervier said, as she stood across the desk. Keyes, gestured over to his right.

"I appreciate that, I'm a busy man. By the way, this is Miles Matheson. My head of security."

They shook hands.

"Detective," Matheson said, although he didn't expect Keyes to introduce him as 'his head of security'. He knew his role as one of Keyes' personal protection officers from time to time, but this was usually overseas. Keyes essentially needed him around for a while, during the analysis stage of the weapon he had recovered in Greece.

"I mean no offence, Mr Matheson, but what I have to say is strictly confidential," Mervier said.

"This is a confidential area, detective. He's alright. Anything discussed will be kept between us. He's ex-MI6, so, I can pretty much guarantee his discretion," Keyes reassured.

"Very well," she accepted.

"North Yorkshire police, just slightly out of your jurisdiction, here in Northumberland, Detective Mervier?" Keyes enquired.

"I am attached to a special crime unit, we collaborate regionally with your local constabulary," Mervier replied, although she truly knew that she couldn't routinely or independently operate officially, outside of her borders, without the inclusion of the neighbouring territory.

Vincent Keyes nodded and sat back in his chair.

"So, tell me, what have I done now?" the chief executive asked.

"I am not here to investigate you, or some of your activities that Legionshield are rumoured to be involved with." She was well aware of the corporation's reputation.

"Why, detective. It sounds like you've got me down as a corrupt arms dealer, or something. Tell me, how are the Phantom D-2000 riot shields doing, ever since we generously supplied you with ten thousand units?" Keyes said obnoxiously.

"I understand they're serving their purpose effectively and the force are always appreciative," Mervier answered, telling him what he essentially wanted to hear.

"That's good to hear. Well, you can tell your chief commissioners that we plan to ship out another five thousand Phantoms next month. Courtesy of Legionshield, of course, it always satisfies me, that we will continue to support our national police, and make a difference," Keyes went on.

She could sense a hint of sarcasm within his boast. And a subtle reminder, to the police, as he believed, he could keep them from sniffing around his affairs, by supplying them with state-of-the-art hardware.

"And I'm sure my colleagues are profoundly grateful. Like I said, Mr Keyes, I am here on another matter, I was hoping that you could help me, or offer some advice or insight, at least," Mervier got down to business.

"Well, you got me curious, what can I do for you, detective?" he leaned forward. He had her undivided attention.

She then proceeded to pull out her mobile phone and scrolled through some images before she settled on one, she was about to show.

"I am investigating four murders that occurred last Sunday night, in York. Four young local miscreants. Two were brutally killed by an individual with super-human strength, and the two others had been…turned into stone."

She then paused, waiting for the two men to process the unbelievable statement she had just disclosed. She got the reaction she was expecting. Matheson and Keyes exchanged puzzled looks, and then Keyes was presented the image on Mervier's mobile phone. He raised a brow as he swept his blond fringe away from his eyelids. He focused in on the image of a woman holding an unusual-looking object.

"You heard me right. They were horrifically transformed by this suspect…using this." Mervier said, pointing to a close-up image of the sceptre.

Matheson came over, and looked quizzically at the image, with Keyes, who was equally befuddled.

"It looks like an old mediaeval mace," Matheson commented, "And who is the woman?"

"I'll come to her in a minute. I was wondering, Mr Keyes, if you recognise or can identify the object, or if this is something your organisation has created?" Mervier asked.

"Well, I'll be honest. I've never seen anything like this before, detective, in fact, it looks a bit primitive, compared to what we usually produce," Keyes said.

"I'm just reaching out. I know your facility tries to specialise in manufacturing wild and wonderful weaponry. Even, some conspiracy theorists have speculated, alien technology, maybe I'm just clutching at straws, but I thought something like this would interest you," Mervier then switched the screen.

"Sorry, I can't help you, although it sounds remarkable," Keyes looked at the screen again. She noted that he looked at the image with great interest and surreptitiously licked his lips.

"Okay, what I'm about to show you is highly classified. This hasn't got out to the press. The police are informing the public that this is just gang-related, whilst I uncover what's going on. Have a look."

She then showed him the recorded footage of the incident.

Keyes was completely enthralled as he watched the video. When it had finished, he took a moment to digest what he had just viewed. There was a momentary silence in the office. Matheson was equally flabbergasted. Looking at the mace, reminded him of the deadly bident's energy, blasting into the ground underneath his feet, on the island, that had sent him crashing into the rocks, and killing two of his mercenaries in the process.

This weaponised relic was phenomenal.

"Incredible," Keyes said, after what seemed to be forever, without comment.

"Definitely not one of yours?" Mervier asked, again.

"No, but I wish it was," Keyes murmured, transfixed at the screen.

Mervier rolled her eyes, realising that this was probably a bad idea, coming here, and now she had inadvertently invoked a spark in the inquisitive executive.

She whipped it away from his viewpoint and scrolled back to the still picture of the woman.

"And, for what its worth, I don't suppose that you recognise her?" Mervier enquired.

"Not the most descriptive of images, detective Mervier, is this all you've got?"

"I'm afraid so."

"Well. It looks like you've got yourself, a real-life superhero here. Or a supervillain?" Keyes grinned.

"She is responsible for the deaths of those young men, so I don't care if she is some kind of vigilante. Murder is murder."

"Indeed. Unfortunately, I don't recognise her. Matheson?"

Matheson shook his head.

"Again, I am most likely looking at this all wrong, but I do remember reading that your bioweapons division once developed some kind of unsanctioned super-serum for government spies, a formula which increased strength and agility?" Mervier mentioned, digging up a bit of Keyes' past projects.

"That was a long time ago, detective. The LS Alpha serum was an experimental drug that had severe adverse effects. We shut down the project before it went live. The company has suffered the consequences of that misfortune, it's all in the past," Keyes explained, annoyed that she reminded him of what had nearly crippled his corporation.

"The reason I'm grabbing at straws, if maybe, one of your disgruntled scientists could have taken a stash. I don't know. It may not explain the object, but would certainly explain the suspect's freakish strength?" Mervier was trying everything she could.

Keyes really did feel that he was under scrutiny, and being personally investigated now. His cooperative demeanour faded. He crossed his arms.

"Detective. I have over 150 employees here at this complex. Only a score is directly assigned to the special projects division. Each one I know personally, and they are meticulously vetted. All of them are dedicated, loyal, and are magnificent assets to science. I can tell you now, with my hand at heart, that not one of our gifted scientists would openly take any sample or secret technology, and field test it on a group of local scum, in the middle of the streets. For what gain? To implicate us? Is that why you're here?"

"Like I said, I'm just investigating. I've got to look at every possible theory. I'm sorry if you feel accused of anything. That is not my intention," Mervier said, although she didn't trust the businessman.

But Keyes' words felt sincere, and why would he put himself on the chopping block? His job was clandestine development, and he wanted to avoid attracting authorities and rival firms. Not invite them in, by engaging or endorsing common criminality, in the city streets. But he did see where she was going with this.

"Listen, detective, I can look into it. And you are welcome to peruse the personal files of our associates that are in the division, if it helps?" Keyes started to cooperate.

"Thank you, Mr Keyes. It could be useful."

"But I think you're barking up the wrong tree," Keyes remarked.

"Detective," Matheson stepped forward again. "I appreciate your need to look into this scientifically, but have you considered looking more outside the box?"

"Meaning?"

"Let's face it, I think everyone in this room has experienced somewhat, extremely supernatural phenomena, have you approached anyone that may offer some alternative insights into what this could be?" Matheson advised. Mervier knew who was referring to.

"Yes, I have. Her phone is off-line. Look, I had never believed in the paranormal, magic and monsters, up until a few weeks ago. I just want to look at this with a clear, realistic mind first," Mervier replied to the former MI6 officer.

"Perhaps, more of an open mind?" Matheson suggested.

"In the meantime, if you can think of anything else that may help this investigation, and in the worst-case scenario, if your organisation is involved without your knowledge, you could possibly vindicate yourselves gentlemen by contacting me." Mervier handed over a card to Keyes, and another one to Matheson.

Keyes got out his mobile phone and started to type a text message. Whilst he was typing his message, he spoke but kept his eyes on the screen.

"Oh, I have a great interest in this, detective. So, I would like to stay involved, to help you, of course."

"I'm pretty sure that I know your agenda, Mr. Keyes. I can honestly say right now, if we do manage to recover this powerful object, it is a murder weapon. Police evidence, and it will stay in our custody, is that clear?" Mervier adamantly said,

Keyes looked up after hitting 'send' on his phone.

"Detective, if you find this woman, you will find the illustrious weapon. Providing you know what you are dealing with. This is a truly devastating device, which we really don't know what else it can do, we have the expertise, the technology and the resources to research and study the mace, if that's what it is."

"I can't allow that."

"Okay, then I believe our meeting is over, detective, I am sorry I cannot help you any further, but the offer is there, should you need it," Keyes forced a smile, and pressed a button on his desk.

A moment later, the security officer walked in and stood to attention.

"I appreciate your time. Gentlemen," Mervier acknowledged them both, and walked out of the room, escorted by the security guard.

Matheson and Keyes then moved over to the window and looked down at the car park. Keyes was very enticed by what he had seen and rubbed his hands together like some kind of clichéd criminal mastermind. Matheson noted this and sensed the cog wheels turning in the executive's head.

"You have a new assignment, Miles," Keyes said, as he continued to observe down at the car park.

He watched one of his ground floor security operatives attach something underneath the detective's vehicle. The CEO then walked over to his desk and tossed a small black digital device over to Matheson. A tracker.

"Vincent, there is a strong possibility that nothing may come of this."

"Even if there is a remote chance of recovering this, and her, I cannot afford an opportunity like this to slip away." Keyes replied, as he saw Mervier get into her vehicle.

Matheson just shook his head, disapprovingly, and left the office, leaving Keyes smiling deviously.

"Good man."

CHAPTER 9

THE GORGONEION TABLET

Osbaldwick
North Yorkshire
8.30pm

It was a warm evening at Ophelia's hilltop cottage. The sun was slowly descending, creating a dramatic orange hue in the Yorkshire skies.

Ophelia and Madison had spent a few hours in the city centre's department stores, shopping for supplies, a quick stop at Madison's flat, and time for Ophelia to make arrangements with her mother to house-sit once again, from tomorrow morning.

In the meantime, Madison was in the kitchen, throwing together a small salad bowl, whilst Ophelia was placing a few garments inside a small-sized suitcase that was resting on top of the sofa. Anubis was checking everything out, with his tail wagging. 'Shooting off again', the dog was possibly thinking.

"What time is your Mum coming round?" Madison shouted from the kitchen, even though Ophelia was a few yards away, stuffing a couple of sleeveless summer t-shirts in the pack.

"I told her, about eleven o'clock tomorrow morning, knowing her, she'll end up showing at eleven at night," she mused.

"Well, I'm sure the place will be in safe hands again," Madison said, picking and grazing on the fresh peppers she had just sliced.

Ophelia looked at her faithful Doberman and smiled.

"Definitely."

Ophelia then made her way over to her digital safe, disguised as a hi-fi speaker. Opened up the front plastic panel which revealed numbered keypads. She pressed in the seven-digit code, and the safe beeped. Inside the secret cavity were a few pieces of expensive jewellery, a small bundle of cash in euros, and English banknotes.

But she bypassed all this and reached for the round piece of stonemasonry that she and Madison had rescued from the spa chamber on Katamarai island, before it had caved in.

Madison entered the living room carrying a salad bowl and sat down on the comfy sofa next to the suitcase. As she poured a copious amount of olive oil dressing over the salad, Ophelia took out the stone tablet from the safe and placed the suitcase on the floor. She took a seat next to Madison, and examined the ancient piece, cross-referencing it with the pamphlet she received earlier.

"Beautiful, isn't it?" Madison said, as she started eating her salad supper.

Ophelia traced her finger over the carvings, gliding them across the inscribed contours and lines of the ugly face that stared back. Ophelia couldn't tell if Madison was mocking the face on the stonework or marvelling at the piece herself.

"To a certain extent yes," Ophelia answered. The face, although captivating, was a little chilling too. A forked tongue was sticking out from the hideous face. The letter 'S' was inscribed eight times on top of the head, which represented snakes for hair.

Medusa the Gorgon.

"For thousands of years, the Greeks worshipped their Gods with so much reverence. They built temples and statues in their honour. Even today, it is common for devout disciples, covens, and zealots to idolise other mythological deities, including Medusa, or what she represented," Ophelia said, inspecting the tablet.

"Her name means to 'guard' and 'protect'. Contrary to popular belief and how modern-day media portray her, Medusa is interpreted as an apotropaic symbol, to ward off evil and negative forces," Madison added, with her own knowledge.

"That's why she features on shields and temples. Similar to the 'oni'. The Japanese demon masks that are displayed in traditional abodes, to cast out evil, and act as a sacred guardian of one's personal domain," said Ophelia.

"A duality. A terrifying monster, and a protective symbol. She is also reinterpreted as a symbol of female empowerment, girl power, eh?" Madison said, chuckling, as she prodded another mix of salad pieces, and consumed them.

"I'm not an expert, but it'll be good to get some insight into this. However, this is what fascinates me, Mads." Ophelia turned the tablet over and looked at all the ancient symbolic engravements.

"According to my rudimentary studies, it looks like Linear B markings, used in the Bronze Age to write Mycenaean Greek, a fair few thousand years ago," Madison suggested, as she focused intently on the tablet. Ophelia was quite impressed with her knowledge.

"That is a find in itself," The curator stated. Her gaze then moved over to the inscribed image of the sceptre, which was next to the markings. "This, here. You recognise it?"

Madison zeroed in, as she placed her plate on the coffee table. As she started to study it, the doorbell chimed, making them both jump from their seats. This, of course, set off Anubis, who started to bark at the front door of the kitchen.

With their concentrated silence interrupted, Ophelia sprang from her seat and approached the new door of her kitchen. She had a much better security system in place. An internal control pad had been installed in the kitchen, and new CCTV cameras were mounted around the cottage and her gardens. The system was synced in with an app on her mobile phone.

Ophelia clicked onto the app icon 'Security: Home.' Pressing the necessary camera number, the live feed display came up on her screen. The front camera, high above the door, was statically aligned to face down on the porchway. Another camera was concealed in the rose bushes, at the side of the door, to capture the faces of any visitors.

It was Detective Nicole Mervier, standing outside.

CHAPTER 10

THE SACRED SCEPTRE

"Detective, this is a surprise. Please come in." Ophelia greeted Mervier, as she opened the door.

Mervier looked tired and was still dressed in her ¾-length leather coat. Her black blouse underneath looked crumpled. She stepped into the kitchen and thanked her.

"Hi Ophelia, it's been a long day, I need to discuss something very important with you," Mervier said, with a serious expression.

"Of course, I'll put the kettle on."

The door closed.

What the detective didn't notice was a black Range Rover, pull up into a small turn off, halfway up the hillside near Ophelia's cottage. Miles Matheson was behind the wheel. He had stealthily tracked the detective's Mercedes all the way from Hexham, and it didn't surprise him that one of her first ports of call was the residence of one of his own clients – Ophelia Winters.

He looked torn. The Black Knight Syndicate boss turned his engine off and peered upwards. He couldn't see the cottage fully from his vantage point, but he didn't venture any further up. After all, he was the one that had supervised the installation of her new sophisticated security system, and was fully aware of where all the cameras, overt and covert, were placed.

Already, he felt he was betraying his long-standing client and friend. After all they had been through together. He rubbed his eyes. It felt it had been a long drive. The former MI6 officer had been hired to track the detective, and if it was for the greater good of recovering a very deadly relic, and the apprehension of its, even deadlier owner. Only then would he feel a little bit better. He exhaled deeply, and texted Keyes, of the update. He couldn't lie. Besides, for all knew, he himself could have been followed as well, to ensure he was doing his job without deviation.

Meanwhile, back at the cottage, Mervier was sat on the couch opposite the two archaeologists. She had explained almost everything that had occurred on that fateful night in the city centre a few days ago.

Madison was aghast.

"Oh my God, I was there, just before what happened, Zach had always been a bit of a prick but didn't deserve to die." Ophelia rubbed Madison's shoulders. This had really affected her protégé. Madison hadn't been up to date with current affairs recently, so wasn't aware of the incident. Ophelia had read something in the paper, but considered it as drug- related, and thought nothing more of it. At least the police and the press were successful with the cover story, and the public was buying it.

"Like I said," Mervier said, "You're not implicated, but I do find it unusual, almost a coincidence that you were there moments before their brutal deaths."

"You said something about an exotic weapon?" Ophelia asked.

Mervier brought out her mobile and was about to go through a repeat of what she did at Legionshield. She had already mentioned to Ophelia about the attack, and how a mysterious super-powered woman had killed two lads using unarmed techniques, and the last two were 'petrified' to death by an exotic weapon but didn't go into detail yet.

"This is a close-up of the relic. The weapon. I thought this would be your field of expertise."

It was the sceptre. Ora very identical version.

Ophelia was amazed. Mervier noticed that the curator had the same expression on her face, as she did when she saw the Bident of Hades for the first time, live.

"This is what it did." Mervier showed her the recorded footage of the incident outside the Saxon Inn.

Like she did with Keyes, she gave Ophelia and Madison a moment to process what they had just viewed. Both were absolutely shocked at the power that had been unleashed from the sceptre.

After Ophelia's initial reaction, the curator nodded and reached over to the pamphlet.

"I have seen something like this. Or something very much alike." Ophelia said enthusiastically. This made the detective's eyes widen, and she placed her coffee mug down on the table. She had Ophelia's fullest attention.

Ophelia opened up the flyer and handed it over to Mervier. The detective compared the image on her mobile to the full colour picture, that was featured on the glossy paper.

"My God, they're identical." Mervier gasped in disbelief. "I'm glad I came here now."

She felt she had made a breakthrough, or at least some dots were being connected. But not everything was adding up at the moment.

"Bearing in mind, there could be duplicates of this, replicas. We don't know. But this is strange," Madison added, trying to puzzle the whole thing out as well.

"What is this?" Mervier asked, looking at the pamphlet.

"Oh, that's an invitation to a fund-raising event on Friday evening, Madison and I were planning on attending to seek some answers, amongst other things," Ophelia replied, unsure now if this was a good idea.

"Who's the host?" Mervier said, as she continued reading the message on the leaflet.

"British peerage, it seems. A Countess Dumas, she lives in an isolated castle, in Somerset," Madison said, even though Mervier's eyes were reading the rest of the invitation.

"When did you get this?"

"This morning, why?" Ophelia asked.

Mervier didn't answer immediately. Instead, she looked at the photographic image of the host on the pamphlet and placed her thumb over the countess' eyes and nose, just exposing her mouth and jawline. The detective then glanced over at the pixelated image of the hooded woman on her mobile screen and compared the stills. Ophelia was attentive to all this.

"Detective?" Ophelia said, disturbing Mervier's concentration.

"We may have a suspect."

"What" Madison was astonished. "Surely not?"

"I admit, a bit of a stab in the dark, but let's look at the facts, don't you think this is all a bit of a convenient coincidence?" Mervier tried to piece this together.

"Looking at it now, I can see how suspicious all this appears," Ophelia said.

"Either I am paranoid or over-determined to redeem myself after our last encounter with unexplained phenomena, and deadly mysterious foes, but I could be onto something here." Mervier then handed back the pamphlet to Ophelia.

"What would a countess be doing, randomly walking in the city streets, that is full of crackheads and muggers, miles away from Somerset, in the middle of the night, and then, stumbling across a group of druggies, only to kill all of them, even if it was self-defence?" Madison said, rising from the sofa.

She went over to the kitchen and poured two glasses of wine from the fridge. She handed one to Ophelia, who then proceeded to take a couple of sips. She appeared quite taken back, by all this.

"What if she wasn't randomly there? That's, 'if' the woman in the invitation is indeed your murderer?" Ophelia said, still trying to comprehend everything.

"What do you mean?" Madison asked, taking a large gulp of chardonnay. She was still getting over the fact that she was personally at the scene of the crime, before it happened.

And then the penny dropped.

"Wait. Are you suggesting, she was there for a reason? That, I am involved in this, somehow," Madison worriedly asked.

"Do either of you know this woman? She could have been following Madison for some reason," Mervier probed.

Madison was flustered, and she momentarily looked over at the gorgoneion tablet on the sofa's armrest. The young woman then cast her mind back to the experiences on the island.

She vaguely remembered that when she was in her disorientated state in the Athenian spa chamber, a similar looking tablet was perched on the shrine: green robed maidens preparing her, for the sacrificial ritual: her encounter with the sorcerer on the plateau, the battle, and her rescue.

Madison then hazily recalled when she was escaping the collapsing chamber after Ophelia had killed the sorcerer, and their confrontation with the maidens. One of them, a priestess, had entered the chamber and exchanged words with Ophelia. But Madison didn't focus in on the woman, and in an act of desperation, had pulled Ophelia away, as she seemed to be in a state of hypnosis, and then both of them had escaped. She remembered removing the tablet and placing it in Ophelia's backpack before the chamber would have buried it forever.

Ophelia concurred, although she was, at the time, weakened from the mercury poisoning, and seemed incoherent when the priestess communicated with her during those final few moments, before the chamber collapsed.

"It can't be them, Nicole," Madison exclaimed, "All of them would have perished underneath the temple. Ophelia and I were very weak and were lucky to get out alive. If it wasn't for that secret tunnel, we would have been buried along with them."

"There's no guarantee of that, Mads," Ophelia replied.

"It's not them, and that woman is not her!" she said, pointing to the pamphlet.

"Speaking of coincidences, there is something else, Nicole," Ophelia declared, and unwrapped the stone tablet from its protected bubble cover.

"What is it?" the detective asked.

"An old stone Greek relic. Maybe our host will recognise it. Shed some light. Madison and I took it from the Athenian temple a few weeks ago, just before it collapsed.

"What's the meaning of the relic?"

"I honestly don't know," Ophelia admitted. "Some carvings on the tablet are very similar to the symbols on the invitation."

Mervier had a closer look, and noticed the rough inscriptions of the gorgon's face, ancient text markings, and what appeared to resemble a mace.

"Is that what I think it is?" Mervier asked, looking at the carving. In particular, the mace.

"Possibly, but there are so many archaeological pieces that look like this, and with similar inscriptions," Ophelia answered.

"You were right about the bident. Would you know anything about this, no matter how far-fetched?" Mervier asked the burning question.

"I'm no expert," Ophelia began, "But when I first examined the tablet, I noticed the inscribed mace. Ancient scholars and historians spoke of a magical Greek sceptre that was forged by the Gods, thousands of years ago, and the stories over time became mythical. Just like the Bident of Hades. The sceptre, or mace, was a gift to their devoted acolytes," Ophelia explained.

"Okay, and the tablet itself?"

"Maybe, a symbol of the coven's followers. Madison knows more about this than I do. We cannot decipher the markings."

"What do you think they could mean?" Mervier asked, probing for more answers. She didn't care if they sounded completely out of this world, after what she had previously witnessed.

"It's too early to speculate, maybe a poem, or a warning," Ophelia guessed.

"A spell?" Madison intervened, "A curse?"

Madison finished her glass and made her way to the fridge again for a much-needed re-fill.

Mervier turned towards Ophelia. The detective's face changed again to a serious look, whilst Madison was in the kitchen.

"Ophelia, whoever this woman is, she possesses extraordinary powers and has an incredibly destructive device. We are not strangers to those. I don't intend to let this one go. You've identified 'what could be' the murder weapon. We have a 'potential' suspect. A lot of this connects. Why, I don't know yet," Mervier summarised.

"Well, it looks like my trip has turned sour," Ophelia said, a little perturbed.

"Not necessarily so," Mervier responded.

Ophelia looked at her quizzingly. After what Mervier had just revealed about this amazing artefact, and her last comment, she sensed that she was about to be thrust into another dangerous adventure.

But one that she could properly prepare for. No deceptive stragglers this time, like Isaac Kane, pulling the strings from the shadows. She trusted Nicole.

"Right, let's get down to business, this is my plan," Mervier said, with a sense of determination.

CHAPTER 11

"WE MAY HAVE SOMETHING BETTER"

Keyes Residence

Newcastle-upon-Tyne

Northumberland

10.00pm

Situated on the outer city limits was the lavish palatial home of Vincent Keyes. The flat-roofed private complex looked like a scaled-down version of his business centre.

He had a few acres of land that consisted of a futuristic two-floor mansion that overlooked the twinkling city in the horizon. Adjoining the main household was the pool house, and another structure that was his gymnasium. A smaller building was adjacent to the pool house, which was an equally impressive guest house.

Vincent Keyes was walking around his main living room in his comfortable lounge top and shorts. A huge flat screen that looked like a mini cinema was attached to the large wall. It loomed over the numerous couches and chairs.

The CEO was on his mobile, and in the process of having a discussion with his PA, Vanessa. His mounted television was displaying the latest news on a satellite network. The sound was muted, but the images on the screen were reporters and spokespeople talking about the latest killings in York, and the police were announcing that two local youths were still missing from Sunday night.

Keyes grinned, as he quite rightfully knew, that the two 'missing' boys were, in fact, now statues. Victims of a mystifying witch that he fully intended to catch, and the wondrous weapon that she wielded.

"Like I said, Vanessa. The police believe that one of our scientists may have gone rogue, and I don't know, taken one of our prototypes and gone on a goddamn rampage, but we know that's not true. I wouldn't worry about it. Anyway, I am cooperating. I let the tenacious detective have access to our personnel files. She'll uncover nothing useful. Let them fumble around in their investigation. I've got her tagged anyway."

He looked up at the screen, and it looked like the police were keeping the truth under wraps. Keyes was just waiting for a glimmer of a break-through to pursue his latest project.

"Now, what are the results of Dr. Delanski's analysis on the bident?" he asked, picking up a mini-basketball, and shooting it through the hoop that was affixed to the side wall.

"Truly astonishing, Mr Keyes. He said that the metal is of an unknown origin, neither steel, tungsten, titanium, nor anything else, nothing on the periodic table; The shaft, however, is mainly forged of bronze," Vanessa replied. He detected by her tone, that she was bewildered.

"Fascinating, indeed, but it's clearly not indestructible as we found shards of the material at the excavation site," Keyes added.

"It has baffled the lab team. But Delasnki believes he can possibly reverse-engineer, and modify the spear, and create something from the shards. What he has in mind are just pre-conceptual ideas. Could take some time. This is the strangest and most powerful metal that we have encountered. A lot more research needs to be done."

"Understood. Let's not pressure our good doctor, I'm sure he will come up with some ingenious creation, but we'll put that in the bag for now, as we may have something better soon," Keyes teased gleefully

"Really?" Vanessa asked, quite inquisitively.

"One step at a time, Vanessa." He threw the ball again through the hoop and switched off the flatscreen with the remote control. He went over to his ultra-modern ensuite kitchen, opened his fridge, and took out a bottle of Budweiser.

"In the meantime, do an inventory check of all our meta-bionics, and check if any of them are missing, just as a precaution. I've got a call coming through."

"Will do. Goodnight Mr Keyes," Vanessa replied.

Keyes ended the current call and tapped the screen to receive the incoming one.

It was Matheson.

"Miles, I have been waiting anxiously."

"Well, you probably know where I am anyway," Matheson started.

Keyes picked up a gadget from one of his tables, as he swigged back some lager. It was another tracker device, and it beeped. He liked to keep tabs on his own agents as well and had managed to bug Matheson's Range Rover. Keyes knew that Matheson wasn't stupid, but he did it for that extra layer of security, and Matheson's safety in case he ran into trouble.

"What's the update?"

"As suspected, your detective has been at Ophelia Winter's residence now, for a good hour at least." Keyes could sense Matheson's exasperation. He clearly didn't want to be there.

"That's a good sign."

"It could be a social visit. Look Vincent, we could be just chasing shadows here," Matheson moaned.

"This actually could all fall into our lap, with a bit of luck."

"I dislike spying on one of my own clients."

"A little contradictory in terms, coming from an ex-spy, wouldn't you say, Miles?"

"I feel that we're wasting our time. That's all. I could get compromised here. How long do you need me to hang here?"

"As long as it takes."

"For crying out loud," Matheson cursed.

"I'm prepared to throw in another quarter of a million for your committed work on this."

"I'll report back when I have something to report," Matheson said begrudgingly, before hanging up.

Keyes put his mobile down and picked up the basketball. He tossed it through the hoop one last time. With a satisfied smile, he took another swig of his beverage, and gulped it down.

"That's my boy."

CHAPTER 12

AN INTREPID TRIO

Ophelia placed the stone tablet gently in bubble wrap. Whilst she was wrapping it, she noticed that the wide eyes of Medusa's inscribed face were depressed into the stone. The eyes looked back at her – she felt a chill, like the hag-like face was somehow warning her. Shrugging it off, Ophelia slid it carefully inside the internal sleeve compartment of her small suitcase.

Mervier had devised an interesting plan which would only be kept between the three women at this stage, as this was completely unofficial.

Madison needed clarity, and walked in with her suitcase, as she had planned to stay the night anyway. She had another glass of wine in her hand.

"So, you want us to stick to our original plans, and attend the gala, but with you in tow?" the young woman asked.

"Right, the invitation said you are permitted up to three guests. This is a great chance to find out what is really going on here," Mervier said.

"I'm sure the countess is expecting professionals in our field," Ophelia interrupted, pointing to herself and Madison.

"Yeah, if the police intervened at this stage, it could prove catastrophic. Look what happened at the museum, even if we're wrong about this woman, and I think we are, which I hasten to add, it would be humiliating. I don't think she would admit police, off duty or not, even if she is guilty," Madison said with concern, "And we don't want a load of blues and twos storming in."

"Don't you think we haven't learnt since then? We need to keep this low-key. Covert. You will be safe, and if you are concerned over your own security, and feel more comfortable, you could reach out to your mercenary buddies, and they can monitor you from afar. If the shit hits the fan, then they can bail us out of there. But if you do that, the numbers must be a token strength. Three or four at the most, not a whole platoon, we don't know what we're dealing with yet, apart from what I've already collated," Mervier advised.

"The idea entered my mind only as a precaution," Ophelia agreed.

"What guise would you play, Nicole?" Madison asked.

"I could be one of your archaeological crew. No biggy. It's not the first time I've done undercover work, girls."

"And if our hosts or other guests ask you a difficult question about our vocation, or enquire about your line of expertise, you can't just impersonate a generic archaeologist, Nicole, they'll twig straight away, especially if they're experts themselves," Ophelia explained. She had a point.

"Fine, then I'll be your chief of security, or something, how's that?"

"That would explain her demeanour," Madison said, turning to Ophelia. "No offence, Nicole."

Mervier just grinned, and nodded.

"This could all amount to nothing, but basically, treat it like one of your field trips, a harmless investigation. Like you said, you would like some answers of your own, from the wisdom of this woman. I, on the other hand, want answers too. It's a perfect ploy."

"Feels like you're using us," Madison said. Ophelia could second that, but deep down, knew wholeheartedly this needed to be investigated.

"I'm sorry if it appears like that, or if I'm gatecrashing on your invite. We do have a hidden agenda. And so might she. But look at it like this, ladies, we're gathering intel, we're not going in there hard and heavy." Mervier tried to reassure them.

"Basically, an undercover operation, she's either luring us in, and we're taking the bait, or she's inviting the cat to the pigeon, without realising," Ophelia added.

"Hopefully the latter, either way, we'll get some answers," Mervier responded stoically.

"Welcome to my expedition, detective," Ophelia smiled reluctantly.

They shook hands. Madison placed her hand on top of their interlocked handshake, as if they were performing a mudra, or an oath.

A sisterhood.

"I am looking forward to working with you both, and thank you, let's finish this one together," Mervier said fittingly, sharing this bonding and heart-warming moment of solidarity.

Outside, further down on the hillside slopes, Matheson was still parked on the roadside verge. He felt he was inconspicuous, as there were a few vehicles parked on several verges on the road that snaked to the top, which were most likely visitors or friends of the small local community in the area.

He nearly jumped out of the seat when his mobile buzzed.

"Shit," he cussed, as he saw the caller ID. It was Ophelia.

Surely, he couldn't have been rumbled, he thought. He was well out of sight of her property, as he could barely see beyond the crest of the hill where she lived. He had no choice. He answered it.

"Hey, Ophelia."

"Miles, sorry for the late call, are you okay?" Ophelia's voice said. She didn't sound unusual.

"Er, yeah. I'm good, thanks. What's up?"

"Are you in the area?"

His insecurities went into overdrive. Was this a test? She may have seen him, or Mervier may have noticed him following her. His mind raced, but he couldn't pause for too long.

"Kind of," he answered, looking around at his surroundings. He felt guilty as it was, spying on his friend. "Are you alright?"

"Yeah. I know this is a bit sudden, but you guys are superb at scrambling fast."

Matheson was very curious, but surmised that this could be the break-through Keyes was hoping for.

"What's going on?" Matheson asked.

At that point, he noticed the tracker buzz to life on his advanced GPS gadget. The lights on Mervier's, Mercedes were seen casting a bright glow from over the ridge line on the hill, and her car appeared from the corner. He mimed another profanity, as he scootched low into his seat, whilst pressing the mobile to his ear.

"I need you and the team, again." Ophelia got to the point.

Matheson had to contain his elation at this news, as the detective's car was descending the hill at 20 mph. Luckily, it was dark, as her lights got closer and closer. He shuffled in his seat, and ducked right down, over the gear stick, and half lay on the passenger seat, completely hidden from view.

"That's great. What's the job?"

Mervier's car ambled past the verge where he was parked, but showed no signs of slowing down or stopping. He peered up, and looked behind his seat. The Mercedes had turned right, and drove out of sight. He exhaled a sigh of relief.

"It's a strange one."

"What's new these days?" he chuckled. He could relax, knowing Mervier was gone, and Ophelia didn't seem aware of his presence.

"Covert surveillance."

"Okay," was all he said, frowning. Clearly, Mervier's visit was a productive one, and already, she and Ophelia were making plans. Fortunately, the Black Knight Syndicate would possibly be a part of that.

This had certainly come on to his lap. He was still in turmoil about what to do, as the tracker was beeping farther and farther away. Should he be following his quarry? Or maintain his position. He started his vehicle, and made a U-turn off the verge, then drove in the same direction as the detective. After all, that was his current assignment.

"When for?"

"Friday afternoon."

"This Friday?" Matheson asked, noting that it was Wednesday night.

"Yes. Again, sorry about the short notice. We can go into details later, but this assignment is kind of twofold. But I just need a small surveillance team, no more than four, to monitor us as we visit a certain place."

"Okay. Location?"

"Ravenscliff Castle. Near Minehead. Somerset."

Matheson drove down the hill, and managed to see Mervier's car reach the bottom, and head towards the borders of the small village. He kept a reasonable distance, and followed.

"Got that, we'll get a team together. I'm on the road at the moment, but we'll touch base tomorrow, Ophelia."

"Great. Again, sorry for the short notice. You know me."

"It's okay, I'll get Spears on this too. He's malingered for too long, since the island," Matheson said, smiling.

"Thank you, Miles. It's much appreciated, as always." Her words were soft, sincere and true. This wrenched Matheson's heart but at least he would be there with her, in allegiance, rather than playing the cloak and dagger routine, against the very ones that trusted him.

Keyes, however, would have his own agenda that would utilise the syndicate, and possibly betray Ophelia. He had to put that thought out of his head, and concentrate on the job ahead.

"It's always a pleasure. You take care Ophelia. I'll contact you tomorrow."

"Goodnight, Miles."

The call ended, and Matheson drove into the night. His face was emotionally torn.

He had to update Keyes.

The Black Knight Syndicate were specially requested again. But, he wondered, on whose side, this time?

CHAPTER 13

THE LAB

It was the following day, inside Legionshields' top-secret laboratory, located on the sublevels. Half a dozen scientists and engineers were in their assigned sectors of work, conducting a variety of experiments on the metal shards from the broken bident, and examining endless amounts of analytical data from their work stations.

Keyes was holding the Bident of Hades in his hands, like a great trophy. It had undergone numerous inspections and experimental tests during the last twenty-four hours.

Dr Delasnki was in the process of compiling some results from his computer. A 3D schematic was featured on the screen that displayed a technical read-out of the relic, along with scrolls of scientific data.

"The metal is out of this world, Mr Keyes. We took a sample, and attempted to melt it. Tungsten is the strongest known metal, as you know, and it is used a fair bit in our hardware. Its highest melting point is 6,192 degrees Fahrenheit. It took treble that to have an effect on the sample."

"Come again?" Keyes placed the bident down on the table, with a sense of disbelief.

"Basically, as hot as molten lava. 18.5 thousand degrees Fahrenheit."

"Incredible, as if it was forged from the depths of hell, itself," Keyes looked transfixed at the data.

"Our technology does not go to the extremes of such testing, but it did take some time to smelt into liquidated form, inside the mega-furnace."

"But can we work from that now? It's not indestructible."

"Not far from it though, but we can move forward, and apply some upgrades, so to speak," Delanski replied. Keyes grinned. His face was elated.

The CEO patted the chief scientist on the shoulder.

"I'll leave it in your good hands, doctor."

Keyes sat down and looked at a nearby computer, accessing it with his own passwords. A classified file appeared on the screen that displayed many sub-documents. He typed in additional passwords. A small list of clients came up.

He glossed over them briefly. It was literally a rogue's gallery of wealthy private customers that consisted of contractors, secret societies, and agencies. The face of an African tribal warlord appeared, followed by a Central American revolutionary group. Each one had an inventory of previous orders that ranged from smaller melee devices, to the most advanced weapons systems.

Keyes scrolled down and noticed the last one – Isaac Kane, from the Institute of Historical Research. The cover for his clandestine sect, the Order of the Crimson Claw. Now, vanquished.

"Well, Mr Kane, weren't you a naughty boy?" he said, looking at the screen.

Keyes looked at the special equipment that Isaac Kane had previously contracted Legionshield to manufacture and distribute for him, and his sinister cult.

Blue-prints of crimson gauntlets, all with their assorted deadly refinements: reinforced chest plate armour, half-face armoured masks, and surgical sharp blades, were displayed on the screen in front of him.

At that moment, Vanessa and Hugo approached him. She looked over his shoulder, and saw Keyes typing in more commands on his keyboard. He then permanently deleted the entire file.

"So, nobody can trace this stuff back to us," Keyes said.

"He was one of our wealthier clients," Vanessa added.

"All good things must come to an end, Vanessa. Shame, but he got a little too ambitious in his cause. Anyway, we've earned enough from him." Keyes switched off his computer, and turned around in his chair.

"What is it?"

"We've done a full check of our powered bionics, they are all accounted for, sir," his PA reported, checking the log entries on her digital tablet. He acknowledged her with a nod.

"So, we're left with how to explain our vigilante's superhuman strength and agility? Perhaps a rival firm?"

"We have well-paid inside agents within the ranks of our competitors. We would know about it," Vanessa said confidently.

"Okay, then a woman of incredible athleticism, or a martial arts master? I don't know, whatever she is, she's inhuman," Keyes pondered.

"Not physically possible, even drug enhancers couldn't have the effect of what you described."

"And that is why this woman is just as valuable to us, as well as the mace. I would love to get into her DNA," Keyes muttered. His eyes stared into space. He was fully immersed in his scheme.

"What's the plan, sir?"

"Matheson reported last night, and as I anticipated, the detective is on to something, and has joined forces with a notable expert in this field to investigate. We also have a location," Keyes replied.

"What would you like us to do?" Vanessa asked, keen to be involved with this new project.

"I have extended every resource that Matheson requires. He is now working with this expert, Dr Ophelia Winters, and has arranged a small team of his mercs to undertake the necessary objectives," Keyes said.

"Very well," she answered.

"In the meantime, we will keep a close eye on things from our side. I'll make the arrangements," Keyes added.

"Can you trust the Black Knights?" Hugo asked, "I could deal with this."

"I'm sure you could, Hugo. But we'll let Matheson's men do the dirty work, if and when the moment arises. That's what they're paid to do. Besides, this curator trusts them."

"Yes sir."

"Don't worry my friend, I will have other tasks for you," Keyes assured.

It was now time to put his plan into effect.

PART TWO

CHAPTER 14

RAVENSCLIFF CASTLE

Coast of Somerset
Friday 8th May.
6.00pm

A small convoy of three vehicles were travelling down the winding road of the beautiful southwestern countryside of England.

They were inland, but only a mile away from the high cliffs of the Somerset coastline, and getting closer to their destination.

There was a tranquil peacefulness in the evening air during the final part of the long five-hour drive from York. The single road was surrounded either side by lush fields and patchy woodland areas, as they ventured on.

The looming turrets of a keep could be seen in the near distance.

The procession was led by Ophelia Winters, who was driving her classic and beloved racing green Morris Minor. Madison was seated next to her, admiring the view of the endless rural landscape. Behind them was a black Mercedes, driven by Mervier.

A little further back, bringing up the rear, was the last vehicle in the motorcade. A dark khaki Land Rover Defender. Matheson was driving, and he felt a little better in his mind that he was accompanying Ophelia on her latest expedition, rather than deceivingly tracking and spying on her.

Sitting in the passenger seat was Nathan Spears, with his elbow sticking out of the open window, taking in the sights, but really looking for any signs of habitation. The place was well and truly remote. He had taken on the assignment with no second thoughts, and even though he had almost fully recovered from the severe wounds he sustained on Katamarai island three weeks ago, he was deemed combat efficient, and fit for duty.

Seated behind them was a clean-shaven male of mixed race. Mohammed Straker, a former marine commando, who had recently retired from the armed forces. He was now a member of the newly formed Group Alpha, from the Black Knight Syndicate. Next to him was a long-time member and survivor of the last engagement on the Greek island – Ashley Fox. He was controlling a remote control, and a small laptop was resting on his legs.

Stacks of holdalls and equipment were behind them in the spacious rear compartment and boot of their Defender.

All the mercenaries were wearing black combat fatigues, and woodland-camouflaged tactical vests.

Matheson had briefed his men when they all rendezvoused at Ophelia's yesterday, and essentially told them it was a surveillance operation, and to be on stand-by for an immediate rescue and evac, should the women get into any physical danger, from foes that were unknown at this time.

He did declare and openly admit Legionshield's interests, but as far as his team were aware, they just had to keep an eye on things from a concealed point, and stay in comms. This was already arranged by Spears, as he had supplied all three women with the latest covert technology, such as hidden earpieces, and tiny voice transmitters concealed in various pieces of jewellery that the ladies were wearing – courtesy of Legionshield Industries.

"There's a good OP coming up," Fox advised, OP meaning 'Observation Post'. He looked down at the satellite map section on his laptop. A smaller screen also displayed a live aerial shot that his overhead drone was transmitting back to him.

High in the sky, a couple of hundred meters away from the lead vehicle, the almost invisible and quiet drone flew towards a dense thicket of trees and bushes that was the size of a football pitch. Very close to that was an old ruin of a long-abandoned lighthouse.

Another one of Legionshield's contributions to the expedition, with advanced stealth technology and concealed weapons systems.

"Alright ladies, the castle is just over that ridge," Spears spoke into the radio transmitter attached to his vest. "We're going to divert here, and set up our position."

"Do you mean where the lighthouse is?" he heard Ophelia's voice through his headset.

He smiled to himself. He was happy, he was working with her again, and this time, more preparations had been put in. However, the initial briefing was quick and bullet-pointed, and they still knew that they were heading into the relative unknown. But they had prepared the best they could, under the circumstances.

"That's correct, good to see the comms still work. Just don't remove your jewellery, or cover them," Spears said.

"The range and signal should be good, the castle is only two hundred meters from the OP, Ophelia," Fox added, as he spoke into his transmitter.

"Well, I guess we'll find out once we're in there," Ophelia replied.

"We've got you tracked, anyway, like Spears said, don't remove your pendants, that includes you, detective," Fox advised again.

"Roger that, guys, just don't shoot my car to shit, this time, if it goes tits up!" Mervier responded from the vehicle in front of them. This created a few grins from the mercs.

"Well, don't get in our way, this time," Fox replied, chuckling to himself.

"Okay, we're coming up to the turning, be careful, ladies," Matheson announced, as the first two vehicles turned right at the fork in the road.

The Defender, immediately swerved left, came off the road, and drove past the dilapidated ruins of what used to be a lighthouse. The vehicle made its way past the small clearing, and disappeared into the woodland area.

Out of sight.

Meanwhile, Ophelia and Madison continued on the single narrow road, and onto the rocky terrain. They were now at least 200ft above sea-level, on the coastal cliffs, and started to approach the brooding-looking 12th-century fortress ahead, that was perched on the precipice of the crags. The Mercedes followed close behind.

Ravenscliff Castle was a foreboding sight as they drove through the open mediaeval gothic barbican, and into the outer courtyard that was surrounded by an old stone curtain that was 20 feet high. The circular keep that was situated at the back of the domain, rose 80 feet into the air, and had a majestic, yet eerie presence.

The land was only a few acres, but impressive, nonetheless. The women looked apprehensive but were awe-struck by the architecture.

"This is it," Ophelia said, as she slowly drove up to the gatehouse portcullis which led to the inner courtyard. The portcullis was open.

"Already waiting for us," Madison said.

"Where are the other vehicles?" Ophelia noted, as she drove through the iron portcullis, and noticed the outer courtyard, devoid of any other transport.

The large open-aired area of the castle grounds was enclosed by more grey walls and was protected by a dozen hideous-looking gargoyles. Their grotesque stone faces were looking down at and across the vacant courtyard. Each one was inside its own cavity, and appeared to be eight foot in height. The terrifying mythological statues seemed to have been constructed only a few feet from the base of the wall, and in different poses. Some were crouching, huddled, proudly upright, or ready to pounce.

They gave Madison the chills as the Morris Minor did a full circle in the courtyard, seeing if there was any other driveway on either side of the keep, that towered in front of them.

"Well, this doesn't look haunted, at all!" Madison exclaimed sarcastically.

"There's no one here. Unless, we're early," Ophelia said, logically. Madison checked her wristwatch. It was 6.15pm.

"The invite's not until eight," Madison reminded them both.

"Either way, I would have thought, the guests would arrive early to get refreshed, look around and stretch their legs," Ophelia stated. She stopped the car, and switched off the engine. Mervier pulled up beside her, and did the same.

The detective stepped out of her vehicle, and walked over the pebbled and cobbled-stoned surface to Ophelia's Morris Minor. Ophelia raised her eyebrows, as they both looked around at their new environment.

There was a barren stillness that enveloped them. Seagulls that squawked in the air seemed to be the only sign of life. The distant sound of waves crashing into the sea cliffs was also heard. They resonated from far below, behind the keep. This added to the feeling of isolation.

The two archaeologists stepped out of the car. Madison went over to the boot of the car to collect their small overnight suitcases. Both were wearing smart but comfortable casual summer clothes.

"Well, I guess this is a good time to check our comms," Mervier suggested, quietly. Their voices did seem to echo within the enclosed walls of the courtyard.

"You receiving guys?" Ophelia said, speaking. Her small flamingo locket around her neck, had a mini-transmitter and body-cam inside. The small eye had been hollowed out for the miniature lens. There was an unnerving pause. Ophelia examined the surrounding walls. She felt that she was being watched, and not just by the mercs.

Then a male voice reassured her, from over the hills.

"Loud and clear, Ophelia," Spears replied.

"Thank you!" Ophelia replied, with a clear hint of annoyance.

"Just setting up our den, the drone's going to do a quick discreet fly-by." Fox's voice was heard.

Only moments passed, until the drone swooped in overhead, and stayed at a good height to avoid detection. It banked and flew above the courtyard, did a quick circuit, but stayed away from the keep and its arrow slits.

"I've got you," Fox said through Ophelia's covert earpiece. The device had been inserted into her left ear, and was very well concealed under her brown shoulder-length hair that covered them.

Then, the large door of the keep opened up.

Two women emerged from the arched door and approached the newly arrived guests. The drone silently ascended, and kept hovering above. The women didn't seem to notice, fortunately. Ophelia's heart was pounding. She didn't want this to be over before it had begun, as the result of poor piloting, from the mercs, or worse still, getting caught spying on their hosts.

The two women graciously reached their three guests, and both performed a dainty curtsey. They were tanned, and wore elegant matching, white sleeveless blouses, and baggy jade green harem bottoms, with white Grecian sandals.

"Welcome to Ravenscliff castle, ladies," the first woman said, with a Greek lilt in her tone.

"Thank you. I am Dr Ophelia Winters, this is my assistant, Madison Trent, and my chief of security, Nicole." Ophelia smiled, and was reciprocated by the two women. They both had dark hair, and appeared in their late twenties or early thirties.

"You honour us with your presence, ladies," the second woman said, as if this was scripted, but they were very welcoming and charming. Madison noted that they had not introduced themselves personally.

"I'm sorry, and who are you?" Madison asked, smiling, trying not to be rude. She studied their faces closely, but couldn't recognise them.

"We are humble servants to the countess. Please, follow us, and we will introduce you to her, she has been eagerly looking forward to seeing you." The first woman spoke, addressing all of them.

Mervier thought, 'I bet she has, and I too.' But she remained silent, offered the two Greek women a courteous smile, and continued to let Ophelia take the lead.

"Thank you. By all means, lead on, the pleasure is all ours," said Ophelia politely.

The servants bowed respectfully and gestured to the three women to follow them into the castle keep. They entered, and the door was closed behind them with a daunting shudder.

The portcullis then immediately slammed down behind them, sealing off the courtyard from the outside.

CHAPTER 15

THE DEN

The mercenaries had quickly established their observation position, within the dense trees and foliage of the woodland thicket.

It had a good clear view of the castle barbican, 300 metres away from their concealed den. The Defender had been covered by military netting, and parked within the perimeter of the thicket.

The men had set up a tripod with a small optical scanner, which kept monitoring the castle exteriors. This was manned by Straker. Meanwhile, Fox was sitting next to him controlling the state-of-the-art drone. Both of them were on the edge of the woodlands.

Spears and Matheson were organising other equipment from the Defender, which included G-36 carbine rifles, and ration packs.

"Well, they're in," Fox reported, "Signal's still good." The mercenary piloted the drone back to the camp, after collating as much data as he could from the castle and its surroundings.

Matheson and Spears joined the others.

"Portcullis came down pretty sharpish," Straker added. He looked through the scope of the scanner, and enhanced the image of the ominous criss-cross iron gates that had slammed shut.

"The barbican and the walls are roughly 30 feet high. The 'cullis itself looks like iron. Those gaps appear to be less than half a square meter wide, too small to slip through," Straker continued.

"Well, I didn't expect a portcullis to be easily breached, Straker," Matheson replied as he pulled out a pair of binoculars, and took a glimpse of it.

"What about security, Fox?" Spears turned to his longest-serving associate. Fox landed the drone and deactivated its power.

"The drone circled the castle twice and I couldn't see any surveillance cameras, mounted defences, or any other point of access except for the barbican, there's only the main gate that leads into the keep, that's it," Fox reported.

"For a member of the peerage, she doesn't seem to be overly concerned with security," Matheson voiced an opinion.

"The place looks well-fortified as it is," Spears looked over the shoulder of Straker.

The former marine was analysing all the data from his scanner, as technical schematics of the castle were displayed on his screen, which were transmitted from the drone, as well as his own observations.

"In case we need to breach, we have sufficient payload on the drone to blast through," Fox advised.

"Well, there goes stealth and secrecy," Straker said.

"Could we set up closer?" Spears, suggested.

"This is the only area that offers some form of concealment," Matheson replied, "Besides, just because we couldn't detect any cameras from the outside, doesn't mean there are any others elsewhere that we haven't seen."

Matheson couldn't risk compromising the team at this early stage.

"I'm sure the girls will let us know anything of interest from the interior," Spears, mentioned. The women were the eyes and ears.

"Okay, Straker switch to the covert body-cams," Matheson instructed.

Straker controlled the small laptop in front of him, and the screen flickered to life. Three images appeared. One from each of the women. They had infiltrated the castle.

The initial plan had been well-prepared. Mervier, Madison, and Ophelia had selected random objects to wear. Clear, live-feed images from their concealed mini-hidden cameras, were sent back to Straker's equipment.

"They're just in the grand foyer. All images are clear," Straker reported.

Straker's computer screen was divided into four sections. One displayed a sequence of algorithms, various data, as well as a tracker location. The other three were the points of view from each body-camera that were attached to the women, with their name featured above on the screen.

The mercs were observing the image via Ophelia's flamingo locket. A similar image was coming from Madison's broch on her lapel, but from a slightly different angle. They were following the two Greek servants into a large gothic entrance hall, that had great mediaeval pillars, and flanks of flame torches, that flickered in the darkness, illuminating the cavities of the walls.

It was only Mervier who was trying to feed them as much information as she could. The detective knew surveillance all too well, and was surreptitiously turning her head and shoulders, quite frequently. She was wearing a necklace with a crucifix pendant. The centre of the pendant had a diamond in the centre which was, in fact, the lens of the secret covert camera.

Mervier's images were made up of a 360-degree view of the entrance hall. This included the old great oak entrance door behind them. It had been secured by a large wooden beam that was placed across the door by the servants. Above that, there were no cameras. To her left and right were beautiful tapestries, and portraits of many historical figures from times past. Most likely the family's ancestors.

"Okay, we got a good view, ladies. Don't respond to this, but I just thought I'd let you know that the portcullis came down the moment you entered, don't worry, it is old iron. We got the tech to penetrate it, if required." Straker reported, "You're all doing well."

Straker was tasked with directing and updating the three women during their activities from inside the castle. The signal then experienced a slight distortion due to the stonework, but returned to clear images. The mercs kept observing.

CHAPTER 16

THE COUNTESS

Ophelia gave a momentary look of worry after Straker mentioned the portcullis, but with the knowledge of the mercenaries, maintaining good coverage of their movements from the outside, gave her some reassurance.

Meanwhile, Mervier came up to the side of Ophelia, and discreetly winked at her, reinforcing that fact. Simultaneously, the two servants stopped in their tracks at the foot of a grand stone staircase that led to an upper balcony, fifteen feet above where they were standing.

A large coat of arms was draped over the balcony. Above that, was a luxurious, huge black iron candelabra, containing countless lit candles, that illuminated the balcony – revealing the glamorous woman.

Countess Dumas.

"Welcome to Ravenscliff, ladies. I have eagerly awaited your presence, thank you for accepting my invitation," spoke the countess softly, as she looked down at her guests.

The attractive and tanned European lady gracefully made her way down the stone steps, and smiled pleasantly. Her long, silky straight black hair was worn in a pony-tail. The countess was wearing a cream off-the-shoulder summer blouse and a white long-split skirt that emphasised her toned thighs.

She appeared to be in her late forties, and carried herself with much elegance and style, as she reached the bottom of the staircase.

"I am Countess Dumas, it is an honour to finally meet you, Dr Winters." The sophisticated woman looked Mediterranean. Now she was face to face with her guests, and had a hint of a Greek accent, with traces of French.

Ophelia smiled and ensured that her locket was facing the direct line of sight of her host. She knew the mercs would be continuing their observation of the entire area, and this lady. The curator didn't know the correct protocol, but she offered a respectful bow and a subtle half-curtsy. She also noticed that the countess was wearing shaded eyewear. They could see her beautifully shaped eyes, but couldn't identify their colour.

"Please, call me Ophelia, Countess. It's a pleasure to meet you, thank you for your kind invitation," Ophelia said. They shook hands. The host's hand felt warm, soft and slender.

"And, you may call me Elina," The countess said warmly, "I'm quite out of touch with all the formalities these days."

"That's alright, may I introduce you to my lovely assistant, Madison Trent?" Ophelia gestured to the young blond person that stood beside her.

Elina gently shook Madison's hand, and smiled at her. Her gaze lasted a couple of seconds, which made Madison feel a little uncomfortable, as if the countess was looking deep into her mind. After, what seemed longer than normal, Elina spoke to the young archaeologist.

"A pleasure, my dear Madison."

There was a pause.

Madison could hear the countess' voice in her head, as if she was telepathically speaking to her. The young woman seemed transfixed. Lost in her host's eyes. It was like she was in a hypnotic trance.

"Madison?" Ophelia said, breaking her protégé out from her unusual silent gaze.

Madison blinked and then tried to compose herself, like she had been suddenly disturbed from a day-dream – this also broke Elina's concentration, as she glanced sharply at Ophelia.

"Oh, I am terribly sorry, I am very pleased to meet you, Elina," Madison said, mildly embarrassed. Ophelia noted this strange behaviour of her assistant, as this was very unlike her usual bubbly self.

Elina then turned to Mervier, who appeared confident.

"And, this is my security chief, Nicole Mervier," Ophelia said.

The two women shook hands.

"Security?" Elina raised her brow, surprised, but retaining her smile.

"I was involved in a horrific incident a few weeks ago, so I really don't go anywhere without my personal protection. I hope that is alright," Ophelia explained.

"Of course it is, and I am very sorry to hear that. Well, I can assure you that you are all perfectly safe here on the cliffs, we are very isolated, and away from the hustle and bustle of Somerset's more disconcerting areas, which are very few, I hasten to add," Elina replied.

"It's just precautionary," Mervier said, smiling genuinely. She tried to focus on the woman's diamond-shaped jawline, but the countess disrupted her concentration.

"Nicole Mervier. French descent?" Elina said.

"Yes actually, from my mother's side," the detective answered honestly.

"Ah, me too. Well, Greek-French, I kept her name after my husband died a few years ago, as you can probably detect from my unusual accent," Elina, declared.

After the pleasantries were completed, the two servants stepped forward, and Elina acknowledged them both.

"My dedicated servants are here to tend to your needs, and will escort you to your quarters. I am sure you will find them to your satisfaction, they are on the keep's top levels, and have beautiful sea-views over the cliffs," Elina, conveyed to her guests, like a proud hotelier.

"Thank you, tell me, what time are the other guests arriving?" Ophelia asked.

"They will be here soon. You are quite early," Elina responded, as she nodded to her servants.

"Oh, I thought I heard the portcullis close when we entered, and we didn't see any other vehicles, or yours for that matter," Mervier said, which slightly annoyed Ophelia. They had just entered the castle, and the detective was playing – detective.

"You have very conscientious security, Ophelia, I can understand why you hired her," Elina said, "But, like I said, you are at no risk of harm here, in my sanctuary."

"I appreciate that," Ophelia said, "Nicole can be quite tenacious."

"I'm sorry, I guess I notice these things, I don't mean to be rude." Mervier butted in apologetically.

"No need to apologise. You are just doing your job, I suppose. I do not drive, and my servants live here with me, in the castle. Once a month, we get supplies delivered from town. We are very self-sufficient here, the portcullis was lowered to prevent curious tourists from dropping in," Elina explained. "It happens from time to time."

"Oh, okay. I didn't know you received visitors, I didn't even know that this place existed, to be honest," Ophelia admitted.

"Not many do," was Elina's response with a quaint smile. "Ladies, I am sure you have many questions, and I do apologise for the short notice. All will be revealed soon, I would just like to say that this will be a truly wonderful time for us, to share our stories and knowledge in our unique field of study." Elina bowed and the servants beckoned the three guests to the staircase that led to the magnificent balcony, and its upper levels.

"Thank you for your hospitality," Ophelia finally said, as she started to follow the obedient servants.

"You are welcome, Ophelia. Ladies, the banquet commences at eight o'clock, in the grand hall. My servants will collect you fifteen minutes beforehand. In the meantime, enjoy your stay here at Ravenscliff."

Elina then turned around and headed towards a large archway at the bottom of the entrance hall, passing many statues in the process.

The three guests were escorted up on the balcony, and as they peered to their left, they saw the stone floor ascend higher, which led to the guest accommodation levels. Ophelia was still taking in the grandeur of the gothic interior as she followed the Greek servants.

They were careful not to communicate with each other just yet, as Elina's girls were only a few feet ahead of them. But their body-cams were getting a lot of good and useful imagery of the castle's internal lay-out for the mercenaries, so far.

Meanwhile, the countess glanced upwards as her guests disappeared around the corner of the high balcony. She grinned deviously. She now had them.

She turned to a portrait of a snake-haired woman, dressed in beautiful ancient Greek robes. An exotic gold necklace was hung across her neck, with a mantled green amulet in the centre. The face was of a ravishing beauty that looked in her early twenties. It was a glamorous depiction of the mythological gorgon – Medusa.

"It won't be long now, mother," the countess uttered.

CHAPTER 17

THE QUARTERS

The evening was gradually getting darker, and Ophelia made her way to the exterior stone balcony of her spacious and dimly lit room.

A gentle breeze blew through her hair, as she stood on the balcony. She had a stunning panoramic view of the Bristol Channel, which was an inlet of the Atlantic Ocean.

Below her was a sheer 200-foot drop to the base of the sea cliffs. On either side of the balcony were two more balconies that jutted out from their respective rooms.

Ophelia inhaled the sea air deeply. The evening skies were dramatic, as the sun started to disappear. It, cast warm hues of orange and pink shades in the horizon. This evoked a sense of calm, and the curator felt soothed by its embrace.

She observed further out to sea, from her high vantage point, and saw a fishing trawler, at least two miles off-shore slowly making a pass across the channel. She felt alone, even though she knew her two associates were with her, inside this eerie castle. Ophelia kept reminding herself that she was still being monitored by her surveillance squad.

A knock on her large wooden door disturbed her from her thoughts, and she turned around and entered her castle room.

The interior of the castle guest room was traditional, but looked haunting. It was slightly modernised to accommodate a handful of electrical amenities that had been installed. A lamp next to her four-poster king-sized bed was already switched on, and it irradiated an ambient orange light within her quarters. Opposite it, was a small ante-room that was converted into an en-suite bathroom.

"Come in," Ophelia said, making her way over to the door.

Both Madison and Mervier entered, closing the door behind them, with a whining screech.

The servants had left a few minutes ago, and after the women had surveyed their rooms, decided to meet up in Ophelia's.

"Lovely rooms," Mervier said, looking around. Her quarters were exactly the same as the others, and she glanced at the balcony that overlooked the ocean, "Apart from the only fire escape," she added sarcastically, "Also, our mobiles still have no signal. No surprises."

Madison seemed somewhat hazy and slouched onto Ophelia's bed. Ophelia turned to the detective.

"I guess we will wait until the countess's servants come for us," the curator said.

"It's best we don't start snooping around yet, keep up the guise of guests. I've scanned our rooms. Nothing untoward," Mervier whispered, as she brought out from her jacket a small gadget, and started waving it over various ornaments, the mantle clock, paintings and the lamp.

"Checking for bugs?" Ophelia asked. Mervier brought her finger to her own lips, indicating to Ophelia to soften her voice.

She understood, and nodded. Mervier continued a sweep of the room, and nothing bleeped on her detector. As she bent over a dressing table chair, her coat parted, and Ophelia could see nestled on the side of her belt, a holstered pistol. She hoped the servants or the countess wouldn't notice earlier.

"Madison, now we're alone, did you recognise her, any of them?" Mervier whispered as she carried on with her room check.

Madison shook her head, a little fazed. Ophelia noted this, and unzipped her suitcase, bringing out an elegant black evening dress. She hung this over a peg on the wall, as there was no wardrobe.

"Are you alright, Mads?" Ophelia asked, a little concerned. Ever since the introductions, the young archaeologist seemed unusually quiet – subdued.

"Yeah…just tired. Surreal. Like, I've just come out of a dream."

At least she was coherent enough to speak, and understand what was being asked of her. It was as if she was suddenly overcome with a feeling of melancholy.

"Listen, if you are not feeling well, maybe you should not attend the banquet, and rest here?" Ophelia advised.

Madison rubbed her eyes, and took a deep breath.

"No, no. I want to go. I need to go. I'll be okay. I'm probably a little tired from the journey, I just need a good shower, that's all," Madison replied.

"Are you sure?" Ophelia double-checked.

"Yeah, I'm all good."

Mervier had completed her sweep, and placed the device back into her pocket.

"All clean here," she reported.

Ophelia had unpacked her evening wear, and then removed the bubble-wrapped stone tablet from the inner lining of her suitcase. Madison slowly came around, and noticed Ophelia placing it inside her large handbag.

"Are you taking that with you to the banquet?" she enquired.

"It's not going to leave my sight. Besides, it'd be good to get a reaction from our host if I showed it to her," Ophelia said.

"I told you. That woman is not the one we encountered on the island. Or her servants, I'm sure of it," Madison said angrily.

"Then, maybe, it's somebody we haven't seen yet?" Mervier surmised, as she looked around the paintings and murals on the walls.

"Or maybe this is a wild goose chase?" Ophelia exhaled, almost in denial.

"Too much of this connects to this woman. This is no coincidence, you know that. The invite, the tablet, this mace, not forgetting the murders, all leads here, I swear my life on it," the detective said, adamantly.

"I hope that won't be the cost of the truth," Ophelia glanced at Mervier.

At that point, she heard a male voice inside her earpiece.

It was Nathan Spears.

"Ladies, are you receiving?"

"A little muffled, Nathan, but it's good to hear your voice," Ophelia responded.

"Okay, as long as we got comms. From the body-cams, there doesn't seem to be any other way in to the castle, except for your balconies. But I can see why they don't need to be secured," Spears reported, clearly acknowledging the sheer cliff face that they were situated above.

Everyone knew that would be a suicidal climb to get into the keep, as there was no other way round to the rear of the castle, except a death-defying rock climb in the darkness.

"Yes, I understand." Ophelia replied, feeling trapped once again.

"Don't worry, we'll figure something out. If you need extracting, use the code we agreed on." Spears reassured, "Keep the body cams and PTTs on you at all times."

"Seriously?" Mervier interrupted, as she looked at the en-suite bathroom.

"You know what I mean," Spears replied, with a hint of a laugh.

"Speaking of which, we need to start getting ready soon, I'm sure our illustrious host will be prompt," Mervier said, as Ophelia placed the tablet back into her large handbag.

Madison and Mervier made their way across the carpeted room and exited, leaving Ophelia alone again to her thoughts.

The curator then moved over to the balcony and noticed the skies turn darker. The previous calm that had enveloped her seemed to change to dread and anxiety.

The fishing trawler that she noticed passing a while ago, was barely seen in the increasing darkness of the sea, but it was still there in the distance.

But the vessel appeared still, rocking in the waves.

Like it was watching her.

It was only visible by its small silhouette, and tiny pinpricks of light that were emitting from its hull, like stars.

She turned around, placed her earpiece and locket on the dressing table, ensuring the locket was facing the door, and headed towards the en-suite bathroom.

CHAPTER 18

THE SALTY STAR

The 80-foot fishing trawler had anchored two and a half miles away from the cliffs where the castle was perched atop.

The current was moderate, and the waves lightly rocked the boat in its stationary position.

The crew consisted of four experienced fishermen and their captain. Rhys Griffith. He was a sea-faring veteran at sixty years old, with an unkempt beard, and long dark and grey tussled hair, that blew in the evening wind.

His boat, 'The Salty Star', had been hired by an arrogant, yet obscenely wealthy American, and left its harbour port near Bristol, a few hours ago. From the bridge of the trawler, he looked at his scanners, and then peered through the windows at his customer, on the deck below.

Standing on the portside of the vessel was Vincent Keyes. He was looking through his infra-red binoculars, and staring across the sea, and up at the cliffs. The haunting silhouette of the castle keep was seen at the very top of the cliffs.

From his image enhancer, he had just seen a small figure of a woman standing alone on a high balcony, near the top of the keep. It seemed for a fleeting moment, to Keyes, that she was looking out at the sea - at him.

This must have been Ophelia Winters, but her presence there was only for a few seconds, before she turned around and disappeared back into the dark inner sanctums of the castle.

Hugo approached him from behind, and stood next to his boss.

"This is the place, alright," Keyes confirmed.

"What about the coastguard?" Hugo asked.

"There's nothing suspicious about a local fishing trawler in this channel, Hugo. Relax tell Griffith to remain here until further notice, he's being paid enough," Keyes asked.

"Yes sir." Hugo turned and headed towards the bridge of the vessel.

Keyes then lowered his binoculars, and turned to face his own crew. Eight dark-clad operatives bearing the Legionshield emblem on their jumpsuits, were arranging various pieces of bulky equipment onto the deck.

They started to assemble the frameworks together, and several parts were the chassis of the combat jetpacks that Keyes had seen being tested earlier. A couple of technicians that accompanied their colleagues began installing the weapons systems into the packs.

As the preparations were underway, Keyes reverted his attention back towards the castle.

The darkness rolled in, and the clouds turned grey.

CHAPTER 19

"WE SHALL BE DINING ALONE"

As expected, the servants were promptly on time to collect their guests from their rooms. Ophelia, Madison and Mervier were all dressed in elegant evening dresses. They were being escorted towards the grand hall, and passed many assorted artefacts that were displayed on the intricate architecture around them.

As they reached the entrance of the grand hall the women were greeted by their host. The countess was wearing an exquisite long flowing jade green dress and wearing wonderful pieces of jewellery. One of them that caught Ophelia's eye in particular was the emerald tiara that Elina wore on her beautifully groomed dark hair. A bracelet that was worn on her upper arm resembled a gold coiled snake.

"Ladies, you look lovely, please come in and make yourselves comfortable." Elina smiled.

"Thank you very much. Like-wise, it's not often I get into my glad-rags," Ophelia replied politely.

As they entered the very spacious dining area of the hall, they looked at all the tapestries on the walls, and the vast collection of mediaeval weapons from different cultures that were ceremoniously displayed as museum exhibits.

As Elina escorted them towards the table, Ophelia noticed they were passing a life-size stone statue of a man in a pose – the details were quite astonishing, as his expression seemed intense.

"An ancestor?" Ophelia asked.

Elina glanced at what tickled Ophelia's interest, and smiled.

"My late husband," the countess replied casually.

They continued walking to the large oval table situated at the far end of the grand hall, where three more smartly gowned maidens were waiting, bowing their heads.

"Oh, I see, a beautifully crafted sculpture," Ophelia added. So many thoughts were going through her head at this point. She deduced that her companions were thinking the same.

"I like to think he's still with me, and looking over me," Elina added, with a little sadness in her eyes, behind her tinted glasses. The countess took her place at the head of the oval table, and remained standing as she waited for her guests to take their seats.

"Understandable. I did read that he died in a sailing accident, I am sorry that you lost him in such a terrible way," Ophelia said remorsefully, still unsure if she was being deceived.

"A truly tragic and untimely demise, indeed. But please, I don't want to dwell on the past, it's the future we must look forward to," Elina said.

"Of course, I'm terribly sorry, I didn't mean to…" Ophelia cut herself short, as she then turned to face the table.

There were only four dining spaces prepared on the table. And four chairs.

No other guests.

Ophelia paused, as she stood behind one of the chairs allocated for her. Madison and Mervier took their positions behind their cushioned chairs.

The centrepiece of the table was a beautiful Greek ornament, which in fact was an ornate fountain. It created an ambience of calm and tranquillity.

The seats were symmetrically arranged, so the countess was at the head, Mervier at the foot, and both Madison and Ophelia on the sides. The fountain didn't impair their viewpoints of each other.

"Where are the other guests?" Madison enquired, a little worried.

"Ah, yes. Unfortunately, it appears that nobody else has accepted my invitation. I knew I was sending them out at too much of a short notice, I haven't hosted in years," Elina responded quickly. "We shall be dining alone, more intimate."

The three guests exchanged looks of concern, but immediately tried to conceal that in front of their hostess.

"Ladies. It's not about the number of people that are here or not, but the quality of the company we already have, I feel, please, take your seats." Elina gestured to them, and they reluctantly sat down, followed by the countess.

The moment they had settled, the servants started bringing in silver platters of delicious-looking food in.

A prawn dish appetiser, with a beautifully arranged garnish and sauce, was placed before each guest.

Another servant glided over and popped the cork to a bottle of some expensive champagne, then commenced to pour the bubbling beverage into their slim glasses. Mervier held her hand over her glass.

"No, thank you, just water please." She turned to her hostess, and smiled, not to be rude. "I don't drink."

"That's not a problem," Elina, then motioned over to her servant, who went back into the kitchen. She returned with a pitcher of chilled water with lime segments, and a smidge of mint.

"Ladies. May I propose a toast? To history, and bringing it back to life!" She raised her glass. They all took a sip from their glasses. Ophelia pondered on those words.

The small banquet had started.

The guests were still apprehensive, and Mervier glanced down at her own black leather handbag. She had packed her 9mm Glock, just in case.

Even though it was a generally pleasant atmosphere inside the hall, Ophelia felt unease and scanned her eyes at the marvellous pieces of antiques and weapons that were proudly presented behind Elina. Her gaze was fixed onto a dozen mediaeval maces and sceptres of different designs.

One in particular, though, looked exactly like the relic that was featured in the pamphlet.

She hoped the others noted it too.

CHAPTER 20

THE MERCS PREPARE

Under the cover of darkness, Spears and Matheson had sneaked up to the barbican, whilst being monitored by the overhead stealth drone that was piloted by Fox, back in the den.

"How much would you say, will be enough to blow up the gates?" Matheson enquired, holding his G-36. Explosives were not his speciality. He was there to cover Spears as he prepared the explosives.

"No more than two C-4 charges should do the trick," Spears said, "Probably."

Even the ex-SBS operative was uncertain, as this was something he was not entirely familiar with, but with his basic understanding and experience of ordnance, it theoretically made sense.

"If this fails, and we blow up the whole thing, and create a blockade, we'll be in worse shit than before by sealing off their escape, or our access," Matheson had confidence in his long-serving associate, but was sceptical of this contingency plan.

Spears attached the charges right in the centre of the portcullis, looking through the small gaps for any signs of sentries or servants inside the outer courtyard. The only things that were aware of what they were doing, was the drone hovering overhead, checking for these things, and the dozen gargoyles that were in their niches on the other side.

"Well, if that occurs, we'll go to plan B." Spears, said completing his work. "Fox, you read?"

"Received, you're all clear." Fox responded through Spears' headset.

"And what's plan B?" Matheson asked, as they prepared to leave.

"Well, this *is* plan B actually," Spears replied, not exactly inspiring confidence in his boss. Matheson rolled his eyes.

"Listen, Miles. What I have rigged here should be enough to blow a hole, big enough for a vehicle without taking out the rest of the barbican. It depends on the sturdiness of these old gates, trust me – to an extent," Spears tried to reassure him.

"Christ. Okay. Let's go."

The two mercenaries then quickly darted away from the barbican, and into the darkness of the valley that led to the woods. The drone followed and maintained its aerial position, looking over at the silent courtyard.

Meanwhile, back at the den, Fox was in his fixed position piloting the drone, whilst Straker was seated on the crest of the thicket monitoring the dinner party inside the grand hall. His eyes moving from one divided screen to another, and taking note of the different angles that the women were projecting from their covert body-cams.

"What are they talking about?" Fox asked, as he flew the drone back in their direction. Next to him was a small mess tin of beans and sausages, bubbling away in its camping stove. Luckily, it wasn't emitting any significant light.

"Just archaeological bantz. They're now settling down for dinner, looks a lot better than the shit we got here," Straker said, as he motioned to the contents of the ration pack heating up behind him.

"Well, I'll just order us a take-out. Sounds good?" Fox said sarcastically.

"That sounds lovely, chow mein for me." He retorted, whilst observing the main course being served on camera.

"To be honest Straker, I don't know what we're doing here. This could be a big waste of time, but that detective thinks that she seems to be on to something," Fox said, changing the subject.

"Well, as long as we get paid, consider this easy money," Straker answered, as he tried to focus in on the banquet.

Spears and Matheson finally broke through the series of bushes that encircled the thicket, and met up with their two associates. The drone came in too, and Fox landed it safely beside him.

"Ah, just in time for dinner, gentlemen," Straker said.

"All set?" Fox asked.

"Yup. Hopefully, we won't be needing to use 'em. But they're good to go," Spears confirmed.

Matheson made his way over to the cooking pot, and dipped his fork inside, scooping up a mouthful.

"It's okay, Straker, I'll take over, get some scoff," Matheson said.

"Thanks boss." Straker was relieved, and made his way to his backpack, and unwrapped a protein bar.

"What's new?" Matheson asked Straker, monitoring the live feed coming through from the women's body-cams.

"Audio's not great. Keeps breaking up, but they're just talking about the countess's history of work."

"Okay," Matheson exhaled. He then went over to the Defender alone, sat down in the driver's seat, and pulled out the military grade satellite-phone from his tactical vest.

Matheson called Vincent Keyes. He had no knowledge that he was only a few miles away on a boat, but his boss insisted on regular reports throughout the surveillance.

He felt that this surveillance operation will be a long night.

CHAPTER 21

THE TRUE MYTHOLOGY OF MEDUSA

The evening had reached the latter part of their main course, which was freshly cooked salmon, asparagus and a delicious dill sauce.

Ophelia had enjoyed her meal, but continued to gaze around the gothic banquet room, taking note of the various paintings of ancient scenes from Greek mythology. She also took an interest in the marble, stone and wooden models and monuments of characters from Greek folklore.

Elina had just reminisced to her guests of her archaeological exploits with her late husband, until she saw Ophelia looking at a nearby bust of Medusa. She had a beautiful face, but had a crown of snakes that resembled long, flowing hair.

"I see you are captivated by my unique collection of gorgoneion memorabilia," Elina said.

Ophelia seemed distracted, and as if pricked by a pin, returned her attention to her host.

"Oh, I do apologise. Yes, the whole mythology of Medusa has always fascinated me, I like how she is represented there," Ophelia replied, referring to the bust in the corner of the room.

"Thank you," Elina smiled, as she faced the curator.

"My latest studies in folklore and mythology are focused on Ancient Greece. I find it truly incredible, although a little fantastical.

Saying that, you could say the same about any ancient culture," Madison mentioned, as she took another sip of champagne. Ophelia was glad her young colleague and friend seemed more coherent.

"I have spent, what seems, many lifetimes researching and uncovering the truths of such stories," Elina said.

Mervier switched her look to the bust. Then averted her eyes to the mace that was displayed on the wall behind Elina. Her heart skipped a beat, as she finished her meal. She felt one hundred percent that what she was looking at was *the* destructive weapon. And despite Madison's protests, the host was the prime suspect.

"I know it is a tale of beauty, jealousy and tragedy, Medusa although popularised as an evil, vengeful and hideous monster, was a victim," Ophelia said, woefully.

Elina rose from her chair and slowly approached the bust. She softly brushed her fingertips down the writhing marble snakes that adorned its head, as if she was in mourning.

"I'm glad you think so, Ophelia," Elina said, as her servants cleared the plates.

"Hunted and killed by what people considered a true Greek hero," Madison added.

"Or so it seems, but the truth of the tale is somewhat different to what ancient scholars, poets, historians, and even the modern-day media portray." Elina replied, as she turned to the archaeologists.

"Every legend evolves through the ages, and has numerous versions," Ophelia announced, as if she was addressing a classroom of students.

"What if I told you ladies, that there is some truth to the tale, and in time it has turned into an epic myth," Elina revealed, as she glided across the room. Her guests followed her with their eyes, absorbed.

"We have encountered many myths that have turned out to be quite genuine," Ophelia answered, reflecting back on the elixir, as well as some of the relics in the vault of her museum.

"Then let me enlighten you."

Countess Dumas had the undivided attention of her guests, and most likely the audience that were outside the castle, who were observing through the ladies' covert cameras and listening devices.

"According to your Greek mythology, Medusa was born of three gorgons, daughters of the sea deities Phorcys and Ceto. Her sisters Stheno and Euryale were immortal, and Medusa was mortal. She was a high priestess of the temple of Athena, and known widespread for possessing extraordinary beauty that captured the attention of all men."

"Sorry to interrupt, but yes, we are aware of her origins, Elina," Madison said, not meaning to intrude, but the knowledge she had was documented in many places and in countless literature.

"Maddy." Ophelia turned her attention to Madison, as if she was gently scolding her for interrupting.

"It's okay," Elina replied, as she walked over to her chair, and sat down.

"I'm sorry, but as far as the tale goes, she caught the eye of the sea God, Poseidon. He violated the sanctity of Athena's temple, and, overwhelmed by his desire for Medusa, he forced himself upon her." Madison continued, matter-of-factly.

"That is correct, Madison, but what the true tale does not reveal is what happened afterwards, before Medusa was cursed by the jealous Goddess, and turned into a monstrous creature." Elina replied, which seemed to silence Madison.

"Please go on," Ophelia said.

"Like you said, Ophelia. Medusa was a tragic victim of rape. By a powerful God or supernatural entity. But, as a result of their union, she conceived a child." Elina startled everyone.

The three guests were speechless. This was, indeed, an astonishing revelation. Ophelia frowned, and spoke.

"Do you mean, when she was beheaded? Her blood spawned Pegasus and Chrysaor, according to legend."

Elina grinned, and shook her head.

"No. There are parts of the legendary story which are known to the world, that delve into the realms of fantasy, which is now taken as myth. That is one example. Although all of it, like any myth, sounds unbelievable and far-fetched, I admit."

"So, was she pregnant?" Madison asked, intrigued.

"Athena hadn't punished Medusa yet. By the command of Poseidon, she was permitted to carry the child to full term, until she gave birth to a normal healthy daughter – Marzanna Medea, she was born as a demi-goddess," Elina explained, to the astounded faces of her guests.

"Well, that's a version I didn't expect to hear," Ophelia exclaimed across the table.

"It is the truth. Shortly after the birth, the Goddess Athena, still consumed by anger, cursed Medusa, transforming her into the monstrous being that you are familiar with today. But with phenomenal powers."

"Turning any living thing into stone, to those that dared to look into her eyes." Mervier came into the conversation, momentarily glancing at the marble bust.

"And, an eternal existence of being entombed in her gruesome form. She was immortalised, like her sisters, and banished from society to live in solitude. She and a handful of loyal priestesses formed a coven, and took refuge on the island of Sarpedon, located in the depths of the underworld, where she would remain imprisoned forever."

"What of her baby daughter?" Ophelia asked.

"She was entrusted to the coven, and was raised as a mortal acolyte, it was decreed by her divine father, Poseidon, that when she reached the sacred age of sixteen, she would be bestowed with a great gift of longevity, and possess certain powers to protect the coven that were sworn to protect Medusa."

"Was she immortal?" Madison asked.

"She was a demi-human. She could be killed like any other mortal human, but gifted – or cursed to live for an extreme length of time. She didn't possess the same deadly abilities as her mother. After her sixteenth year in this world, she aged just one year, for every 340 years of a normal human being."

"Incredible," Madison gasped.

"Well, I am sure the Guinness book of records would love to hear from her," Mervier quipped, although she got a laser look from Ophelia.

"Again, a myth to most. But contrary to popular belief, Medusa was never killed. She knew that her life was a never-ending curse, although she yearned for a normal life, to be a mother and loyal worshipper. Instead, a life of existing as a monster, hunted for years."

"So, Perseus failed. Was it all a lie?" Madison asked.

"A fabrication. Storytelling. There was no Perseus. There was a time in the Mycenaean period of 1497 BCE, where King Cranaus of Athens dispatched popular Greek heroes at the time to take her head, for his own military and political gain. The brave warriors who sought to prove their valour and courage, attempted to slay Medusa and eradicate the coven. However, all of those that hunted her became victims of her vengeful and divine wrath. They never returned home. Over time, the hunt for Medusa ceased, and the island was deemed too dangerous to visit. But the threat still lingered for centuries that followed. As far as the legend goes, poets created the heroic tale of what you have always known today – until now, of course. That is, if you believe?" Elina completed her tale.

There was an atmosphere of incredulity from the three guests.

"A compelling story, I grant you that, Elina, you've certainly given us a new insight into an ancient myth that the world has been fascinated with for 3,500 years." Ophelia spoke, breaking the silence.

"Myths and legends are full of surprises. Take that as you will, ladies, I did say that tonight would be enlightening." Elina replied, raising her glass again, and then taking a sip.

"Shame there is no proof of this," Madison voiced her opinion. "Are you suggesting that Medusa actually exists?"

"I'm not saying she doesn't, but isn't that the beauty of unearthing secrets of ancient origins?" Elina answered.

"You sound like someone I used to know," Ophelia uttered under her breath, remembering Isaac Kane.

Despite the guests' views and opinions of this new take on the ancient myth, they were still intrigued. Ophelia thought of the mercenaries listening in to this bedtime story. She also pondered why Elina was so passionate about sharing the story.

"I am quite impressed with your armoury collection. I take it they are from the Mycenaean era?" Mervier asked, trying to bring her investigation back on track.

Elina turned her head over her shoulder to see what Mervier was pointing to. The wall of ancient and mediaeval weapons.

"From many eras in history, Nicole. A few pieces date back over 3000 years old."

"May I?" Mervier asked getting up from her chair. She ensured she took her handbag with her. A reassuring notion that her Glock was close to hand if need be.

"Of course," Elina responded, and gestured for her to have a closer look.

Mervier made her way over to the wall of ancient weapons. Ophelia gritted her teeth again, and decided to get up too. Madison followed and all approached the wall. Elina rose as well and made her way to where Mervier was approaching.

Before she could reach for the mace, Elina immediately held out her hand to stop the inquisitive detective.

"No!" Elina abruptly said.

The detective whipped her hand back the moment Elina spoke. Ophelia and Madison came up behind their curious associate, and were about to pull her back, but Mervier smiled at her host.

"I apologise, where are my manners?" Mervier said.

"It is a very sacred relic, I cannot allow anybody to touch it, but by all means, you can look," Elina advised.

"May I ask what it is?" Mervier asked.

"Yes, there was a picture of it on the invitation, or something very similar," Ophelia added.

"That's right. That is known as the Skeptron of Hephaestus," Elina revealed. "Or sceptre."

"The Greek god of artisans and blacksmiths," Madison said, marvelling at the unique object.

"Unearthed a few hundred years ago, at a site near Mount Olympus of all places," Elina replied.

"Legend says that he crafted many wondrous and divine objects and weapons, each with extraordinary powers," Ophelia recalled, as she once again cast her mind back to the Bident of Hades.

"Indeed. This particular sceptre was alleged to have been forged at the time of King Cranaus, and was wielded by ancient kings as they rode their chariots into battle, as a symbol of majestic power. They believed it would bring them luck and protection on the battlefield, a bit like the Christian spear of destiny," Elina gazed upon its beauty.

Her guests were enthralled, and Ophelia took note of the emerald crown stone, and then at the haft of the beautiful wand. It had what appeared to be a red bloodstone forged into it.

It was the weapon Mervier was looking for. Or a very identical replica.

Ophelia recognised it as well, and she felt that she was in the lion's den.

A sense of nervousness gripped her, and she stepped back.

The three women tried to exchange concerned looks after closely looking at the sceptre, and Elina noticed their reactions, although they really tried to compose their expressions, and keep their cool.

"Tell me, do you believe this possesses supernatural properties?" Ophelia enquired, unsure what to do or say. She glanced around her, and saw that they were the only people in the room. But she also knew Mervier was armed, and her mercs were hopefully monitoring everything right now.

Her worries were now escalated, as Elina gently reached for the sceptre, and removed it from its display hooks on the wall. She cradled it in her arms, as she faced the three women.

Ophelia tried to discreetly step back cautiously. She knew that all it would take now, was for Elina to effortlessly touch any of the three women with it, as they were all in proximity.

That's if the mysterious Countess was truly the suspect, and the sceptre she was now holding, was the true magical weapon in question.

There was a suspenseful silence as Madison and Mervier shared the same concerns as Ophelia. Mervier would have no time to reach for her Glock now.

They believed in the power of the bident. They certainly believed in the power of the sceptre too.

They were overcome with fear, and were inches away from the sceptre's crown.

Ophelia knew the secret password to utter, in case of emergency, and for the Black Knights to respond quickly. She parted her lips, and drew in a breath.

Elina smiled, and then held out the opulent snake-encrusted wand, towards them.

CHAPTER 22
FORWARD POSITIONS

The Black Knights were all crouched in the foliage, and anxiously observing the scene. Matheson dashed towards the Defender, as Straker monitored the multiscreen on his laptop.

All the three bodycams on the screen were facing the looming sceptre that intimidatingly gained closer to the women.

"Why did Mervier have to mention that now?" Fox said, angrily. He didn't care if she heard him through her earpiece. This jeopardised the entire operation. The mercs knew the ladies' disguises were compromised. Hopefully the merc's presence hadn't.

"She knows the password, what is she waiting for?" Spears said, hoping that she was listening.

But would it be too late?

All it would take would be a second for the sly countess to touch any of them with the supernatural sceptre, before they could react.

"We better get to forward positions." Straker responded, "Get that drone in the air."

Fox opened up his portable equipment case where the drone control console was.

At that point, the Defender screeched up to the clearing where the three mercenaries were huddled. He shouted through the open passenger windscreen, his right hand on the wheel, his left was holding the sat-phone.

"Get in, let's go!" Matheson shouted at his team.

Without hesitation, Spears, Fox and Straker gathered their kit, and jumped into the vehicle.

"She hasn't said the go code yet," Fox said.

"We're moving closer. If we get compromised, we get compromised," Matheson replied.

The Defender left the OP, and lifted dirt as it approached the castle. Seconds later, the drone was airborne and flew high above and ahead of the vehicle.

Meanwhile, on the Salty Star, Vincent Keyes, whilst holding his sat-phone, was still standing on the deck of the old boat that was still floating in the channel. He was facing the dark castle in the distance, and then he looked behind his shoulder at his eight determined- looking operatives fastening themselves to their jetpacks.

Hugo's bulky frame managed to slide into the chassis of his jet pack, and he nodded to his boss.

"We have verification," Keyes said with a distinct grin on his face. "Recover the sceptre, and take her alive, the others are expendable."

"Yes sir."

"Deploy the air reapers, and hold positions until I give the command," Keyes ordered.

CHAPTER 23

A DIVINE DEMONSTRATION

"Don't be alarmed, ladies," Elina reassured, as she allowed the anxious-looking women a closer inspection of the mystical baton. She then lowered it, and approached a small table near the wall display.

"I was going to wait until tomorrow, but allow me to perform a small demonstration of the sceptre's enchanted power, if you would like to follow me?" Elina said, kindly.

A sense of relief overcame the three women. Ophelia was aware that the mercs were enroute, and this could have disastrous consequences if they burst in now.

"Spears, wait." She uttered into her locket. This was overheard by Elina, who spun around as she reached the small oval table that contained a large number of stone insects, from scarab beetles to moths and butterflies.

"I beg your pardon," Elina asked, quizzically. She was taken aback by the unusual response of the curator.

Ophelia heard Spears' voice through her hidden earpiece. He had received her message.

"Got that, just clear your throat, and we'll abort and hold position," Spears said.

Ophelia distinctly cleared her throat, with a raspy sound.

"Got that," Spears acknowledged.

Elina tilted her head slightly, whilst she looked at Ophelia, as if she was scrutinising her.

"Spears?" she asked. The earlier sense of relief from Madison and Mervier was short-lived, and they remained quiet, until Ophelia spoke.

"Yes, sorry Elina. Spears. I was referring to the beautiful spears you have arranged on the wall. I just noticed that I recognised a few. I have some similar ones in my vault. Especially the doru, used by the hoplites," Ophelia said, thinking quickly.

Everyone turned towards the same wall, from where Elina had removed the sceptre. Elina smiled as she saw what Ophelia was glancing over at. A small collection of leaf-shaped bladed spears that were neatly displayed next to five Greek aspis shields, and four Corinthian helmets with horsehair crests.

Nobody saw Mervier exhale a discreet sigh of relief.

"Oh, yes. Again, Mycenaean, and all of these were recovered from what was the Phoenician states, Now, modern day Lebanon," Elina explained, distracted.

Elina then returned to the table, and the women gathered around too – still mindful of the sceptre.

"As professional preservers and protectors of certain unique artefacts, I am sure you will appreciate the divine qualities of this incredible and divine treasure. Ladies, this is no illusion."

All three women looked on with bated breath, as Elina positioned the sceptre's haft near one of the small detailed stone butterflies that was laid on the table, like an ornament.

The bottom of the sceptre that contained the bloodstone, touched the insect sculpture.

A second later, their eyes were greeted with the most amazing sight.

The stone butterfly magically transformed. Small rocky fragments disintegrated away from the insect, revealing beautifully coloured wings that fluttered to life. It was now organic, and flew into the air above them.

Ophelia, alongside her two companions, were mesmerised.

The butterfly danced in the air, circling the group. Elina appeared enraptured, as she watched the reborn insect flutter towards the ceiling. Full of new life.

It was a beautiful and breathtaking sight.

Elina's audience were transfixed, and then looked at their host. Was she a witch? Sorceress? Stage magician? Mervier frowned.

"A neat trick," the detective said.

Ophelia had seen magical objects perform great feats of terrifying power, but this truly astonished her.

The sceptre was indeed the one they were looking for, but was imbued with additional magical properties. As well as turning living things into stone – it could miraculously do the reverse!

Madison had a million questions right now. In fact, they all did.

"I assure you, Nicole. It is no trick. But believe what you will." Elina replied, respecting her opinion.

Ophelia looked around the banquet hall, and noticed the many models, busts and sculptures that surrounded them. She also took note of the two huge stone rattlesnakes that formed part of the décor, on either side of the banquet hall's entranceway.

There was another stone statue of a hoplite soldier, in one of the darkened corners of the room that was holding a real leaf-bladed xiphos sword and wooden aspis shield. A chill went through her.

"Remarkable," she averted her attention back to the wondrous countess.

"And the crown of the sceptre?" Mervier asked, curiously. She was keen to get a reaction. Elina turned away and seemed to ignore the question. Mervier nodded to herself.

"So, could this essentially reanimate anything back to life?" Madison posed the question, as Elina made her way over to a small collection of stone statues that were placed in front of the enormous fireplace.

"The powers of the sceptre are restrictive. It can only transform stone representations of sentient and in some cases, non-sentient life into a state of animation, and to obey the commands of its revivor through one's mind, the gift of a new mortal existence, but can only survive for as long as the one that granted them life," Elina said, with an aura of mystique.

"So, as an example, could you transform the entire terracotta army to life, and have them do your bidding?" Madison asked.

"In essence," Elina chuckled. "But why? I am not a blood-thirsty warlord."

Mervier had to cynically grunt underneath her breath.

"Could it resurrect the dead?" Ophelia asked nervously, reflecting once again on the sorcerer that she had killed less than a month ago.

"Absolutely not. It is not a bewitched wand with the ability of bringing the deceased back to life, the sceptre will only work on pure stone creatures, of any form."

"What do you mean, of any form?" Mervier enquired.

"Everything from mere humans to the creatures of the natural world like you just witnessed. This doesn't preclude, of course, forms of the unnatural world, any form that is fully articulated in stone can be reanimated," Elina declared.

The women were in awe of this information, and Mervier stood at her position behind the small oval table, as Elina stopped at the fireplace. The detective's right hand stealthily slid into her handbag, and she felt a bit more at ease when her palm rested on the handle of her concealed handgun. She kept her hand in her handbag.

"You wield great power, Elina," Ophelia stated, "Although awe-inspiring to witness, it is also terrifying. I've seen this happen before. I've seen the chaos and devastation that comes with artefacts like these. The potential for this sceptre is immense."

"Where's the devastation in bringing life to the world?" Elina said.

"It depends on what you're bringing into the world," Ophelia replied, seriously.

"Of course. It is down to true ethics. I am not seeking power or fame. I am like yourself. I like to preserve and safeguard what history and folklore does not truly reveal to the world, in a world, that would bring out the true darkness of such opulent treasures, and the ones that control them," Elina spoke back, with a sorrowful tone.

Ophelia shook her head. She couldn't believe Elina's words. The curator had heard a similar declaration from her former nemesis. She finally knew that all the cards were on the table now, and felt the charade was over.

The investigation needed no other evidence. Even from the get-go. Mervier was aware of that too, and gripped the handle of her Glock from within her handbag.

Elina had revealed so much. It appeared as if she didn't really care that she had been identified or implicated, in any way, of the crimes committed in York.

It felt to both parties that everybody in the room was fully aware of everyone's agenda and their true purpose in attending the meeting. But it was only a matter of time who got the upper hand, or whose veil was dropped first.

Ophelia knew, and suspected that Elina did too, that it was time for this pretence to stop. But nobody made a move.

Just yet.

"And am I expected to trust those words, after experiencing one man that recited the same statement, and left a path of death and destruction in his wake?" Ophelia said, emotionally.

"I can understand your concern, Ophelia. Which is why I restricted the guest list to just you and Madison. I was hoping that your notable Professor Shaw would have accompanied you as well. No offence, Nicole. But your presence here has been delightful, nonetheless."

Elina lowered her tinted glasses, and glanced at Madison. The countess had to hasten the proceedings. The two made eye contact, and Madison felt lost – almost hypnotised by her bright jade-green eyes.

The young archaeologist heard Elina's soft voice in her head.

"I know you have it. Tell me where the tablet is?"

As Ophelia and Mervier took a few steps back, they were contemplating what to do next. They felt they had been rumbled, but at the same time, they were wondering if Elina was aware that they knew?

"With due respect, this is no gala, is it?" Ophelia asked, as she peered at her eyes before she placed them back. Madison was still in a temporary haze and looked at Ophelia's large handbag that was still draped across the chair next to the dining table.

Elina noted this, and smiled at the young woman. She tipped her head down, so her eyes looked over her spectacles, and fixed her eyes on Madison again. Ophelia didn't know what was happening during this unusual exchange.

"Have you brought others that will bring harm to us?" Elina's voice echoed in Madison's head.

Madison parted her lips. Hypnotically seduced.

"Yes," she replied softly.

Elina smiled, and tilted her head back, and adjusted her glasses. She placed her other hand on a stoker from the fireplace, and like a lever, solely moved it in the opposite direction. A slight rumbling was heard from the far walls of the banquet room.

This momentarily distracted Ophelia and Mervier as they glanced behind them and tried to deduce where the echoing sound emanated from the darkness.

"Ladies," Elina said, bringing their attention back to herself. It was only Madison that appeared completely in a surreal daze. "I invited you down to simply share tales and a chance to finally meet such an esteemed figure in our special vocation, such as yourself. I always knew that I wasn't the only one. And to thank you."

"I don't understand," Ophelia answered.

"Besides, we really didn't get a chance to get to know each other," Elina said.

"It was you, wasn't it, in the chamber, on the island?"

Elina smirked.

CHAPTER 24

MARZANNA

Countess Elina Dumas slowly took a few steps forward and approached Ophelia, who started to retreat a couple of steps.

Mervier had to decide what to do, as she saw Elina stop a few feet away from the curator. They felt threatened, but the charming Countess exhibited no threatening behaviour. In fact, she remained humble and sincere.

"This was all an elaborate plan to lure us here," Ophelia said, stroking her flamingo locket. Any minute now, she would have to say the password and the Black Knights would crash in and rescue them. But she needed answers. She held off from the command, much to Mervier's dismay.

The detective really wanted a confession. For all she knew, Elina may not be the killer, and the suspect could still be roaming the halls of the castle, or a servant that they hadn't even seen yet. That's why the gun wasn't pulled out yet. Either Elina would need to make a hostile gesture, commit an aggressive act or reveal information that would prompt Mervier to affect an arrest. She strongly felt that she had the weapon. But this weapon displayed a different kind of magic. Maybe it possessed other marvellous abilities, such as turning souls into stone.

"You were invited. But I sense your motives for coming here are not all innocent, Ophelia."

"You got me intrigued."

"You want this, don't you? To add to your collection." Elina was still holding the sceptre.

"As you said, I would like to ensure the protection of such powerful artefacts, and prevent those abusing that power."

"And what makes you think I would take advantage of its true properties?" Elina replied, sternly.

"We both know my concerns, you were affiliated with the Order of the Crimson Claw, were you not?" Ophelia had to reference the recent past.

Elina circled the group of women and stood next to the hoplite statue. A new sense of dread enveloped Ophelia.

"We had little time in that chamber, but I do recall explaining to you that they were originally the protectors of my coven, before they went rogue, and grew in strength, almost overwhelming us, so I thank you for putting an end to their devilish deeds."

"Who are you, Elina? Wait a second," Ophelia paused for a couple of seconds. "E. Dumas. I should've guessed, an anagram of Medusa," Ophelia deduced.

"Like I said, I took my mother's name, even by an alias," Elina revealed.

"You're an ancestor?" Ophelia asked, incredulously.

"I am Marzanna Medea, daughter of the true Medusa," she declared.

This was unbelievable, and Ophelia stood there, frozen, as if she had been turned into stone herself. Mervier's palm was sweating from inside her handbag, as she nestled her fingers across the hand grip of the pistol.

Ophelia cast her mind back to when Elina spoke of the birth, thousands of years ago, and how she was protected by the temple's devoted worshippers. The gift of extreme longevity. This would make sense how she had lived all these years, through countless generations, developing into adulthood, planning, manipulating, accumulating wealth, living and surviving all her life.

She was a living ancient. But living now, as an introverted peer of the realm. Secretly, an elusive high priestess of a once forgotten coven of witches.

A woman with a mythological lineage that was no longer a myth.

"You have lived for over 3,500 years?" Ophelia gasped. It was surprising that she hadn't gone insane. But maybe she was, the curator considered.

"Believe me, it comes with its challenges, and I have seen and experienced more than you can fathom. The gift of prolonged life can also be a curse. But my longevity comes at a price."

"What is it you want?" Ophelia said, backing up. She had to be mindful and distance herself away from this powerful woman, and her equally formidable sceptre.

Elina, now revealed as Marzanna, remained standing next to the ancient Greek statue of the soldier. Her wand, hovering ever so close to the mighty sculpture. This escalated the tension, and Ophelia's heart was pounding through her chest.

"What I truly want is peace and serenity. To protect my mother from the ones that prey upon us, and to restore her back to her true glory."

"What?" Mervier broke her silence.

"And the key to this was taken from me back on the island." Elina snapped her fingers, which made Mervier and Ophelia jump.

Madison reacted immediately, and, still in a trance, obediently glided over to Ophelia's handbag and retrieved the stone tablet from it. Ophelia was shell-shocked, as her young companion walked straight past the two stunned women, totally disregarding them and then handed over the tablet to the awaiting hand of Marzanna.

The gorgoneion tablet was back in her possession. She gazed down at it with adulation.

"*Join us,*" Marzanna said to Madison telepathically. The young woman nodded and took her place next to the high priestess.

"Madison!" Ophelia gasped at her friend's betrayal.

"The coven must stay strong for us to fulfil our destiny." Marzanna said.

"You've bewitched her!" Ophelia shouted at her.

"So, that is what all this is about, Countess?" Mervier asked.

"I do not possess the powers of my mother, but, as a compensation, I have been gifted with more than just a prolonged lifespan. Which brings me to this thing, as you so eloquently put it, Nicole."

Mervier's breathing became racy, due to the adrenalin coursing through her body, and she was losing patience. She allowed Ophelia to take the lead and have full jurisdiction of all the decision-making, but the detective had to supersede soon, before it was too late.

"If you don't say it, I will." Mervier turned to Ophelia, as she forced her words out through gritted teeth.

"Alerting your hunters? Fine. Let them come, witness your friend's demise, and face your own horrific fate, you must trust me. I mean you no harm, providing you abandon your true mission, and hear what I have to say," Marzanna said, earnestly.

Ophelia raised her hand to prevent Mervier taking any rash action. Mervier cursed under her breath. She was aware that the mercs were listening in and were close by – waiting to storm the castle. But any immediate excitable action would undoubtedly result in a disastrous outcome.

Ophelia and Mervier couldn't provoke this woman. She clearly had the upper hand, and the women knew their lives would abruptly end, long before Spears and his group would reach them.

"Just release Madison," Ophelia implored. She was getting used to saying that recently.

"I will. I don't want you to misunderstand me and my motives, I am trying to do the same myself, Ophelia, but I fear my efforts will be futile."

"Try me." Ophelia stared at Marzanna. Not once, affected by her entrancing glare.

Marzanna held the sceptre intimidatingly, and remained in her position. The statue to her left, and a hypnotised Madison to her right.

The young woman appeared to be looking through Ophelia as opposed to at her, like some kind of obedient robot, ready for the next command.

Marzanna concluded her tale.

The myth that is now fact.

CHAPTER 25

THE LEGACY OF THE GORGON

Marzanna opened her arms passively, and spoke with soft sincerity.

"You see, I have no intention of harming you or your friends. I could have poisoned you, and effortlessly taken the tablet from you, once I found out where you had hidden it, but no, I used my powers of persuasion to achieve that," Marzanna explained as she motioned to a catatonic Madison.

Ophelia knew that they could have been killed, or taken captive once they arrived.

"I had two or three weeks to plan, and without the knowledge of where both of you resided, developed this idea. It took a while for me to track down Madison in York. I only knew of your general location, based on what happened with your museum at the hands of the Crimson Claw. One night, I followed her, with the intention of peacefully reclaiming the property that she stole from me, and to find out where it was, Ophelia."

"You killed those boys."

"Survival instinct. They got in my way. And Madison, unbeknown to what happened, slipped away into the night. I knew I wouldn't get another chance, so I created this event."

"To which we took the bait," Ophelia cut in.

"It was the only way I could be reunited with the tablet."

Mervier now had all the evidence she needed. A full admission from her suspect.

Enough was enough.

She pulled her gun from her handbag, which had stayed inside its leather shelter for what seemed like an eternity.

"No wait!" Ophelia shouted.

Before she could align her gun at Marzanna, the sudden sharp sound of the crack of a whip echoed in the chamber, and coiled around Mervier's neck like a black snake.

The detective dropped the weapon, and it harmlessly clattered onto the carpet. Her hands reached up and desperately tried to pry her fingers underneath the coils of the whip to get an airway.

Ophelia whirled around to see one of the green-robed maidens holding the other end of the whip. She was almost concealed in the darkness, standing in a human-sized open cavity that used to be a small section of the stone wall. The curator looked at the stoker at the fireplace, which was, in fact, the lever that opened the secret hidden wall space.

Mervier fell to her knees, and felt the whip increasingly tighten around her neck the more she struggled. She gasped for air, as she continually tried pulling on the coiled weapon.

Marzanna held up the sceptre, and the maiden kept a firm hold. The high priestess glanced momentarily at Madison, as if the young woman was speaking to her with her mind. Marzanna peered back at the helpless Ophelia, who darted over to the detective, to try and help her release the coil.

"Halt!" Marzanna raised her voice. Ophelia spun round. She contemplated scooping up the Glock which was only a few yards from her.

"Should your friends outside breach my domain, you will all perish, I swear. I didn't want it to come to this, Ophelia. For generations, we have been hunted, and every time they have all met with a gruesome fate. Don't be one of them!"

Ophelia fully realised it was check-mate, and she had no choice. She nodded, with a look of defeat.

"Kick the weapon towards me." Marzanna commanded.

Ophelia reluctantly stepped towards the Glock, and toe punted the handgun. It was kicked across the carpet and rested at the feet of Madison. Marzanna motioned to her new acolyte, and the young woman obediently scooped up the pistol, and aimed it at Ophelia.

"Maddy, no." Ophelia cried out to her.

Madison was incoherent to her pleas, and retained her threatening pose. Marzanna signalled to her maiden in the darkened crevice of the wall, and with a flick of a wrist, the whip was uncoiled from the detective's neck. The maiden retracted the whip back.

Mervier coughed and spluttered once the whip was released. Her hands rubbed her throat as she wheezed for air. Ophelia placed her hand round her shoulder, attempting to comfort the detective. Both subdued women looked up at their captor.

"What's the importance of that thing, why do you need it so much?" Ophelia asked.

"I was about to reveal this, before I was rudely interrupted," Marzanna said, looking at Mervier, who was still on her knees.

"The gorgoneion tablet is actually a sacred talisman, created by the coven," the countess announced.

"A talisman?" Ophelia said, assisting Mervier to her feet.

"To you a relic, or the part of a temple's frieze. To us, a symbol of life, crafted by the will of the Gods. Ancient, as well as powerful."

"That I don't doubt," Ophelia replied.

"It is my legacy, to preserve the salvation of our bloodline. A gift from my father, for when I reach my physical birth age of half a century, the talisman will be used as part of a ritual that will bring back the return of my mother, after an eternity of being entombed."

"So, you can unleash her wrath upon the world?"

"She has been denied a life. Devoid of love and prosperity. The incantation that is inscribed on the talisman will remedy that. The Gods decreed that, at the moment of her release, the curse would be lifted, and I, myself, will return to that of a normal mortal woman. Something, that I have always truly desired since I turned sixteen, when I was bestowed the powers of a demi-god."

Ophelia and Mervier listened intently to this astonishing revelation.

Marzanna spoke with emotion.

"Why fifty?" Ophelia enquired.

"I have possessed these unique powers for thirty-four years. The age of my mother, when she was cursed by the goddess Athena. The ceremony must take place when I turn this age, not far from now, otherwise both Medusa and I will be afflicted and cursed for the rest of her days, and her thirst for vengeance could be catastrophic if it fails. It is the command of Poseidon. A chance. The *only* chance."

"And the sceptre?" Mervier croaked. She was still hell-bent on bringing this woman in, and the weapon.

"Like the bident, uniquely constructed by the Gods, and entrusted to the Coven of Gorgo, to protect our heritage. Our very existence."

"I can't let you disappear with it, Countess, you have committed murder," Mervier said, massaging her bruised neck.

Marzanna shook her head.

"As I wasn't gifted with the devastating powers of my mother, Poseidon perhaps felt pity for what happened and as his offspring, he ensured my survival by compensating me with what I have possessed for over three millennia. His lesser gods forged many magical weapons. Some are still out there to be discovered. However, this remains with me, until such time, we are no longer threatened by the hostile forces that have pursued us over endless time."

"You are not being hunted, Marzanna. I came here for answers."

"And you have them. So, call your troops off, or they will suffer, just like others."

"How do I know that you're telling me the truth?" Ophelia asked. She had been duped before, and found it difficult to believe her words – no matter how sincere.

"You have to take my word, for what it's worth. My only purpose is to save Medusa. My mother. You are free to go, with the promise that you will not pursue us. I have what I wanted. Let that be an end to it, as far as you're concerned."

Mervier's eyes scanned the room, and time was ticking. She glanced at Ophelia.

"She's lying," Mervier said, eyes fixated on the woman, who remained stoic.

"Then prove your intent, release Madison from your spell." Ophelia demanded, still distrustful of this mystical woman.

At that moment, one of the maidens appeared from the far door, which led to the kitchen. She approached Marzanna, and whispered into her ear. Marzanna nodded, and handed her the talisman.

"Prepare the boat," she uttered to her maiden, who disappeared with the other into the crevasse in the wall. Once they vanished into the darkness, the wall sealed itself shut.

Mervier was aware that the maidens had gone. She gripped the strap of the handbag that had slipped down her arm during her ordeal with the whip, and slowly moved forward.

She was only two or three metres away from Madison and Marzanna.

The detective also noticed Madison's head slumped down, she dropped the gun, and collapsed onto the floor in a heap. Mervier wondered, was she released, or did the spell wear off?

Was she dead?

"Madison!" Ophelia cried. Madison was still. Lifeless.

At that moment, Mervier spoke loudly into her concealed mic.

"Flamingo!"

"Wait!" Ophelia shouted, but it was too late.

CHAPTER 26
ENTERING THE FRAY

A huge explosion followed.

The portcullis was blown to pieces, and huge chunks of stone rubble from the barbican crashed to the ground.

The mercs had waited endlessly for the word, and were sitting in their Defender fifty metres away from the smouldering remains of the iron portcullis. Billows of smoke and dust rose from the debris, as Spears peered through his binoculars from the passenger seat.

Straker and Fox were in the rear seats. Fox had his computerised equipment on his lap, as he controlled the drone that hovered over the courtyard.

Once the smoke cleared, Spears noticed a huge gaping hole in what was left of the castle's portcullis, but the ground was littered with debris.

"It's clear!" Spears said, and Matheson hit the pedal.

The Defender accelerated fast towards the jagged opening. Uncertain what they were charging into from beyond the entrance.

Simultaneously, from the trawler's point of view, a massive orange glow was seen from beyond the castle in the distance. It lasted a few seconds, then darkness returned.

Vincent Keyes was watching from the deck, and it was now time. He flipped open his small portable I-pad, and his screen displayed the aerial images of the castle, from Hugo's on-board camera that was attached to his jetpack.

His air reaper assault group were already airborne, and they started to make their descending approach towards the courtyard.

"About goddamn time," Keyes growled.

CHAPTER 27

BETRAYED

Both Ophelia and Marzanna felt the other had gone back on their word, as the sound of the explosion outside shook the foundations of the castle, startling both.

"You have betrayed us!" Marzanna scowled, and instantly placed the bottom of the sceptre onto the stone statue of the hoplite warrior, whilst Ophelia rushed forward to check on Madison, who was lying prostrate on the ground.

Mervier threw her handbag at Marzanna, and clipped the handle of the sceptre, disarming the countess. The powerful weapon clattered harmlessly on the ground a few yards away from Ophelia.

"The sceptre!" Mervier shouted at Ophelia who, whilst trying to check for signs of life in her young associate, responded to the detective.

Ophelia dove for the sceptre, whilst Mervier sprinted towards her fallen Glock.

And then the unbelievable happened again.

The ancient Greek warrior moved. It had come to life.

First his head, and then his arms. Fragments of rock crumbed away from his stone body, and his reanimated eyes opened to reveal pure blackness. The head turned stiffly towards the two women. They looked in horror, as the warrior stepped off its stone pedestal.

Every time the stone-grey parts of the warrior's body moved, granules of stone seeped into the ground like multiple mini-waterfalls, as a result of the metamorphosis. Its joints were slowly loosening, dispensing more loose specks of rock. It became more mobile.

This distraction afforded Marzanna to scoop up the sceptre before Ophelia could reach it. The daughter of Medusa raced over to the entrance and was joined by four maidens in green reptilian-styled gowns. Each one carried a short recurve bow, and a quiver of arrows.

"We're under attack," one of the young maidens warned.

She turned to Ophelia, who was scrambling to her feet in the middle of the banquet room, now being approached by the seven-foot reanimated hoplite statue. It, or he was brandishing a large straight razor-sharp bronze sword, and carrying a wooden shield. The warrior wore a Corinthian helmet and a bronze muscle cuirass breastplate.

"It didn't need to be this way," Marzanna said solemnly to Ophelia with saddened eyes, but she felt that she would be relentlessly hunted, "You leave me no choice. I'm sorry."

Marzanna touched the two stone serpents with the reverse end of her sceptre, like she did with the hoplite soldier. At that moment, particles of stone fell from the surface of the snakes on the wall, their forked tongues lashed out from their heads, and both thirty-foot rattlesnakes, the size of mega-pythons slithered off from the wall and blocked the entrance.

Marzanna made her way into the grand foyer and signalled her four maidens to join her. They approached the large bulky wooden door to the courtyard, preparing to engage what intrusive forces had blasted their way into Marzanna's sanctuary.

Meanwhile, Ophelia and Mervier had more than enough to contend with, as they faced their new opponents that were once statues – now brought to life by the sceptre.

Two giant snakes slithered towards them, and an ancient Greek soldier was hacking and slicing the air, as he attempted to slash the women with his deadly sword. His strokes were clumsy and laboured, as if he had been awoken from a deep slumber.

Which wasn't far from the truth.

They were trapped, and Madison was still comatose, or dead on the floor. One of the brown giant snakes, the size of anacondas, slithered closer to the young woman, and its eyes blinked. Its jaws widened, ready to devour her.

Ophelia raced over to the armoury wall, and immediately grabbed one of the doru spears. Obviously not skilled at spear fighting, but it was worth a try. She screamed at the snake that was almost on top of Madison, and it sharply redirected its attention to the armed curator.

Ophelia threw the spear like a javelin at the snake and it was an impressive throw. It struck the huge serpent below its jaws. It remained embedded for a few seconds, and then the snake hissed aggressively, recoiling back, as if it actually felt pain.

Mervier grabbed her Glock, and cocked the weapon, took the safety off, and fired off several rounds of her seventeen into the same snake, before the slow, sluggish hoplite warrior closed in.

Bullets slammed into the snake, and as the projectiles smashed into the head and body of the writhing serpent, large holes were created from the 9mm slugs. Weird crystalised dark sandy blood poured out from its wounds. The snake collapsed onto the ground. It appeared to be half-organic, and half sedimentary rock.

Whatever it was, it appeared dead, as it stopped moving.

Ophelia quickly raced over to Madison, dodging the incoming swing from the warrior's sword. She grabbed her under the arms, and proceeded to drag her away from the approaching second giant rattlesnake-python-anaconda, hybrid.

Mervier fired more shots into the clunking warrior. Four shots ricocheted off his breastplate, and two penetrated his shield as he rose it to deflect. The rounds struck harmlessly into his chest armour again.

Ophelia dashed to the armoury wall again, and grabbed the nearest xiphos sword.

She quickly noticed herself in the reflection of a polished shield. A ruffled-up woman, wearing a dinner dress, and holding an ancient Greek sword. Not that it mattered, this empowered her. She took the aspis shield too and faced the warrior stomping towards her.

Mervier fired four more shots into the hoplite's body, trying to target beyond the armour line. Two got through into his neck, and the same bursts of sandy-blood-like substance oozed out from his new wounds. But the warrior didn't slow down his stride. At that moment, the second snake attacked Mervier, and, like a rattlesnake, tried to lash out at her with its deadly fangs.

She fired the remaining shots into its tough skin, but the snake quickly slammed its head into her, knocking her across the room. It then coiled around her, like a python.

Ophelia couldn't help her, as she was engaged in a ferocious duel with the warrior. Luckily, she had speed and agility on her side, as the former statue moved quite zombified with slow movements with his sword swings.

However, the blows raining down on her were heavy and powerful. Her shield took the brunt of his overhead and diagonal cuts coming down, splintering the archaic shield that she desperately tried to keep hold of. She couldn't find an opportunity to counter. Now, she wished she had studied swordplay.

Ophelia reacted when she found an opening, and struck low. Her sword hacked small chunks of flesh-stone from the warrior's shins. But, with each stroke of her sword, she was met with either a block from a shield, or a counter attack from her seemingly invincible opponent. Her energy was ebbing away, whereas the reanimated soldier didn't show any signs of fatigue.

The soldier slammed his shield against hers, and the force of the charge sent her crashing onto the floor. Her shield flew across the room in several pieces. Ophelia still maintained her grip on her heavily dented sword. It wouldn't be long before that would be shattered too, she thought. As he raised his sword for the final death blow, she clambered up and raced over to the armoury wall once again, avoiding the deadly cut.

She tried to think quickly as she looked at the choice of weapons on the armoury wall, just as the warrior loomed above her.

Mervier was getting crushed to death by the deadly embrace of the gargantuan serpent that had coiled itself around her body. She grunted, and tried with all her might to pry herself out of the giant snake's pulverising crush. The detective could feel and hear her bones cracking and grinding each second. One of her arms was free but could not reach her Glock. Not that it mattered any more. She had run out of ammunition.

Mervier nearly passed out. Was this the end, she thought? Her eyes started to close, and her arms felt numb. She had lost all her strength, and started to lose consciousness. The python's head rose above her, and its jaws opened – ready to devour her.

She looked up at the giant snake's mouth, and prepared for her horrific demise. Swallowed alive by a magically reanimated overgrown serpent.

All of a sudden, a doru spearhead pierced straight through the mouth of the snake from the other side of its head. The serpent writhed and let out a deafening hiss. Its black eyes dilated as wide as its jaws, and loosened the crushing grip on Mervier. She fell and rolled onto the ground.

As the detective looked up with weary eyes, she saw Madison standing above the lifeless snake, holding the spear deep into the back of its head. The same spear that was used on the first monstrous reptile.

Madison had come round. And appeared back on their side. Marzanna had indeed broken her hypnotic spell.

But the fight was far from over. As Mervier was crumpled on the ground, with suspected broken ribs, Ophelia was still struggling to defeat the Greek warrior near the armoury. Madison leapt off the lifeless snake, and raced over to help her friend.

CHAPTER 28

CHAOS IN THE COURTYARD

Meanwhile, inside the outer courtyard of the castle, another battle was just getting started.

The mercenaries' Defender had just ploughed through the small chunks of rubble and iron wreckage that had collapsed from the explosion, allowing an accessible hole for the vehicle to drive through.

Once they entered the courtyard, Matheson swerved the vehicle to a grinding halt, next to Ophelia's Morris Minor. Three of the Black Knights exited the vehicle, except for Fox, who remained in the back seat, manning the drone overhead.

There wasn't a moment to lose, and Spears sprinted towards the huge oak door at the front of the keep. As soon as he and Straker started to break into a sprint, he saw the door open quickly.

The four maidens armed with their traditional toxotai bows emerged from the doorway, and fanned out, allowing their high priestess, Marzanna, to step out. They created a semicircle formation around her, as she made her way over to one of the small niches in the stone wall, only a few meters away from where she materialised.

"That's her!" Matheson pointed. He noticed that she was still carrying the sceptre.

Marzanna scowled at the mercenaries as they advanced. She signalled to her four maidens, who started nocking arrows to their intricate bows.

"Take cover," Spears shouted, as the maidens released the first volley of arrows at the approaching mercs.

The arrows flew accurately in the direction of Matheson, Spears and Straker. They all dove to the ground, evading the lethal arrows. They sailed above the mercs, and struck the opposite wall. As they started to pick themselves up, the maidens widened their formation, and had already prepared their second set of missiles onto their strings.

Four more arrows whistled across the courtyard. The three mercenaries rolled and dove again, dodging the incoming bolts of death. They were pinned and not gaining any ground.

Enough time for Marzanna to reach the first niche in the wall, which contained a grotesque-looking stone gargoyle.

"Sentinels arise, destroy the intruders," she emitted from her lips.

Marzanna placed the end of the sceptre firmly onto the gargoyle. A strange vibration occurred, followed by a brilliant light. She kept the sceptre held in place whilst the light embraced the entire sculpture – and, like a conduit, the light streaked across the entire circumference of the stone wall like a lightning bolt.

As soon as the ethereal light connected to a gargoyle in its niche, the glow expanded, enveloping each stone sculpture completely, and then moved on to the next one in sequence. Within seconds, all twelve gargoyles had been touched by the mystical light, and Marzanna finally removed the sceptre from the first statue.

The mercs didn't notice the majestic light that had previously encircled them in a matter of seconds, as they were too pre-occupied with dodging wave after wave of arrows.

But Fox did notice from the drone's camera.

He panned in, and saw the most terrifying sight.

"Guys, heads up!" Fox shouted into his mic, completely in awe.

All twelve gargoyles miraculously came to life. Their hideous faces flinched first, and then their heads moved. The terrifying monsters broke out of their niches, and particles of stone spilt from their dormant joints, once they were fully reanimated.

Each snarling gargoyle simultaneously launched out of their crevices, and flew into the air. Their bat-like wings flapping in the night air, showering excess stone and dust onto the ground.

"The gargoyles are alive!" Straker shouted.

"Well, this is new!" Spears looked up, and they circled the mercs, preparing for a bombing dive run.

"Blast 'em!" Matheson wasted no time, being dumb-struck.

The moment they aimed their G-36 carbines into the air, the horde of grey gargoyles made their first dive. They swooped in fast and low. Their sharp talons open, ready to snatch and tear apart their victims, who were taking firing positions on the ground.

The mercenaries let rip. All three fired short controlled bursts into the air. Bullets thudded into several gargoyles, and tore off small fragments of rock from their muscular, powerful bodies. But this didn't seem to affect them too much.

One gargoyle dove and evaded another burst from Straker, then circled and flew straight for him. Straker fired back whilst retreating. Round after round, smashing into multiple parts of the winged demon. His rifle was spent, and he turned and broke into a run, trying to get cover behind the Defender.

At that moment, the drone launched a small missile at the ferocious creature, and scored a direct hit. The gargoyle was blasted into dozens of pieces. A tar-like substance also splattered across the ground, along with the monster's rocky remains.

Fox was controlling the drone, within the safety of the Defender.

This agitated the rest of the flying horde. Two of them flew straight for the drone. Fox activated the small twin machine guns on the drone's undercarriage and laid a heavy barrage of fire at the approaching monsters. The rapid fire obliterated one of them, sending shards of its decimated body crashing into Mervier's brand-new vehicle.

"Whoops!" Fox muttered under his breath, but realised he couldn't swerve the drone out of the way in time, as he saw on its camera, the second flying creature filling the entire screen within a matter of milliseconds.

The gargoyle smashed into the drone at full speed, utterly destroying it. The wreckage plummeted down, and landed full force onto Mervier's car, further crushing its roof and shattering the windows. The creature then circled again, and locked its eyes on its nearest target on the ground. Nathan Spears, who was firing continued bursts at the deadly flock.

Marzanna and her maidens stayed close to the entrance of the keep, as they observed the battle intensify around them.

She was temporarily distracted when she looked up and saw a further group of men in jetpacks soaring overhead. They immediately opened rigorous fire with their mini chain guns that were attached to the packs.

Huge chunks from a couple of the gargoyles rained down as a result of the powerful barrages that were launched by the air reaper's superior weapons.

This also surprised the mercenaries on the ground. Fox leapt out of the Defender and noticed the new players entering the chaos.

"Who the hell are these guys?" Fox shouted. Matheson, who was closest to him, reloaded his rifle.

"Legionshield."

"Who the hell invited them?" Fox said amidst the din of the firepower from above.

"Does it matter? They came at the right time!" the leader replied, "We gotta get inside the keep. Get the girls outta there."

At that point, the bottom half of a destroyed gargoyle fell from the air, and directly on top of Ophelia's Morris Minor, crushing it into a pulp. She wouldn't be happy about that. If she was alive, Matheson thought.

Spears hammered another clip into his carbine, when one of the gargoyles landed on the ground. It stomped fiercely towards him, a few yards away. The mercenary switched to fully automatic, and laid a continuous volley of fire into it, tearing pieces off its body with each step it took. Spears backed up as he emptied his magazine. The gargoyle still advanced, growling and snarling.

It then leapt into the air and was about to pounce on the retreating merc, when he quickly ditched his rifle, and rolled to the side. The gargoyle landed with a thud where Spears had previously stood.

He scrambled up and pulled out his automatic pistol, firing 9mm slugs into the gargoyles already battle-damaged head. Two further shots struck its eyes, and the gargoyle winced back, blinded. It flailed its arms, trying to swipe at Spears with its deadly claws, but Spears dodged each swing, and picked up some debris from the portcullis that was strewn across the courtyard. A piece of sharp iron, the size of a cricket bat, was his own weapon.

The gargoyle could sense Spears' movements and launched in the air again. Spears side stepped and swung the iron bar with everything he had across its neck. The force of the strike took the gargoyle's head clean off, and the monster's headless corpse collapsed onto the cobbled stones.

Marzanna surmised that the battle could go either way, as she saw at least half of her reanimated protectors get destroyed. She then signalled to her archers, and they tried to aim for the skies.

Arrows streaked upwards at the constantly moving aerial targets. One arrow managed to strike one of the air reapers in the shoulder that was unprotected by his exo-armour. He shrieked, and lost control of his jetpack. As he tried to recover, a gargoyle suddenly slammed into him with full force, and the pilot screamed as he smashed directly into the high wall of the keep. The jetpack exploded with a deafening bang, and the remains of the reaper and the pack plummeted to the ground.

The maidens continued this tactic as they saw four gargoyles in a midair battle against the air reapers who were banking and manoeuvring high above the courtyard. They were firing high-velocity rounds and lasers at the demons.

Another air reaper met his end when a gargoyle grabbed the chassis of his pack from behind and threw him into the walls that surrounded the bailey. The jetpack exploded in a massive ball of flames.

At that point, one of the maidens released an arrow. It harmlessly bounced off the pack of the reaper that was descending towards her.

A laser beam blasted out from the jetpack's mounted dorsal gun and accurately hit the young acolyte in the chest, scorching her gown. She froze, as she felt the deadly effects of the super-intensified laser pierce her heart.

Marzanna stopped in her tracks as she witnessed this shocking moment.

"Carissa!" she cried.

Her young disciple fell to her knees, dropped her bow, and then crumpled dead to the ground. Her eyes were still open, looking blankly at the battleground.

"No!" Marzanna screamed with anger.

The high priestess leapt high into the air with supernatural speed, as the air reaper started to ascend, and when she was close enough thrashed the pilot with the crown of the sceptre, making contact with his unprotected leg.

The air reaper's body instantly turned to stone mid-flight, except for his light armour. The jetpack whizzed out of control and crashed into the keep's half-opened door, destroying it. His stone body was smashed into pieces when he impacted.

Marzanna landed on her feet, and whirled around to notice another reaper soaring in towards her.

"I want her alive," came through the reaper's earpiece as she targeted the woman.

A single laser blast from the dorsal gun streaked at her.

The reaper was Hugo, and the laser shot glanced at her arm, scoring and searing her flesh, but not severely injuring her. It was enough for her to drop the sceptre.

As Hugo landed, he immediately detached himself from the jetpack, and he let it tumble to the ground. The hulking menace approached her. Her three surviving maidens were approximately twenty meters away and were already being fired upon by Hugo's wingman who was hovering above. The maidens desperately dove for cover.

Hugo revealed a bulky crimson gauntlet on his wrist. He aimed it at Marzanna, and without hesitation clenched his fist. A huge weighted net was launched out of the gauntlet. It ensnared the wounded woman, bringing her to her knees. He pressed another button, which electrified the net. High voltage coursed through Marzanna's body, causing her to convulse uncontrollably on the ground.

He had her at his mercy.

⌖

CHAPTER 29

HER SIGNATURE MOVE

The living statue warrior brought down his sword again, and Ophelia blocked it with an old antique mace that she had managed to wrench off the armoury wall. She held it with both ends and buckled once again to her knees. The warrior pressed hard and Ophelia was losing strength.

The blade was an inch away from her face, as she struggled hard to suppress the force coming down on her.

Madison let out a huge war-cry, and launched into a flying side-kick. Her foot made contact to the side of the hoplite warrior's armour, and he stumbled back a step, allowing Ophelia to escape from her hapless position. Madison's foot felt the impact too, and when she tried to recover her footwork, she stumbled.

But she bravely adopted a fighting stance as the clunky warrior spun around to face her. Ophelia then swung the mace hard at her unstoppable opponent, and he raised the shield, parrying the blow. It bounced off harmlessly: The shock vibration caused the curator to drop the weapon.

At that time, the warrior thrust his weapon straight at Madison in an attempt to run her through with the blade. Madison jumped back reactively, landing on her good leg. She hobbled back further, realising she hadn't the ability to fight as effectively as she wanted to. She picked up a chair next to her and threw it at the soldier, who raised his shield. The chair broke into several pieces, and the formidable warrior continued to advance on the girl.

Ophelia darted behind the warrior and ripped down a large coat of arms flag that stood prominently next to the fireplace. She quickly ran towards him with the material in her hands, whilst the warrior relentlessly continued to slash and hack at the withdrawing Madison.

Ophelia vaulted into the air, and threw the huge cloth over the Corinthian helmet of the reanimated soldier, temporarily blinding him. She then proceeded to scoop up the sword from the floor, as the warrior spun around, disorientated. His movements couldn't shake off the material that enveloped his top half.

The warrior dropped the shield and sword, and used his hands to pull off the coat of arms that was draped over his head. The helmet came with it.

When the living statue had regained his sight, a battleaxe wielded by Ophelia was the last thing the warrior saw. The blades flashed before his dark nondescript eyes.

The battleaxe decapitated the warrior. The hoplite crashed to the ground, and his head landed with a hard thud, next to the helmet. Finally defeated.

Ophelia stood there and dropped the heavy battleaxe.

"That must be your signature move, huh?" Madison said, catching her breath, remembering when Ophelia decapitated the sorcerer not so long ago.

"It works."

"More effective than mine," Madison said, hobbling on her injured foot.

"I'm glad you're back with us," Ophelia replied.

"I'm so sorry."

They embraced but briefly, as there was more to do, and the sound of battle outside was escalating. Ophelia then picked up the fallen xiphos sword, and dashed over to a wounded Mervier, who was still clutching at her ribs.

Madison hobbled over, wincing every time she took a step.

"It's not over yet. We've got to get out of here. Our friends need help."

"Where's the witch?" Mervier said angrily. She was still seeking justice.

"I don't know. You're in no condition to pursue, Nicole."

"We'll see about it, I cannot allow her to escape," she groaned, as she was helped up.

"Worry about that later, we've got to go, and now!" Ophelia said, adamantly.

The three women, dirtied and dishevelled, headed towards the main foyer.

Into another war zone.

CHAPTER 30

THE RAGE OF THE MAGE

The battle at Ravenscliff castle was in its final stages. The four mercenaries were still trying to find a clear pathway to the door of the keep, but were relentlessly attacked by the remaining gargoyles that swooped down.

Legionshield's air reapers were still engaged in aerial combat with the monstrous creatures. Another reaper had been rammed into, and sent to his doom, landing with horrendous force on the ground below. His mangled body was buried underneath the twisted fiery wreckage of his jetpack.

Ophelia emerged from the open door of the keep, supporting both her wounded companions in each arm.

They looked around at the devastation in the courtyard, and the spectacular light show of lasers and tracer fire above them. Their faces were equally astonished to see flying gargoyles amidst the action.

"Holy shit!" Madison gasped, whilst she hobbled out.

Spears and Fox raced over to them, and the mercs assisted the two injured women, whilst Ophelia glanced over to the other side of the courtyard, and saw her beloved Morris Minor crushed. It was covered with huge pieces of remains that resembled terrifying demons.

The Defender was still intact and looked relatively unscathed. Matheson and Straker had sought cover there, and were firing bursts of fire at the swooping gargoyles that were descending during their continued dive attacks.

"What the hell?" Ophelia shouted when she saw the wreckage of her car. Mervier's was just as damaged. Not that it is the immediate concern right now.

"Where is she?" Ophelia's face darted left from right, searching for the countess.

"We got to get you to cover!" Spears yelled, and lifted Madison onto his shoulder. Fox did the same to Mervier, but she shrieked in agony as the strong mercenary hoisted her onto his shoulder. Her battered ribs feeling each step as he raced across the compound to the Defender. Spears wasn't far behind.

Ophelia then noticed Marzanna twenty meters away, ensnared in some form of net. Still holding the xiphos short sword, she broke into a run towards her and the menace that had her entangled in his special restraint.

"Where the hell are you going?" Spears shouted, as she neared the Defender. She ignored the merc, and closed in on the countess' captor. The sceptre was still on the ground near her.

Meanwhile, Marzanna was still captured and sustaining bad physical injuries from the electrified net that was still attached to the gauntlet of Hugo's right wrist. Marzanna tried with all her superhuman might to pry her fingers through the small gaps in the net, but the powerful current continued to seer through her. Any normal human being would have been killed by now, Hugo surmised. She was a tough cookie.

Suddenly, a short sword was thrown from a few metres away, and struck Hugo's shoulder by the flat of the blade. It didn't cause injury, but just enough impact for him to unclench his fist that had activated the gauntlet's weapon. This resulted in stopping the electrical current, and distracting him momentarily for him to spin around and face his new adversary.

Ophelia Winters stood stoic in front of the hulking brute, unarmed and battle-worn. Her evening dress was torn in several places. Her legs and arms were bruised and sported fresh cuts.

But she stood steadfast.

Hugo was angered, and approached the curator. He also signalled one of the reapers in to intercept her.

Marzanna saw this, and replenished herself. With immense supernatural strength, she ripped apart the net with her hands, freeing herself.

Immediately she launched into the air and threw herself into Hugo. As she grabbed him, he tried to wrestle her off him – but to no avail.

Marzanna was at her most enraged. She tossed Hugo like a rag doll straight into the stone wall behind him, in one of the empty crevasses that once housed a gargoyle. This knocked the wind out of him, but he was still conscious. As he slumped to the ground, the air reaper came in at Ophelia.

The curator picked up the xiphos sword from the ground, and held it defensively, waiting for the attack to come. Its mini-guns were trained on her.

The air reaper flew in low.

Marzanna then jumped into the air, covering the distance from where she was to where the reaper was, within a second. She clung onto the side of the jetpack's chassis and whirled in the air, redirecting the pilot's course. He crashed into the ground accompanied by a scream. Marzanna landed on the ground nearby, and as the wounded reaper hastily unbuckled himself from the destroyed equipment, Ophelia charged forward and slashed at the operative with her sword, cutting his leg joint where it was not armoured. He fell.

Marzanna smiled, and observed Ophelia bravely standing her ground.

As Ophelia knocked the pilot out unconscious with the haft of the sword, Marzanna was attacked by a dazed Hugo from behind. The countess lashed out a flurry of lightning-fast strikes and kicks, like a super-powered martial artist. Too fast for the human eye to register each blow that connected.

But they did, and even though he was wearing strong exo-armour, Hugo was brought down with each crippling blow. Marzanna opened her hand and delivered a powerful palm heel strike into the centre of his chest armour.

The Legionshield henchman was catapulted back ten feet and smashed into the same cavity that he landed in a few seconds ago. This time he stayed here, incapacitated or dead. Marzanna didn't know which, but he wasn't moving.

She then saw one of the other reapers lowering its descent, and starting to fire at the three surviving maidens, who were racing to the keep's door. One of her young acolytes was tragically cut down by the intense firepower of one of the mini-guns. Her back was riddled with dozens of red holes. As she fell, Marzanna once again leapt ten feet into the air, and underneath the reaper.

She grabbed his lower legs, which dangled freely, and pulled hard. The pilot, inside his jetpack, lurched forward, and the firepower of the mini guns sprayed into the ground a few feet below. She had saved her two remaining maidens.

Marzanna spun around again, screaming with wild ferocity, and generated enough force to sling the reaper across the compound, causing him to crash against the wall next to the keep's door. The jetpack took the brunt of the collision, and exploded. The air reaper was instantly killed.

At this point, Ophelia seized the opportunity and opened up her other hand to collect the grounded sceptre. Her fingers were only inches from it, until the end of a whip quickly coiled around the centre of the artefact, and in a blink of an eye, pulled it from the ground into the hands of one of the maidens.

The two maidens stood with Marzanna, and then they approached the door of the keep.

Ophelia was stunned, and looked at them. They were only fifteen meters across from where she was standing. Marzanna and Ophelia looked at each other for a couple of seconds. Both knowing that they had saved each other's lives.

There was a moment of respect. An understanding even.

Marzanna reclaimed the sceptre from her maiden, and her two flanking acolytes nocked arrows onto their bow strings, pulled them, and aligned the tips directly at Ophelia.

Marzanna stretched out her arms, and instantly lowered them. Her maidens obeyed, and gently eased off the draw pull from their bow strings.

"No, let us go," Marzanna uttered softly amidst the sounds of gunfire, lasers and explosions. But to Ophelia, it was audible – the only thing that she heard.

Then, as if on cue, a gargoyle crashed down in four huge pieces in the wide space between the two women. For Ophelia, this was reminiscent of the time when the temple chamber came down in-between Marzanna and herself, on the island during a very similar, brief exchange of looks.

But Ophelia was fully aware, and not hypnotised in any way, shape or form. Marzanna had reached out amicably.

The horrendous distraction spewed dust and smoke into the air when the destroyed gargoyle hit the earth. Ophelia shielded her eyes from the dust. When the dust cleared, she looked towards the doors of the keep.

Marzanna and her two acolytes were gone.

CHAPTER 31

ESCAPING RAVENSCLIFF

Vincent Keyes had been monitoring the battle from the jetpack cameras that were broadcasting their images to his electronic tablet.

Each image displayed the progress of the mission. One by one, various images from his multiple-screen display instantly switched to static, the moment each air reaper crashed or was killed.

Only two of his elite air reapers remained in the air.

He viewed the three screens that were feeding live images. Two of them were embroiled in the aerial fighting that was still occurring. His two surviving reapers were blasting the last remnants of the gargoyle horde from the skies.

However, the third image had been displaying an image which was coming from a grounded undamaged jetpack. It was Hugo's. The image showed the fascinating fight between Marzanna and the jetpack's owner, as well as the live footage of the incredibly powerful woman killing a couple of his aerial attackers.

This excited Keyes, as he had it confirmed that this remarkable woman who claimed to be the daughter of Medusa was, indeed, extraordinarily powerful, and wielded an even more destructive weapon.

He had to get his hands on both.

The last image that the jetpack cam picked up was Marzanna disappearing with two of her faithful servants inside the castle.

Keyes spoke into the ear mic, as he had been in constant communication with his lethal air crew throughout the mission.

"Don't let her get away. She's gone back inside the castle, leave the mercs to deal with what's left of those unholy creatures!" he ordered.

By viewing the images, he noticed that most of the gargoyles had been destroyed. He also saw Ophelia standing there near the keep, holding her xiphos.

"If anybody gets in your way, kill them."

"Affirmative," was his response from one of the remaining reapers.

Vincent Keyes looked anxious, and turned his attention to the castle and the cliffs leading up to it. He pondered. There could be no way of escaping unless there was a network of tunnels leading to the coastline, or worse still, a tunnel that led inland.

The CEO looked across the deck to see who he had left in his expeditionary force. Only a handful of engineers and four security operatives, but no jetpacks were left. Only a couple of small two-man futuristic boats that were attached to its davits.

He then looked through his infra-red binoculars again, and enhanced the images so he could view the cliffs and coastline carefully. Across the dark waters, it was quiet.

He felt his opportunity was slipping away.

That was until he saw a glimmer of slight activity emanating from underneath an overhanging section of the stone castle. It was a part of the fortress, and it appeared to jut out from where the top of the cliffs met the castle's stonework.

Coming out from the bottom of the protruding section of the castle was a large basket, and it was attached to a couple of pulleys that descended 200 feet to the rocky coastline below.

Inside the basket were three women.

Keyes' jaw dropped, and he observed his prime target, and the surviving members of her coven attempting their secret escape.

"You slippery, bitches!" he growled, "I've got you."

He noticed the basket was in a controlled descent, opposite the cliff face.

Keyes spoke quickly into his ear mic as the basket continued its course.

"Air reapers, I've spotted them. They're making a break for it on the cliffs. Look for a descending basket underneath the castle. Intercept them when they land on the rocks below. Do not blast them out of the sky!"

"Roger that, sir."

Vincent Keyes now had a glimmer of hope. It wasn't over yet. Without taking his eyes off the basket, he tilted his head to address his crew behind him.

"Prepare the EELs."

The crew knew this was the name of his new hi-tech sled-skiffs that had replaced the trawler's lifeboats, back at the harbour.

He surmised, as long as he could cut off their escape, there would be no chance of them slipping through his fingers now.

CHAPTER 32

THE HUNT IS ON

Ophelia was still standing above the unconscious air reaper who was sprawled out by her feet.

She was joined by Spears and Straker, who fired numerous bursts into the air, dropping the last gargoyle from its flight. As it landed in pieces, Ophelia glanced upwards at the two surviving jetpacks as they banked towards the trio.

"We're on your side, you, arseholes!" Straker shouted into the air as they came in.

Spears slammed in his final magazine into the G-36 carbine, and shielded Ophelia. Both mercs aligned their rifles into the air, preparing to fire on the approaching reapers – alleged allies or not.

At that point, they banked hard either side, and started to ascend away. Whether they feared being shot at by the Black Knight mercenaries or something else, they immediately changed course. Like they had been recalled.

Ophelia peered down, distracted by the muffled voices coming from the unconscious reaper's headset that was halfway off his helmet. The mercs held their fire.

The curator picked up the helmet from the prostrate jetpack operative, placed the earpiece section to the side of her head, and tried to listen into the garbled communication.

It was a male's voice updating his aerial combatants.

"Roger that, disengaging." One of the reapers acknowledged via the headset.

"Head to the cliff face, our target is nearly at the bottom!" was the stranger's voice.

"Enroute." The second reaper responded.

Ophelia looked alarmed, and her eyes darted up into the night skies again, as the two air reapers manoeuvred over the outer walls of the bailey, flew past the top of the keep, and disappeared on the other side, as if they were flying out toward the channel.

"They're going after her, we got to stop them!" she shouted.

"What?" Spears said, completely baffled.

At that point, the Defender screeched over to the group, driven by Matheson. Next to him was Fox. They had Mervier and Madison in the second row of back seats, still nursing their injuries.

"Where's the countess?" Mervier shouted through the window, still holding her bruised midriff.

"On the cliff face," Ophelia replied, trying to catch her breath, uncertain of what action to take. Does she pursue her, or escape the battleground that was Ravenscliff?

Mervier opened the door to her side, and clambered out of the Defender.

"We can't let her get away!" She noticed a holstered 9mm Ruger sidearm strapped to the leg of the downed reaper. Immediately she drew it, and cocked the weapon.

"Whoa, what the hell do you think you're doing?" Straker said.

The determined detective was relentless, and fixed her eyes on the doorway of the keep. In front of it was the smashed debris of stone carcasses of the gargoyles, jetpack wreckage and a couple of bodies from Legionshield's aerial unit.

"I have a job to do. I'll do it alone if I must. Whoever these people are, we cannot allow them to capture her," Mervier snarled, "There is a secret exit, probably to the cliffs. It's all we have!" The detective remembered the fireplace, and the stoker that activated the sliding wall.

Ophelia was torn. She agreed, to a certain extent, about preventing Legionshield apprehending the countess, but couldn't decide what to do.

There was a momentary pause.

Mervier shook her head, annoyed at the mercenaries' hesitation. Despite her injuries, she broke into a run.

"For God's sake!" Ophelia cursed, gripping her sword. She ran behind Mervier. She didn't have a plan, but maybe would be able to think of something if they were lucky to catch up with her. The curator was warned, or even advised to stay away, but something compelled her to follow Mervier.

Matheson sighed with exasperation at this new development. He signalled to Spears and Straker, and they bolted after Ophelia. Not to catch her, but to assist.

"Secure the area," Matheson said, and Fox climbed out of the Defender, noticing the wounded air reaper, groaning. He was slowly coming round. The merc trained his Glock on him.

Hugo was still incapacitated inside the niche, like a new addition, or a replacement to the gargoyle that once adorned the wall display.

Mervier, Ophelia, Spears and Straker had already made their way into the keep.

Matheson surveyed the area.

The battle was over.

But the chase had begun.

CHAPTER 33

TRAPPED

Marzanna and her two surviving maidens from the battle were inside the sturdy and spacious wicker basket as it continued in its vertical drop.

Its cable wires attached to the top of the basket that transported the escapees grinded. It was mechanically and electronically operated from its chamber high above them. Marzanna looked anxiously over the edge of the basket. She realised she was only 50 feet above the surface of the rocks below. Not far away now.

It was only then that she saw two figures in jetpacks materialising from out of the darkness in the near distance above her. Two of her acolytes placed arrows onto their bow strings. Marzanna scowled at the air reapers closing in.

"Will this never end for us?" she said, angrily.

Her two archers stood in front of Marzanna, and waited until the reapers were in range. It was clear they had won the battle, as there was no sign of her reanimated gargoyles.

Meanwhile, inside the secret chamber 150 feet above the fleeing women, Mervier entered the room, followed by Ophelia and her mercs. It was a simple and sizeable rustic-looking area. It had firm wooden cladding as a floor. Stone walls surrounded them, no weapons or furniture. A plain emergency escape exit.

At the end of the room, the floor had a 10 x 10 metre square gap, and below was a sheer drop to the rocky coastline. Fixed to the ceiling was a motorised pulley contraption, and a strong single cable wire was securely attached to it.

It was moving.

The cable wire hung through the gap in the floor, and all the way to the bottom – where the basket was.

Mervier noticed a metal pedestal next to the gap in the floor. It was a basic control board with a couple of buttons, and a single lever. The lever was fixed to the left, and it wouldn't take a technical wiz to know how to operate the controls.

The bruised and bloodied detective then peered over the edge carefully. Looking down, she saw a small shape of what looked like a basket containing a handful of passengers. She exhaled with relief.

Without hesitation, Mervier immediately went over to the control console, and flipped the lever to the centre panel of the console.

"What are you doing?" shouted Ophelia.

The cable wire suddenly jolted, and stopped moving.

The women in the basket were astonished when the basket stopped its descent. Now they were sitting ducks. The basket swayed slowly left to right. It was dangling precariously above the rocks – only 25 feet from the bottom. Marzanna knew she could jump to safety with her miraculous powers, but the fate of her loyal maidens was another matter.

They didn't possess any great supernatural abilities. Her acolytes were young normal mortals, with great skill sets in ancient weaponry and fitness – but even a jump from this height would certainly kill them. They accepted their fate.

"Save yourself, High Priestess, we will cover you," said one of her maidens.

"You must survive to fulfil your destiny," the second one added.

Marzanna saw the air reapers get even closer, and they were well within range, but they didn't open fire. They maintained their positions, hovering twenty or thirty meters away from the dangling basket.

She also knew she couldn't abandon her faithful sisters of the coven. She treated them like daughters, although she knew she could never conceive herself – which was another one of her curses. Marzanna had already witnessed the deaths of two of her devoted followers. Any more, could trigger her to unleash an unfathomable amount of vengeful wrath – just as Ophelia feared.

She just wanted to escape and realised she was trapped. Marzanna had underestimated her new hunters.

"I stay, and will share the same fate, if it is the will of the gods."

As soon as the air reapers were close enough, the only two armed maidens pulled back on their bows, and released the first couple of arrows, concentrating their aim on one of the reapers.

The arrows skimmed past the jetpack operatives. A narrow miss, but they didn't retaliate. They flew out of their current positions and soared around, like buzzards stalking their prey. They were now moving targets.

"Why aren't they fighting back? They could effortlessly destroy us," a maiden said.

"They want us alive, they're just making sure we don't get away," Marzanna replied.

"High Priestess. I implore you. Escape while you can. We have devoted our living souls to you, all our lives, let us do the same in death." The first maiden pleaded with her matriarch.

Marzanna looked over the edge, and for a moment, even considered leaping into the misty rocks below.

It was at this point in her terrible predicament, that the basket started to ascend.

Inside the control chamber, Mervier had wrenched the lever fully to the right, which started up the machine. The cable wire was now slowly hauling the basket upwards – towards the chamber. The arrest was only moments away.

She was wary of the fight that would shortly ensue once they arrived back inside the chamber, and the risk she was putting them all in, but this was the last-ditch attempt of capturing her and the sceptre.

Ophelia saw a glimpse of the control board behind Mervier, and knew that Marzanna was being hauled up to be captured. She still didn't have a plan.

Should she desperately try to do something to allow her to escape, or accept what fate would have in store for all of them? Either way, whatever decision she made, there was no telling of the outcome.

The detective's mind came up with many potential ways this could play out. At least she had some form of backup with the mercs. If they were compliant, she could use this to her advantage.

"You'll kill us all, Nicole!" Ophelia shouted, trying to make sense of what was happening, realising that Marzanna would most likely go on a destructive rampage, once she emerged through the opening in the floor.

"There's no time to argue, Ophelia, I'm sorry. She is dangerous."

"She just wants to live."

The mercs were totally perplexed. What was happening?

Whilst Mervier glanced down at the rising basket below, Ophelia placed the tip of her sword on Mervier's neck, where her carotid artery was.

The detective was astonished and froze. The mercs were equally flabbergasted.

Meanwhile, inside the basket. Marzanna and her maidens were continually ascending towards the ever-increasing opening gap in the chamber above. They estimated that they were now 60ft above the coastline.

Marzanna needed to make a decision of her own. Even at this height, she could break an ankle.

"I can jump and catch you both," she suggested desperately.

As the maidens looked at each other, considering this crazy idea, a single laser beam pierced the night sky. It struck one of the acolytes in the chest, and she collapsed into the basket. She was killed instantly. Her bow fell over the edge and crashed onto the rocks below.

They were trying to pick off the expendable. And the wicker would offer no shield or protection.

"No!" Marzanna shrieked. Her remaining maiden took aim and released another arrow causing the air reaper that fired the lethal beam to swerve out of the way of the incoming missile. Marzanna was unarmed and could not use the sceptre either.

The basket was now 70ft above the ground. Nearly halfway up.

Marzanna deduced that Ophelia had betrayed her trust, as she knew the location of the secret entrance that led to the chamber, and kept the pursuit up. Or these new enemies now had the upper hand, and forced the information out of the curator. And they were waiting for her inside the chamber.

All of a sudden, the basket abruptly stopped again, causing it to rock side to side.

What was going on up there?

"I can't allow that, forgive me," Ophelia solemnly said, as she cranked the lever to the left with her other hand. She kept the sword tip pressed lightly on her neck, and Mervier dropped the Ruger 9mm.

The cables groaned, and the basket commenced its descent, for the second time.

"You, stupid woman!" the detective growled.

Mervier looked desperately at the mercenaries.

"Guys, do something, can't you tell, she's been hypnotised by this witch, just like Madison had been?" Mervier screamed at them.

They exchanged confused looks.

They pondered, could this possibly be true?

"Trust me, I am perfectly coherent, I'm saving us all," Ophelia said, glancing down momentarily at the basket's progressive journey to the ground.

"Ophelia, listen, this woman is a murderer, and God knows what she could unleash onto this world," Mervier tried her conflict management tone.

"Ophelia, our mission objective is to recover the sceptre, and peacefully bring this woman in, you know that," Straker said. He was aware that Matheson was probably listening to everything going on from their radio headsets.

"Exactly!" snapped Mervier. She was relieved, knowing that she had the mercs on her side.

Ophelia looked at Spears, who chose to remain silent to this point. He had complete loyalty to the woman he had shared so many experiences with, as well as having a romantic interlude in the past.

"Nathan," she said softly. "Please trust me, you know me, I'm not bewitched. All she wants is to survive, like her…mother, and protect herself. To leave a life of forever being hunted."

"And you believe that?" Spears spoke, uncertain.

"I do."

"And if you're wrong?" Straker added.

"Guys, for Christ's sakes, we're wasting time. Don't be fooled by her, we don't know the extent of this woman's powers," Mervier said, trying to convince the men.

Whom to believe?

The mercenaries had to do something.

It was apparent the team were turning on each other.

As Ophelia was distracted by pleading to her mercenaries, Mervier felt the bronze of the metal sword slightly move away from her neck. She quickly flung her arm aside, striking Ophelia's sword arm.

The weapon was knocked out of her hand. It landed on the floor on the far side of the room.

Now Ophelia was unarmed, and the detective, being a seasoned cop, had more unarmed combat prowess than her companion.

She didn't want to fight Ophelia, but the curator herself was knocked back, and nearly fell over the edge of the gap in the floor, to her doom.

The mercs raced forward, but Mervier stretched out and caught the curator's arm before she toppled into the abyss that was beneath her. With all her might, she hauled her back, and as soon as Ophelia was on solid ground, the tenacious detective grabbed the lever again to the central point.

Spears dashed forward and scooped Ophelia up. Straker moved over to the control panel, as Mervier picked up her Ruger, and aimed it at Ophelia. Straker stopped in his motion.

"Back off," Mervier warned. "You've got to trust me. This is the right thing to do!"

Mervier yanked the lever aggressively to the right, but this time, the machinery stalled, and the grinding metal whined. Rattling noises were heard in the pulley mechanism above, and the cable wires shuddered. Nothing moved. The old machine was broken.

"Shit!" Mervier cursed, and desperately tried pulling the stiff lever back to the centre, and then attempted to reset, by pressing the on/off buttons, but nothing was operating. It had seriously malfunctioned or simply died.

Ophelia grinned to herself, but it didn't last long. She didn't know how far from the ground the basket was. The countess could be stuck there for a long time, and completely exposed to whatever was out there attacking her.

This probably exacerbated the situation below.

Marzanna knew that something was occurring above her in the chamber. The basket was starting, stopping and changing its course. But now it had come to an immediate halt. The cables groaned more now and the soothing hum of its mechanisms went silent.

Marzanna and her maiden were left stranded in the basket. She glanced over at the edge again, and although they had been descending for a good period of time, she noticed that they were a good 30ft from the ground.

The air reapers made another approach, blasting streaks of laser beams at the archer that was attempting to aim at the moving targets. They were trapped in their only source of salvation. Marzanna couldn't afford another loss.

She made a decision, and kicked away the door section of the basket off its hinges. The wicker door fell to the rocks below, and toppled into the waves of the sea that crashed off the embankments.

"Cover me, I'll catch you!" Marzanna advised. The maiden was down to her last arrow, so she placed it on her string, whilst keeping low inside the basket.

Marzanna prepared to jump, and smiled at her acolyte, reassuringly.

A laser ripped through the wicker basket, barely missing the crouched maiden. Furiously she broke cover, and aimed at one of the reapers. As the arrow flew through the air, Marzanna leapt from the basket and landed safely on the jagged rocks below with great precision, and an even cleaner landing, like an Olympic gymnast. It was an amazing feat.

The arrow struck true into the reaper's shoulder, penetrating his armour. This affected his piloting as his jetpack dipped to the side. The reaper shrieked in pain, as the arrow remained embedded in his right shoulder. Blood oozed from his wound and trickled down his arm, as he struggled to recover control.

He banked hard away from the cliffs, and started to make his way back to the trawler.

The other reaper kept his position and closed in on the swinging basket.

Cora, the last maiden, looked at her dead sister curled up in the corner.

Another laser blast pierced the side of the basket and blasted straight through the other end. The lethal beam passed just inches above her head, severing a strand of her black hair.

Marzanna shouted out from below.

"Cora. Jump!"

Cora made her way over to the open section of the basket and leapt out into the night air. Another laser beam streaked behind her, where she launched from, boring another charred hole into the basket.

Cora plunged 30ft down, and before she hit the ground, the maiden was caught by Marzanna's awaiting arms. The countess almost lost her balance, but managed to compose herself on the slippery rocks.

The air reaper then started to descend towards them, and made an attack dive.

"Stay on them!" Keyes said, through the pilot's headset. He had been anxiously observing the whole action with his infra-red binoculars, from the deck of the Salty Star.

Marzanna ensured Cora took the lead, and they both hurriedly made their way across the rocky embankment that led towards a small dark opening at the foot of the cliffs. It was a cove. Ripples of waves from the channel washed in.

It was concealed by the darkness. Even Keyes didn't notice it at first.

The reaper was gaining distance, and saw the two women about to enter the cave. He checked his inventory and his chain guns were dry. His laser capacity had been depleted. The reaper switched to another control on his left controller dashboard.

Another muzzle that was installed underneath the dorsal laser aligned itself on the first woman making her way into the cave.

The reaper pressed the fire control button and a small dart whistled through the air, striking Cora's rear shoulder. The force of the impact sent her down with a groan.

Marzanna rushed over to her, and pulled the dart from her flesh. Seconds before she did that, the dart had released a microchip-sized implant that buried itself beneath her skin.

Cora was helped to her feet, and both women staggered into the cave, swallowed up by the darkness.

"Sir, they've entered a hidden cave, and I have zero visibility," the reaper reported to Keyes.

He was the only combat-efficient air reaper that was airborne.

"My weapons are dry, sir, but the 'leech' is active," he added.

"Good work, we are preparing the EELs, return to the trawler," Keyes advised.

The air reaper flew back to the Salty Star.

All was silent.

CHAPTER 34

E.E.L's

From their respective vantage points, Vincent Keyes, from the trawler, and Ophelia's dysfunctional group, from the basket chamber, watched the mouth of the cave.

The silence was suddenly broken as a white 24-metre-motor yacht emerged from the dark maw of the cave. It started to accelerate quickly towards the floating trawler.

Standing on the foredeck was Marzanna, and she was next to a five-foot stone statue of a half-woman, half-fish sea siren looking out onto the sea. The statue's figurehead was holding a metal trident. The yacht was aptly called 'The Siren'.

Inside the small bridge piloting the boat, was one of her two maidens, who had previously left the banquet room with the talisman. Cora was being tended to by the second maiden inside the luxury salon.

Keyes watched intently as the motor yacht was gaining speed. The CEO turned to his crew as they were operating the trawler's davits, they were lowering two flat-looking, eight-foot boats in the water. Each one looked like a sleek black manta ray that had merged with a military bobsled – low, wide and deadly.

"Deploy the EELs, quickly," Keyes barked.

The EELs were the latest creation from Legionshield. Exo-External Littoralcrafts.

They were ultra-low, hydrodynamic sled-skiffs. Built for stealth and speed. They had a raised armoured wedge-shaped bow like a snow-plough, designed to deflect debris, shatter coastal defences, and provide ballistic cover for the crew. It gave the sled a distinct 'head', angular and tough.

The dual cockpit in each one was occupied by two prone-positioned operatives; One was the pilot and the other was a systems officer and gunner. They were encased within recessed compartments like sniper nests and minimalistic panels surrounded them. The cockpit was enclosed with a retractable canopy for low-drag traversal or open operation undercover.

The EELs armaments consisted of dual side-mounted micro-missile pods, and a dorsal laser cannon which was mounted like a dorsal fin on top of the wedge-shaped bow.

Vincent Keyes had these two prototypes designed and manufactured for the US Navy SEALs, for coastal insertion, espionage, rapid extraction and light assault. But now, it was a perfect opportunity for them to undertake their first live field test.

"Intercept them!" he ordered.

He watched the two EELs launch as soon as they touched the water, and soared towards the escaping motor yacht.

He was going to make sure this coven wouldn't escape. Keyes stared at the bow of Marzanna's boat, getting closer, and it started to make a turn to avoid crashing into the trawler.

The EEL's magneto-hydro jets propelled the aquatic sleds across the channel, and one of them fired a small missile from its payload.

It flew across the surface of the water like a torpedo, and skimmed past the lower hull of the yacht's bow. The missile impacted the cliffs near the cave, resulting in a huge explosion which shook the cliffs themselves. The cave collapsed.

"Disable it, don't destroy it, you idiots!" Keyes shouted into his headset, which was received by the sled's pilots.

"Roger that," one of the EEL pilots responded.

Marzanna noticed the sleek military-looking sleds approaching quickly, and laser beams shot out from their dorsal bow guns. The energy blasts struck parts of her hull, tearing into the unarmoured boat. Small sections were blasted off, others disintegrated. She was sustaining damage already.

Any longer, her yacht would be crippled and nothing more than a floating wreck in the water. She had to escape the channel quickly, but these new flat water-sleds with clean-bevelled armour plating would definitely prevent that, with their constant attacks.

They started circling the yacht as it picked up speed, heading out to sea. It had passed the trawler and Keyes continued to observe the sea pursuit.

Marzanna looked frustrated on the foredeck and Cora walked over to her. The maiden's shoulder had been bandaged.

They watched the two sleds whizzing around the yacht. The sleds looked like piranhas taking bites from a larger sea mammal, but in this case, their lasers were tearing pieces off the hull.

The yacht had no manoeuvrability to shake off its smaller attackers and needed to stay on course to reach its maximum speed of 31 knots.

"The boat's taking too much damage, we'll never escape the channel," Cora said, anxiously.

Marzanna pulled out the sceptre from her sash and Cora stood back. Even though the high priestess was immune to its touch, her maidens were not.

"We'll try and slow them down," Marzanna replied calmly.

Without hesitation, Marzanna then placed the bottom of the sceptre onto the statue of the siren. There was a flash of light and within seconds, the mythological siren's outer rocky shell crumbled away – she had been reanimated.

"Destroy them," Marzanna whispered as she focused on the approaching two EELs swerving around the aft, taking pot shots at the lower hull, trying to disable its engines.

The sea siren broke out from her ceramic base and turned her head towards the black meddlesome sleds. The former statue dove into the water and disappeared underneath the waves. Within moments, the reanimated mermaid emerged from the water and fixed her blank dark eyes on the first sled.

She submerged and swam underwater. Her hand tightly gripped the lethal-looking trident. As soon as she was underneath one of the sleds, the siren thrust her trident onto its armoured underbelly.

The tri-forked spears slightly flipped the sled, but didn't penetrate its strong hull. The trident caused nothing more than superficial damage and scraped off the sled as it soared past, recovering its trajectory.

The second EEL was now approaching the siren who was treading water. Laser blasts pierced the surrounding water, and she quickly swam away from the intense beams.

Once the sled passed her position, the sea siren suddenly dove out of the water and managed to land on the canopy of the small flat boat. She was being carried on top and the pilots inside attempted to shake her off, by swerving with sharp manoeuvres.

From inside the EEL, the pilot looked into his screen that displayed the viewpoint ahead of him. The sled had a small camera encased in transparent armour on the wedged bow underneath the

dorsal laser cannon. They were gaining on the leading skiff-sled –
beyond that, was the yacht.

At that moment, the screen showed the siren clambering onto
the bow of his sled, and she was hammering the trident down onto
the forward-facing laser weapon. A moment later, she had blocked
the view ahead, and he was piloting blind.

"Get her off of there," snapped the systems officer to his pilot.

The pilot operated the controls and banked hard to the left,
in an effort to throw off the sea siren - but to no avail.

She desperately clung onto the bow and had secured a good
grip with her hand. The 'tail' half of her body was inadvertently
covering the area where the camera viewport was located. The siren
brought the trident down again, smashing its steel prongs onto the
laser cannon, trying to dislodge it from its mount.

The sled veered off and looked out of control, from the
perspective of Keyes, who continued to monitor the sea skirmish
from the trawler's deck.

The pilot couldn't shake her off the sled, and he motioned to
his systems officer.

"Get out there and shoot her off!" he growled, annoyingly.

He reduced speed and as his co-pilot reached down in his
prone position to grab his holstered pistol, the canopy slid open
above them.

The systems officer immediately got up on his knees and was
greeted with splashes of seawater. He noticed the siren hacking
away at the bow wedge, and aimed his Ruger 9mm at the mermaid.

Two shots were fired and punched into the siren's mid-section.
She shrieked and spewed blackish blood from her midriff. The
live mythological creature suddenly looked at the systems officer

in response and screamed with a high-pitched yell which nearly deafened him.

This was enough to distract him for a moment, as she then plunged the trident deep into his chest, impaling him. Blood spattered across the hull and onto his fellow pilot who was still in his prone position, piloting the sled.

The siren, with great strength, hoisted the man off his feet with the trident, and flung him like a rag doll into the sea.

She turned her attention to the fearful pilot. He hit the controls which activated the retractable canopy, and it started to slide across to close.

Unfortunately, the action wasn't quick enough.

The siren's trident came down before the canopy sealed itself shut, and was thrust into the pilot's back, and went straight through him. The tips of the trident hit solid surface as they pierced through his chest - pinning the dead pilot to his compartment. He remained still in his prone position and his head slumped, as blood spilt from his mouth.

The sled came to a dead stop and the siren removed the trident from the pilot's back. She dived into the water once again and swam fast towards the second EEL, which was continually firing last blasts at the yacht.

Vincent Keyes couldn't believe his eyes. Why the hell did they have to get out of the sled?

"Son-of-a-bitch!" he cursed. He had no other resources to support the remaining EEL which continued to chase after the yacht. It was also rapidly increasing its speed.

Meanwhile, Marzanna raced over to the aft deck and watched the black sled approaching behind. Fortunately, the yacht was gaining considerable distance, and it appeared that the sleds weren't fast enough to catch up. But the sled continued on relentlessly. She wasn't out of danger yet, as the lasers of the attack boat could still reach her yacht.

"Increase speed!" she shouted behind her.

The motor yacht's engines groaned as the boat sliced through the waves, building up speed. The freedom of the open sea was near.

The gunner of the second EEL aimed the laser cannon via his dashboard screen, and fired several bursts at the escaping vessel, which was less than fifty feet away.

Beams of energy streaked across the waters and struck the lower hull of the yacht again. Huge scorch marks were seen on the boat and pieces of the hull were blasted away.

"They're gaining distance, sir," the pilot spoke into his controls.

Vincent Keyes' voice was heard from the comms console.

"Stay on course," he commanded.

At that moment, the sea siren repeated her tactic and launched from the sea to dive onto the bow of the sled, but the pilot suddenly pulled hard on the controls and dodged her. The siren deflected off the bow of the boat and landed in the water with a huge splash.

This redirected the sled, which afforded time for the yacht to increase its distance. The sled performed a U-turn in the water and charged the siren, who was preparing the next attack from the front.

The systems officer programmed the controls and had the siren in his crosshairs, as she swam towards the boat, using a rapid dolphin-type kick stroke.

A missile was launched from its mounted side-pod and skimmed across the surface of the waves.

It then hit the siren when she exposed her position from the water. She exploded into a thousand fiery pieces and small chunks of the reanimated statue sunk to the bottom of the channel, along with the trident.

The pilot manoeuvred the sled sharply and returned to follow the yacht, but it was too far out and was almost at its maximum speed. There was no way the sled could catch up with its quarry now. He reported this to the CEO.

Keyes received the message, but didn't curse or scream at his operatives. Instead, he stood there on the deck of the trawler, watching the yacht speed out into the open sea. He had his backup plan in place.

He pulled out his electronic tablet and flicked on a switch. A small green blip flashed on the digital screen that displayed a technical read-out of the area and coordinates.

Keyes looked over at the yacht, which was no more than a white spec on a dark horizon. His target had escaped for now, but it wouldn't be long before he would reacquire her again, he promised himself.

The Legionshield boss smiled as he gazed across the waters.

Simultaneously, Marzanna looked out from the aft of her yacht and was joined by Cora, who was still feeling discomfort from the wound on her shoulder.

Marzanna smiled as well, as she glanced back at the trawler in the distance, and then at the abandoned castle high on the cliffs.

She had escaped the hunt and was finally safe.

Or so she thought.

PART THREE

CHAPTER 35

"IT'S NOT OVER YET!"

It was the dawn of a new day.

The courtyard of Ravenscliff castle was strewn with debris and rubble. Smouldering wreckage from the jetpacks was extinguished and collected by the ground workers. They had been brought in by four helicopters, in the early hours of the morning, from Legionshield's Northumberland HQ.

The organisation wasted no time with the clean-up operation, and worked quickly before the local authorities could find out what had occurred last night. Fortunately, the location was very remote, and miles away from anywhere. There were only a few minor explosions and bursts of gunfire, which could have possibly been detected by any nearby witnesses.

But the castle had not yet received any response from the emergency services or coastguard.

The corporation's blue helicopters were on the ground, and crewmen loaded several body bags which contained the dead reapers who were killed during the battle, and the two EEL pilots who had been earlier fished out of the channel.

Two additional body bags were placed in a different helicopter, and enclosed in those were the corpses of the maidens who also lost their lives.

The third maiden that had died in the basket on the cliffs was vapourised moments after the missile struck the cave's coastline below it. The fireball that had followed engulfed the basket and her body at the same time.

Amongst the bustle that continued outside the remains of the barbican, Ophelia was leaning on the side of the Defender, sipping a flask of coffee. She had already collected her belongings from her room inside the castle, and also managed to recover her xiphos sword, which she concealed in the Defender. A car blanket was draped across her bare, dirtied-cut shoulders. The curator looked exhausted and dishevelled.

Madison was having her ankle strapped up by Fox on the other side of the Knights' unscathed vehicle, whilst Spears and Straker had the wounded air reaper and a battered Hugo in handcuffs. Mervier was liaising with Matheseon, and appeared to be in a heated argument with a man who clearly looked in charge.

"Release them now, they're with me!" he shouted, referring to the mercenary's two injured prisoners being guarded by Spears and Straker.

This riled Ophelia, and she hadn't yet been introduced to this American. She brushed off her blanket and prepared to march over to the small bickering group to protest – after all, the two Legionshield operatives had tried to attack her. She hoped Matheson had explained that to the executive. At that moment, Ophelia was suddenly distracted.

Her eyes darted skywards as a US Boeing CH-47 Chinook tandem-rotor helicopter came in overhead. At the same time, two large recovery transports rolled up from the road that led to the clearing outside the barbican.

As the Chinook landed, dust and sand blew all over the place, causing everyone to shield their eyes. Ophelia managed to glimpse the logo that was emblazoned on the helicopter's side – Legionshield Defence Industries.

Her eyes rolled.

"As if this party weren't big enough already," she said to herself.

Four people jumped out of the helicopter once the rotors stopped spinning; A woman and three men. One of the men was wearing a suit and carrying a long black metal case. The other two were wearing fatigues that resembled the ones that the reapers were wearing underneath their light body-armour – security.

The woman was Vanessa and her crème long coat flapped behind her like wings.

"Excuse me," Keyes said to Matheson and Mervier, as he hurriedly made his way over to his associates.

The CEO joined Delanski, who was holding the metal case. Vanessa stood with them and surveyed the damaged ramparts of the stone wall in front of her.

"Must have been some gig?" Vanessa said, assessing the area.

"Lightshow and all," Keyes replied, as his eyes looked down at the case.

"Mr Keyes, my lab team have been working all night and I think you'll agree, we have developed quite a remarkable piece," Delanski proudly announced.

"I don't doubt it, let me see it," Keyes asked, ensuring he and the small group encircled the reveal, so nobody could see. Delanski opened up the case.

The Bident of Hades was resting in its convoluted foam interior. One of its twin prongs was shorter than the other, but the metal was no longer dented – in fact, they looked sharper and shinier.

The bronze shaft had been repaired and had a small thin cable running across it that was forged into the centre base of the spearheads. The slim cables were encased in steel for protection.

Two parts of the shaft had leather grips and one of them had some kind of trigger device attached.

"It is still in its experimental phase, but it shows what we could potentially do with it after further study and development," Delanski said.

The head scientist was prepared to lift the bident from its case, until Keyes halted him with a gesture of his hand.

"No, not here, too many prying eyes," Keyes warned, noticing Ophelia only thirty metres away from them.

Keyes glided his hand tentatively down the shaft and noticed the modifications.

"Enlighten me, Doctor."

"We call it 'The Plasma-Rod," Delanski grinned, more than content with his creation.

The men quietly chuckled.

"I like it," Keyes responded.

"We obviously couldn't duplicate the supernatural energy it previously had, but close to it," Delanski mentioned.

"Go on." Keyes was eager to know more.

"Like it says in its name, the bident emits a powerful blast of plasma with a similar destructive force that it used to have, no magic, just raw and pure, super-powered energy," Delanski said.

Keyes glanced at the trigger control on one of the leather grips.

"The only flaw is that you can only discharge half a dozen blasts before it is required to fully recharge, the metal, however, can cut through any armour, including the chassis of an APC," Delanski added.

"How do I recharge?"

"Simply solar-powered. The tips of the bident simulate conductors, but it will take approximately twenty minutes for the rod to replenish its energy capacitators. A truly devastating melee weapon, don't you agree, sir?"

"Have you tested it?"

"Of course, it nearly took out the whole lab!" Delanski replied.

"Astonishing," Keyes said, as he marvelled at his new reverse-engineered tool.

"Who says advanced technology cannot measure up to magic?" Vanessa added.

"Good work, Doctor, you have far surpassed yourself," Keyes praised.

"Thank you."

Keyes looked over at his shoulder and saw Ophelia stomping across the clearing towards him.

"Keep it out of sight, I need to handle this woman," Keyes advised.

At that moment, Ophelia approached the CEO, and Vanessa, along with the two close-protection operatives, marched out in front to intercept her. They blocked her path.

"Excuse me!" the angry curator snapped at them.

Ophelia felt like she wanted to punch Vanessa in the face, but Keyes spoke from behind his human shield.

"It's alright."

Vanessa and the two bodyguards parted, allowing their boss to casually stride through. Ophelia was furious and stood there with her hands on her hips.

Keyes and Ophelia met.

"I haven't had the pleasure of introducing myself yet, Dr. Winters," Keyes said with an unconvincing smile.

"What the hell is going on here?" Ophelia shouted, ready to smack him across his smug face.

"If you give me a chance, my good woman, I'll be able to explain," Keyes replied.

"Go on!" she barked, still enraged.

"It is clear you're tired and cranky, and somewhat battle-worn," he looked down at her appearance.

"You have not seen anything yet, now tell me what the hell you are doing here?" she ranted.

"Well, I have just saved all of your lives to start with – again, and now we are cleaning up your shit," Keyes stated the obvious.

"What the hell?"

The CEO started to walk over to Hugo and the air reaper, who were still in their restraints. Ophelia turned around and tried to keep up.

"Whoa, wait a second." The curator was at boiling point, as he continued to walk away from her.

"Time is of the essence, Dr Winters," Keyes said without addressing her. He eventually made his way over to the mercenaries who were standing next to a very angry-looking Hugo, and the bloodied, deflated air reaper. Matheson and Mervier started to approach the group too.

"I said release them, now!" Keyes ordered Spears. The mercenary scowled at the CEO, and looked over at his senior officer. Matheson reluctantly nodded.

"What are you doing, these men tried to kill me?" Ophelia protested.

Spears obeyed his boss and removed the handcuffs from the two Legionshield operatives. They threw the handcuffs to the ground, and with a self-satisfying smirk, Hugo stared at Ophelia whilst massaging his wrists.

"Nathan, what are you doing?" Ophelia asked, with a shocked expression.

Spears felt defeated and gave Hugo a stern look.

"Hugo?" Keyes raised his brow, allowing Hugo to vindicate himself.

"She obstructed me as I was trying to subdue the witch," he spoke with a deep rasp.

"Kovac?" Keyes glanced over at the air reaper, who, in turn, looked at Ophelia.

"I thought she was one of *them*," the reaper croaked, looking down at his slashed leg.

"Medic!" shouted Keyes, and one of his bodyguards rushed over and produced a portable first aid kit.

"A clear case of misidentification, Dr. Winters, what do you expect them to think, after you attacked them, in a desperate attempt to defend the suspect?" Keyes said trying to justify his operative's actions.

"No, I was defending myself, you moron!"

Keyes turned to his two wounded men.

"Get yourselves fixed," he said, and his two bodyguards escorted them over to the Chinook, leaving the CEO surrounded by the others.

"I'm starting to wonder whose side you are on, Dr. Winters?" Keyes said accusingly.

"Like-wise," Mervier added.

"You still haven't told me who you are, and why you're calling all the shots here?" she asked aggressively, ignoring Mervier's comment.

Mervier noted this.

Matheson stepped forward, trying to keep the peace. He knew too well that the curator was ready to physically lash out.

"Ophelia, this is Vincent Keyes, CEO of Legionsfield," Matheson revealed to her.

"The defence contractor?" Ophelia gasped. She was vaguely aware of this shady organisation.

"The one and the same, and I have an interest in your friend, amongst other things," Keyes added.

"And who the hell invited you?" Ophelia then looked at each member of the group, as if it was a witch-hunt.

"I came to him first, Ophelia, if that's who you still are?" Mervier admitted.

"What?"

"I confess, I didn't know he would be joining us on this operation," the detective glanced at the CEO with a surprised look.

"You got Matheson to thank for that, you see, the Black Knight Syndicate work for me," Keyes revealed.

"I don't understand. This was an unsanctioned operation that was planned by Nicole, and she used my invitation to gain access to the castle. I felt I had no choice but to comply," Ophelia explained, trying to piece together everything.

"I had the detective under surveillance, and it was only a matter of time before she approached you, it was lucky and convenient that you had an invitation in the first place, otherwise, we wouldn't be all here now," Keyes said.

"But I hired you Miles, I trusted you," Ophelia's tone mellowed, as she looked up at a guilty-looking Matheson.

"When you hired him, you hired us, whether you're aware of it or not, however, on this occasion, we, as in Legionshield, took a more proactive role, and by the looks of things, I'm glad we did," Keyes explained, as he observed the damage around the castle grounds.

Ophelia felt alone and was lost for words – to Keyes' delight.

"We were your reinforcements, and as I explained earlier, we came in at the right time, or you would have all perished. You can at least be grateful for that, Dr. Winters!" Keyes snarled, feeling under-appreciated.

Ophelia shook her head in disbelief, and massaged her temples with her fingertips as she knew a headache was imminent.

"I'm sorry, Ophelia," Matheson said sincerely, but he knew it was falling on deaf ears.

"None of this would have occurred if she hadn't pulled your weapon on her," the curator growled, as she pointed at the detective.

"If I hadn't done anything, we could have been killed. They were aware of your boys getting ready to storm the castle. She had already possessed Madison, for all I know, you could still be under her spell," Mervier explained.

"There was no guarantee of that, I was finally making sense of what she was saying, her motives, her…"

Ophelia was cut off.

"Do you hear yourself, Ophelia?" Mervier interrupted, "You're enraptured by this woman."

"You don't understand me," Ophelia started to try and explain, but the detective gave her no quarter.

"Have you forgotten what happened in the basket chamber? You let her escape, and held a blade to my throat?"

"I acted on impulse. This coven just wants to be left alone, they're no threat to anybody."

Ophelia wasn't helping herself, and the mercenaries struggled to believe what was being explained during this heated debate.

"Try telling that to the families of those boys in York," Mervier replied.

"I'm telling you, she is not the bad guy, here, I swear," Ophelia pleaded.

Maybe she was still enchanted or hypnotised, the group thought.

"You obstructed my duties, I could have you arrested right now," Mervier warned.

"After we saved your life in there?" Ophelia snapped back.

"Alright ladies, enough, we got to figure out what to do next," Matheson intervened again, as the atmosphere was already sour, and he didn't want the situation to escalate.

"All I know right now, is that it's not over yet," Keyes said.

"What?" Ophelia glanced at the CEO in disbelief. She had hoped Marzanna and her maidens would escape successfully.

Keyes nodded to his PA, and she stepped forward with a larger and more sophisticated electronic data-pad than Keyes' tablet. He peered down at it.

They continued to track the location of their prey. A blip flashed on the screen.

"They're hugging the west coast of France," Vanessa uttered to her boss.

"They've covered some good distance considering the time. If I were to put a dollar on it, they'd probably slip through the Strait of Gibraltar, and head due east, keep monitoring," Keyes advised.

Both he and Vanessa started making their way to one of the smaller helicopters, but halted when Ophelia shouted at them.

"You're still going after her?"

Keyes and Vanessa spun around and faced Ophelia.

"Too much is at stake, Dr. Winters," Keyes said, "Besides, I've already lost seven good men. I'm going to make sure they haven't died for nothing. Now if you will excuse me, I've got a job to do, you can join us or go home."

Ophelia stayed put.

"She'll kill you all if you continue the hunt!" Ophelia retorted.

"We shall see," Keyes answered back, and he and Vanessa headed back to one of the helicopters. He was joined by Delanski and Hugo.

Ophelia was left standing there with her mercs. She knew that the Chinook was there to airlift the crushed cars that were still in the courtyard, and onto the long maintenance vehicles that had parked up on the road.

She turned to Matheson.

"Who is that guy?" she exasperatingly asked.

"Ex-CIA, we've been in business together for years, listen, I'm truly sorry about all this. I didn't expect it to escalate like this," Matheson said, apologetically.

"We've got to stop him," Ophelia stared ahead, and saw Keyes about to climb into the awaiting helicopter.

"Regretfully, we've got to fulfil the assignment, whether we like it or not, or he could disband us, it's best you return to York, there's nothing you can do for her," Matheson said, tossing her the keys to the Defender.

She felt she had completely lost her allies. And their trust. She was in despair.

"Miles, I haven't been enchanted by her. I swear on our lives, she just wants to live," the curator pleaded again.

They both heard Keyes shout at them from the helicopter, the engines were firing up.

"Miles!"

Matheson and his three mercenaries stood there. He looked at his men for some response – there was a pause.

"You with us or not?" Keyes yelled again, this time louder.

It was time to make a decision.

CHAPTER 36

LOYALTIES

Detective Mervier jogged over to the helicopter, placing her hand on her ribs as each stride still caused her discomfort. "Hey, you're not holding on me, this is still my investigation. Official or not, Mr Keyes."

"You are one tenacious woman, detective, but you are free to join us as long as you understand it's my show?" Keyes smiled.

"She's my suspect and I intend to bring her in – alive."

"She's all yours, I doubt she'll come quietly, but I won't deny you the opportunity," Keyes said.

"I cannot trust Ophelia any more, she's been bewitched."

"I believe that, hop on board." Keyes gestured with his hand, as she started to climb aboard the helicopter.

"Just one thing, Mr Keyes, no more deception, I'm still pissed off that you had me tracked," Mervier scowled.

"A necessity at the time, but you have my word."

As she jumped inside the helicopter with Hugo, Vanessa and Delanski, Keyes glanced over the Black Knights who were still with a crestfallen Ophelia.

"Miles, last chance!" the CEO shouted, "You know the consequences."

Matheson was torn once again, and he waved in Keyes' direction, acknowledging him.

"You do this, we're done," Ophelia said, morosely.

"And so are we if we don't," Matheson sighed.

He had a sworn duty to the job, but he also had a moral commitment to his long-term client and friend. Maybe he could do both. If he was to redeem himself, it would be now.

She looked up at Spears, Straker and Fox. All of them had the agonising decision of staying faithful to the curator, or the job that their careers and livelihoods depended on.

"I'm with you Miles, whatever," Fox said.

"Straker?"

"I need the dollar, sorry, Ophelia, I've got a family to support, and a sick daughter in oncology," Straker answered with no hesitation.

"Nathan?" Ophelia looked at the mercenary, who she was emotionally closest to.

Spears studied her face and wasn't certain if she was herself, or as the detective suggested, enchanted, and possibly still held by the witch.

"Go on without me, Miles, this is not our battle," Spears softly said.

Ophelia smiled with relief, a tear trickled down her cheek.

Spears always had her side, and he truly believed that her words were true and that she wasn't bewitched in any way. After all, he witnessed the countess saving her from certain doom, at the hands of Legionshield's cohorts.

"So be it, look after her," Matheson patted Spears on his shoulder.

"Will do," Spears replied.

Matheson motioned to Straker and Fox, and they rushed over to the helicopter and an increasingly impatient Keyes.

Once they were out of sight, Matheson unzipped one of the holdalls from the Defender, and pulled out a satellite phone. He synced the channel to its setting and ensured that it was fully powered up. He then handed it to Ophelia.

"We'll keep in touch, you do what is best," the Black Knight leader said, giving her a wink.

Ophelia nodded appreciatively.

"Good luck, Miles." Spears shook hands with the former MI6 officer.

"You too."

"Thank you, Miles," Ophelia politely acknowledged.

Matheson then quickly raced over to the helicopter and joined Keyes, as Fox and Straker climbed aboard.

"I'm relieved you made the right decision, that is, if your motives are true, Miles?" Keyes queried, as Matheson and Keyes hauled themselves inside.

"Let's just do the job, and get home alive," he replied.

"I take it Spears is not joining us?"

"That's right," Matheson said.

"Then he's finished."

"Let's hope we won't be, when we catch up with this witch!"

"You lack faith, Miles," Keyes replied as he donned his headset.

Keyes had a lot to organise and prepare for.

"Let's go!" he shouted, as he turned to the pilots.

The final part of the mission had just begun.

The helicopter ascended into the air, spraying more sand across the area. Spears and Ophelia were left standing next to the Defender, observing the aircraft fly into the distance.

They then hopped into the Defender and joined Madison.

Ophelia wasted no time. She turned the ignition on and put her foot down, sending up dust behind them, as the vehicle swerved and accelerated away from the castle grounds.

She had plans of her own to make as well.

CHAPTER 37

CRETE

Monday 11th May

It had taken Marzanna's yacht a long two and a half days at 31 knots to reach the thriving and beautiful southern coastal town of Agia Galini.

As soon as she moored The Siren at the bustling harbour, she and her three surviving maidens had hopped onto land. The high priestess, along with her entourage, had changed into stylish summer clothing to blend in with the locals, eaten at a local tavern and stopped off at various stores around the town for supplies.

Marzanna Medea felt a great sense of relief and peace when the soothing warmth of the Mediterranean sun touched her skin.

The high priestess had also purchased an open-topped jeep from a local dealer, and later in the afternoon, they were driving inland to their final destination.

Meanwhile, at Maleme military airport, Vincent Keyes was sitting in the private lounge of the main operations centre, tracking the movements of the 'state-of-the-art' implant that had been injected into the witch's acolyte. The signal was still strong, and after hours of painstaking monitoring from sea-to-land, his target was finally on the island and making a move.

Legionshield had arrived in an Embraer C-390 Millenium transport aircraft, which was owned by the company. They also had special permission from the Greek authorities, and they were continually grateful for their business and the previous involvement in the elimination of the terrorists a few weeks ago. The CEO and his detachment of operatives had landed in Crete a good twenty-four hours before Marzanna pulled into the harbour, and since that time, they had waited patiently.

In that space of time, his contact, Colonel Finellis, had been cooperative in allowing Legionshield and the Black Knights to land, unload crates of equipment and stay at the airport until further developments.

In the colonel's eyes, Legionshield and their paramilitary syndicate were the unsung heroes of the conflict that occurred a few weeks ago.

Keyes had concocted a story by informing Finellis that the remnants of the terrorist cell were suspected to be congregating somewhere on the ancient island, and they were tracking one of its agents.

This was enough for Finellis to give Keyes his full support. All this was low-key and Keyes refused military aid, except for the use of a couple of logistical vehicles that had parked on the airstrip. As he explained, it was just a handful of resistance that had re-emerged, and the Black Knights were brought in to make 'hard' arrests.

Finellis bought all this bullshit, but he had no reason to query Keyes' story after the events on Katamarai island.

Keyes had changed into urban-style combat fatigues from his company, and next to him were Matheson, Hugo and Vanessa. Behind them, the two mercenaries were doing an inventory check of their weapons.

"Mr Keyes, I appreciate you're in charge of the operation, but as it is on Greek soil, I insist on providing you a small detachment of troops," the colonel said.

"Colonel Finellis, we are not going in hot and heavy, stealth and secrecy is the aim, this is more of a 'polish-up' mission, and their leader is a British citizen and needs to be brought to justice," Keyes said, giving Mervier a momentary glimpse.

"I understand, but there are ways of doing this officially, without creating an international incident."

"Sending the army in is not the way to go, Colonel," Keyes replied.

He was getting tired of this man, and for the last twenty-four hours, Finellis been constantly burning the CEO's ear about politics and the collaboration of both the Greek government and Legionshield for Anglo-US-Greek relations.

"This is very unorthodox, Mr Keyes, but in order for you to execute this operation, I will join you personally, with a small select unit of soldiers – for our reassurance," the colonel insisted.

"Fine, but they are your responsibility. I cannot guarantee their safety."

"Of course."

"With due respect, Colonel, I still run the show," Keyes stated, and walked over to the lounge window that overlooked the airstrip where he viewed the latest activity.

He noticed a larger crate being unloaded from the C-390, and onto a small loading transport.

Two airfield personnel were securing harnesses to it, with the assistance of two company engineers. They peered up to the stencilling underneath the Legionshield logo.

It read: 'A.T.T.A.C'

Armoured Trooper and Tactical Assault Chassis.

Legionshield referred to it simply as the 'A/TAC' – it was a human-sized design, and a revolutionary hi-tech prototype of weaponised combat armour that completely encased its occupant. It was equipped with an awesome array of deadly weaponry for the soldier to operate from within. A fully versatile and mechanised unit for the warrior of the future.

A piece of equipment which would undoubtedly be revealed in good time, Keyes thought.

"I think we've got things in hand," Keyes replied, confidently to the colonel, as he saw the crate being forklifted onto one of the military trucks.

Keyes' gaze through the window was interrupted by Vanessa, who was monitoring the portable global digital tracking device.

"Sir, we have a strong signal, our target is continuing north-west from Agia Galini," she reported.

Keyes walked over to her and glanced down at the scanner's read-outs.

"Okay, we can intercept her en-route, any idea where she possibly could be heading?" he asked.

"She seems to be approaching Agios Vasileios soon," Vanessa enlarged the map on her scanner.

It displayed several main roads and track roads that could deviate to many mainland villages and towns, but the blip maintained its course.

"Vincent," Matheson cut in, "All you have is the location of the woman's servant."

"That's all we have got to stay on track," Vanessa answered.

"Wherever her servant is, she is as well," Keyes theorised.

"And if not?" Matheson asked, fumbling with his satellite phone.

"Then we can find out where the witch is, from her servant once we intercept her, I thought you would have deduced that, Miles?" Keyes replied in a condescending manner.

"Fair enough," Matheson uttered.

"What're the coordinates?" Keyes asked Vanessa.

Vanessa gave him a bunch of grid reference coordinates out aloud, and Keyes continued looking at the screen.

Matheson was typing into his sat-phone during the exchange.

Vanessa expanded her screen-map of Crete, and pointed to it with her finger.

"We are here, and we can intercept within an hour and a half if the target stays and continues without a stop, or we could wait until it reaches its final destination?" she suggested.

"I can't take the risk of losing the signal, we'll get her in transit."

"Agreed," she replied.

"Alright people, let's move, we've waited here too long," Keyes ordered, and already Finellis was on the landline to his squad.

The mercenaries packed their kit, and followed the CEO out of the lounge.

The hunt was back on.

CHAPTER 38

AN OLD COMRADE

Heraklion

North Crete

Elsewhere on the stunning island, Ophelia Winters landed at Heraklion International Airport a short time ago. It was a wonderfully sunny day.

She was accompanied by Nathan Spears and Madison Trent. They were all dressed in summer clothing and carrying light luggage towards the pick-up point outside the main building of the airport.

Ophelia had used her museum contacts to charter a private flight which took the weekend to organise. The curator was representing St George's Museum and was using her position and influence by informing the Heraklion Archaeological Museum, that she was going to attend an event on Tuesday, and with a notable donation – she brought the 3,500-year-old xiphos sword with her that she had 'liberated' from Ravenscliff as the donation, and declared it through customs.

She had flown from Full Sutton Airport in Yorkshire on Monday morning, and it took just four hours to reach Athens. Then the trio jumped onto the next flight to Heraklion, which lasted just an hour.

Spears had also made a few calls during their weekend preparations. During all this time, Matheson had kept them regularly and secretly updated via the sat-phone.

Waiting for the small group at the pick-up/drop-off rank was a Greek man in his late fifties standing next to a small, old and beaten-up livestock truck. There were several holdalls in the back of the battered truck.

He was a little dirty, balding and slightly overweight. His dress sense wasn't good on the eyes either. He was wearing a very colourful Hawaiian-type shirt and khaki cargo shorts and sandals that looked decades old. However, he did appear approachable with the massive smile he sported across his face whilst smoking a cigar.

Spears spotted him from the other side of the road.

"Hey, Nathan Spears, you little shit, it's been a long time, my old friend!" the man shouted, opening his arms in a warm, welcoming way.

"Vassilis, you little arse-ache, great to see ya!" Spears shouted back.

Vassilis wrapped his arms around the mercenary, nearly crushing him in his tight, friendly embrace.

"Whoa, more like big arse-ache now! What is this?" Spears joked, slapping Vassilis' belly.

"Nah, honest living," the larger man laughed.

"Too many kebabs and byres," Spears added.

Madison knew 'byres' was the Greek word for beer as they sounded almost the same when spoken.

Vassilis then turned his attention to the two attractive women that were walking behind Spears.

"Well, well, well, Nathan, who are the 'omortes kopeles'?" Vassilis smiled at Ophelia and Madison, quickly giving them the approving 'scan' with his eyes from top-to-bottom. This made them both feel uneasy, but they both forced a smile.

"Omortes kopeles?" Ophelia looked at Spears, questioningly.

"Beautiful young ladies!" Vassilis translated.

"Something like that," Spears grinned.

"Nathan, my boy, you still haven't made any effort to speak my 'dialektos', huh?"

"You know me, a lazy little shit," he said, laughing heartily.

Spears then introduced the curator and her associate to his Greek friend.

"Ophelia, Madison, meet Vassilis, a pain in the arse," he grinned.

"It's an absolute pleasure, ladies," Vassilis greeted them by kissing their hands.

Madison had to cringe and Ophelia winced, as soon as Vassilis turned to his vehicle, shoving the chunky cigar back into his mouth.

"He's alright, we're old comrades-in-arms, he used to work for the Syndicate a few years ago. Prior to that, he was in the Greek special forces before being recruited by Matheson," Spears said to the ladies, reassuringly.

"And now?" Ophelia asked.

"Now, a retired slob!" Spears said, loudly in a jocular manner, so Vassilis could hear. The merc threw the three small luggage bags into the open back of the truck.

"Now c'mon Nathan, I'm a cattle farmer now, the best thing I ever did was retire when I could. Are you still with the Black Knights?" Vassilis asked as he made his way round to the other side of the truck and hopped in the ripped-up driver's seat.

"Not any more, I guess."

Vassilis frowned as he started the engine. Spears climbed in the long passenger seat. There was just enough room for him and his two female companions.

"Jump in girls, I won't bite," Vassilis laughed, once more. He was a quirky, jolly fellow, but Spears trusted him, and right now, Ophelia felt safe for the time being. The former Greek merc rolled down the windows and allowed the putrid stench of his cigar smoke to billow out.

"I'm more concerned if the seats will bite. This thing is older than I am," Madison uttered sarcastically, as she examined the truck and the torn cushioning.

Ophelia looked at the latest message on her sat-phone.

"You'll be fine, c'mon, we better start making a move," the curator advised.

Vassilis put on his sunglasses and shifted gear. The gearstick whined, and the engine gave off a sickening mechanical sound.

"She'll be fine when we get her on the road," Vassilis assured.

Ophelia looked at the text message from the sat-phone.

"Okay folks, where are we heading?" he asked.

"Just follow my directions, Vassilis," Ophelia replied, as he gunned the cattle truck out of the parking bay.

"As the lady wishes," he responded, exhaling a big billow of cigar smoke into the air.

They left the airport and went into open country.

CHAPTER 39

CROSS COUNTRY

The sunrays were searing down through the open windows of Vassilis' battered truck, as it continued on its journey due south.

Vassilis' driving was a little bit reckless as he sharply turned corners of the windy road, and drove fast over some patches of the surface that were in a bad state of disrepair.

The vehicle bounced and the sound of clunking was heard with each manoeuvre. Vassilis blamed the suspension, or the lack of it, but time was of the essence, and they had to make up some time.

They had been driving for over half an hour, and were entering the more isolated and picturesque areas of the rural countryside.

"So, what exactly are we involved with here?" Vassilis asked.

"It's quite hard to explain, we're just tracking someone," Spears said.

"So, why all the hardware that you asked me to provide for you?" Vassilis motioned his head to the rear of the truck where all the bags were stashed.

"I appreciate that, especially at a moment's notice, we wouldn't have been able to transport our own kit commercially," Spears replied, handing him over a stack of euros.

"Well, I do have a few contacts left, even on the unsavoury side, you still didn't answer my question, Nathan," Vassilis pressed.

"He's my close-protection," Ophelia butted in, "We just need you to get us where we need to be – if we ever make it," she uttered her last words, referring to the hunk of junk she was travelling in.

"I thought you said you were no longer in the game, Nathan?" Vassilis tried again, chewing on what was left of his stub-sized cigar.

"I'm not. This is kind of an unofficial job. We need to get to someone before the Knights do," Spears said regretfully. Vassilis saw his expression.

"They've gone rogue, or you?"

"It's complicated, they're under duress but Matheson is kind of guiding us on the down-low."

"Miles Matheson, is he still knocking around?"

"For the time being."

"I thought he hung up his gloves years ago," Vassilis laughed.

"What did you manage to get?" Spears asked, referring to the equipment.

"A couple of used M4 carbines, Glock 17's, combat knives, binos and a tranquiliser rifle, just as you asked. I didn't question it at the time. I just thought it was another protective expedition."

"It still is, in a sense, although if we don't reach her in time, all this will be more nothing."

"Hostiles?" Vassilis asked as he quickly turned another tight corner, making everyone lurch to the left.

"Hard to tell," Spears replied, as his eyes glanced to his left at Ophelia.

Madison cut in.

"Some may say the person or the group we're trying to save are the hostiles," the young woman said, further confusing the former Greek mercenary.

"What, we're helping the enemy?"

"Not quite, but I can't guarantee the reception we're going to get when I face her again, she probably still thinks I betrayed her," Ophelia added.

This still didn't make sense to Vassilis, as he concentrated on the road.

"You're right, this is complicated," Vassilis said, with a perplexed look.

"Whenever have things been straight-forward, Vassilis?" Spears commented.

"True."

"Next right," Ophelia interrupted, as she continued to monitor the frequent texts being sent by Matheson, from miles away.

The banged-up truck swerved at the cross-junction and took an immediate hard right, then carried on due-west through the Cretan countryside, leaving a plume of sand in its wake.

"So, who's the other party that is also after your 'mark'?" Vassilis enquired.

Spears sighed.

"Our benefactors," Spears said.

"I don't follow."

"Legionshield Defence Industries," Spears revealed.

Vassilis whipped him a surprised look, as he momentarily took his eyes off the road.

"You got to be shitting me, what would a defence contractor have to do with snatching some woman?"

This was getting stranger and he wished he hadn't asked that question, but now he knew what they were possibly up against.

"That's where it gets more complicated."

"How so?"

"Let's put it this way, she possesses something unearthly that they desperately want for their unique weapons programme," Madison answered on Spears' behalf.

"Unearthly?"

"Something beyond the realms of reality," Ophelia added.

"Ah, and you want it as well?" Vassilis presumed.

"If the faction acquires it, or her, then it's game over, we need to save her," Ophelia explained sternly.

"Like I said, complicated," Spears reiterated.

"Don't worry Vassilis, once you drop us off, stay out of sight and wait for us to return to you," Ophelia advised.

"If we return?" Madison uttered under her breath.

"Or just return to your farm, and forget that we had ever met, or had this conversation," the curator suggested.

"I don't want you involved in the actual extraction, mate, I just wanted you to source out some supplies for us and collect us from the airport, then drive us down to wherever she is going, and that's it," Spears said.

Vassilis inserted another cigar into his mouth and lit it, much to his female passengers' annoyance. He was quiet for a few moments, and it looked as if he was contemplating.

Finally, he spoke, and broke the awkward silence.

"I'm not being funny, Nathan, but it sounds like you're going to need as much help as you can get, how on earth are you three, alone, going to achieve this, and bring this woman in, if she could be resistant?"

"You took care of that," Ophelia replied, tilting her head back at the luggage in the back of the truck.

"Ah, the tranquiliser, I see now." Vassilis nodded his head.

"If it has any effect on her?" Madison cut in, looking ahead at the dusty road.

"I'm with you on this, I'm not playing chauffeur, knowing the odds are against you, old friend," Vassilis said adamantly.

"Thanks, man," Spears responded.

"Like the good old days, we're not far now."

They were approaching a region that comprised of stunning white mountains with breathtaking backdrop rocky cliffs and underbrush that covered the valleys.

They were nearing the Imbros Gorge.

CHAPTER 40
FINAL DESTINATION

Only a few miles away, a small fleet of vehicles was making progress. The convoy consisted of two military trucks that were following two Land Rovers down the main road. This led to the spectacular mountainous region of the Imbros Gorge.

"The signal has slowed down, but we have a good fix," Vanessa reported, as she sat in the rear seat, next to Matheson in the lead Land Rover. Matheson had insisted that he rode with Keyes in the lead vehicle, so he could keep track of Vanessa, who was, in turn, tracking Marzanna's movements and secretly relaying information back to Ophelia.

Vanessa didn't even notice Matheson's subtle handling of his sat-phone.

Keyes was driving. Seated next to him was Colonel Finellis. He spoke on his radio to the trucks that were tailing them.

Directly behind Keyes was the second Land Rover, and that was occupied by the Black Knights, and DS Mervier. Fox drove the vehicle and stayed closely behind.

"They must be on foot. We are approaching the hiking trails, but we should encounter minimal civilians in this area. I know of a good entrance point that will allow access to the trucks, it'll be a squeeze, but we should be able to manage, Mr Keyes," advised Finellis.

Keyes nodded. The CEO was now glad that the colonel insisted on joining them in the operation.

"It will take slightly longer to get to, but we'll get there soon enough," the colonel added.

"No problem," Keyes acknowledged, and followed Finellis' directions as they continued round the twisting roads in the mountains.

The colonel had kept his word, and selected six of his soldiers to accompany him on the impromptu mission. They were all huddled up in the second military truck which was at the rear of the procession.

The first truck was driven by Hugo, and four Legionshield operatives were sitting in the back, sheltered by the late afternoon sun. They were hand-picked by Keyes shortly before leaving the UK due to their engineering expertise in some of the hardware that they had brought along.

In the middle of the truck was the crate – the main cargo that Keyes was keen to use later, should the coven try and get the upper hand with their witchcraft. He had the fullest confidence in the ATTAC, as it would be a formidable force against any foe, whether they were magic-users or magical weapons.

The prototype had been custom-built for Hugo, and the bodyguard was very eager to climb inside the chassis and use it in the manner that it was designed for – destruction and superior defence for the operator.

The convoy turned another corner and saw a closed wooden fence. Beyond that was a steep rocky trackway that led deep into the mountain valley. It was barely wide enough just for one vehicle, but as soon as they pulled up, Finellis opened up the fence and signalled the convoy to continue through. The vehicles drove down the trackway slowly and carefully.

⊷⊶◁▷⊶⊷

CHAPTER 41

THE GORGE

Vassilis swerved into the lay-by on the side of the mountain road. There was a fence line that meandered across the crest of the clifftop for many miles.

A gap in the fence was the only access to the steep slope, which was a dusty pathway laden with underbrush that descended into the depths of the breathtaking gorge below. This was used by hikers and the lay-by was the last parking point for visitors.

Fortunately, there were no other vehicles or people around.

Ophelia had received guidance from Matheson's sat-phone text messages to use the alternative access point to avoid running into Legionshield. Furthermore, this route was a short-cut trail that led to the signal's last point of origin.

As soon as the cattle truck stopped, Ophelia and Madison jumped and went straight for their bags and started to quickly undress down to their underwear. Before Vassilis sneaked a look, Spears distracted him.

"According to Matheson's calculations, the grid coordinates he sent will take us here," Spears indicated to Vassilis and showed him the sat-phone's longitude and latitude readings. Vassilis used his own phone to type in the coordinates and enhanced the display.

"That will take us off the main trails, but I believe I know the area, it's seldom visited and about four kilometres into the gorge, due west," Vassilis squinted at his screen.

"What's there?"

"Nothing much. Old rock formations, a couple of streams, a small Minoan ruin, a couple of caves that lead to nowhere."

"Could be the place, alright," Spears responded with a nod.

Meanwhile, Ophelia and Madison had changed into more suitable clothes. Madison was wearing a sleeveless light beige top, jungle green shorts, and hiking boots.

Ophelia was in her 'signature' adventure attire, a dark olive-green t-shirt, camouflaged cargo shorts and hiking boots – both women were ready.

Spears turned to the women.

"We may have a location, and it will give us a head start," he said as he climbed into the back of the cattle truck and started handing down the equipment bags to Vassilis.

"Good, how far?" Ophelia asked, collecting her small Bergen. The hilt of her xiphos short sword could be seen poking out of the top.

"We got to tab two-and-a-half miles through the valley and then we go off trail. Apparently, the signal's stopped, but that's all we got at the moment," Spears replied as he changed out of his civilian shirt and into his desert-camouflaged t-shirt and tactical vest.

Ophelia couldn't help but take a discreet peek at his bare torso as he changed tops. She noticed his broad shoulders were scarred and his upper back still had a couple of freshly healed bullet wounds, which he sustained during the battle on Katamarai island, that had nearly killed him.

Ophelia turned to Madison and glanced down at her foot.

"Will you be alright with that, Mads?"

Madison was still feeling slight discomfort with her foot and ankle, but she was a resilient young fighter.

"It's a little bit sore, but I'll manage alright," she said, with a strong, determined look on her face.

"You'll be okay, angel, we'll help," Vassilis said, laughing, as he collected another bag from Spears.

It sounded a bit patronising in Madison's opinion, and she gave him a laser-look.

"I said, I'll be fine."

"Fiery little one, this one, huh?" Vassilis said to Spears, chuckling.

"She can hold her own," Spears replied, grinning as he cast his mind back to the island, and the image of the young archaeologist, kick-boxing her way through the crimson marauders, wearing a toga. Not something you see every day.

"Let's make a move," Ophelia said impatiently.

Spears looked at Vassilis, as he jumped off the cattle truck.

"You seriously going to wear that?" he asked, glancing at his garish-looking Hawaiian shirt.

"Oh, I'm sorry. I forgot to bring my tuxedo for tonight's spectacle."

Spears dug into his Bergen where his concealed M4 carbine was amongst a bundle of other equipment, and tossed him a spare dark grey top.

"I'm not sure that it's going to fit, but it's better than the stand-out-like-sore-thumb eyesore that you're wearing now," Spears remarked.

Vassilis caught it and grinned, then changed into the top. It indeed was tight around the mid-section, which emphasised his belly more now, but he shrugged his shoulders and then put his

Bergen on. Their travel bags were thrown into the driver's cabin and locked up.

As soon as everyone was ready, they moved through the gap in the fence and started a steady descent down the forty-five-degree slope that led into the gorge below.

It was late afternoon and the sun was slowly going down.

Ophelia's group was deep in the valley of the dramatic Imbros Gorge, and they had been hiking for a while. The gang encountered no other travellers, and better still – nobody from Legionshield. She knew they were ahead of them. According to Matheson's reports. However, the organisation was coming in from a different direction elsewhere in the gorge, so there was no guarantee that she wouldn't cross their path enroute.

Madison took each step in the craggy valley carefully, ensuring she didn't twist her sore foot, which would slow everybody down. She wished she had packed her hiking stick.

Vassilis took the lead as he was the most experienced tracker in the group. He was closely followed by Ophelia and Madison, with Spears bringing up the rear.

As the group continued, Ophelia looked up at the towering limestone cliffs that rose hundreds of metres high, creating a sense of grandeur and scale. She knew she was at the bottom of the valley, and they went off-trail to a more dense, narrower area in the gorge.

They went deeper and the valley became darker. The gorge narrowed to a width of only a few metres during several intervals of their hike, and then opened out once again to other clearings.

The rocks in the ground rose like pillars and were of various shapes, resembling arches, caves and many twisted like geological sculptures. Despite their rocky terrain and surroundings, there were thick patches of cypress trees and vegetation.

It was a thrilling, yet daunting experience as they were alone throughout the whole hike, except for small herds of wild goats grazing on the plant life.

As soon as they brushed aside vegetation from the trees, the group entered a wide clearing and stopped in their tracks.

"This is it," Vassilis said, signalling to the group to join his 'point' position.

They had finally arrived, and it seemed that they were the only ones there.

The group moved forward cautiously.

CHAPTER 42

IMPASSABLE

Legionshield's convoy was bouncing on the rocky terrain in the valley, and brushed past thickets of trees and underbrush, as the trail narrowed to a point from which they couldn't advance any further.

The lead jeep stopped and was facing tall rock formations and trees. The trail ended there.

Keyes looked ahead and beyond their obstacle. The valley continued on, but wasn't accessible even for a quad-bike, never mind the jeeps and trucks that halted behind him.

"It looks like we're on foot now," he clearly stated the obvious.

Keyes jumped out of the jeep and helped Vanessa out, as she viewed her tracker-scanner.

Everybody else got out of their respective vehicles and assembled near the CEO. The party was fifteen-strong, and started to mobilise their kit and weapons, preparing for the final hike.

"We need to go north which is straight ahead," advised Vanessa.

"How far?" Keyes asked, throwing his backpack on.

"No more than a mile, providing the signal hasn't faltered. It hasn't moved for the last hour," Vanessa answered.

"It could be a glitch," Mervier said.

"There's only one way to find out. We haven't got a choice, we've come all this way, I'm not going to stop now, let's see where it leads us to," Keyes said, looking at Vanessa's scanner.

Matheson was watching and hoped that Ophelia had managed to reach the signal first.

"Colonel, prepare your men," Keyes ordered, turning to the officer.

Finellis didn't like taking orders from this civilian, ex-CIA or not, but he relented and whistled to his six camouflaged soldiers.

Keyes signalled to two of his four own operatives, and they followed him, as they made their way over to Hugo. The muscular henchman opened the door, and climbed down the steps from the driver's cabin.

"Get ready Hugo, and wait for my signal," Keyes said.

Hugo nodded and, accompanied by the two Legionshield operatives, darted to the back of the truck and disappeared inside the canopy.

Keyes returned to the main group of soldiers, operatives and mercenaries. Mervier looked at the weapons cache that had been unloaded onto the ground.

She helped herself to an H&K G3A3 assault rifle, she still had her 9mm Ruger. The six Greek soldiers and their colonel were also carrying the same, as they were the standard issue for the Greek army.

Keyes looked at his fearsome fighting force, like a drill sergeant inspecting his troops on parade. Deep down, he knew they were cannon-fodder and expendable, but would probably afford him time and opportunity to fulfil his task without too much challenge.

"What lies deep within that valley, you will have not faced before gentlemen," Keyes said, addressing his Greek entourage.

The men were quiet but looked battle-hardened and ready.

The CEO then took out a long carrier case from the back of the jeep and strapped it to his back, it was no secret that it contained the modified Bident of Hades.

"Be cautious, alright people, let's move out." Keyes signalled to his group, and led the way through the thicket of vegetation with Vanessa, Finellis and his two other operatives, who were holding American AR-15 assault rifles.

The six soldiers followed them in line through the trees that led to the rocky passageway in the valley.

Mervier felt more at ease with the Black Knights, and they waited until the last of the six soldiers disappeared into the tree-line.

Matheson glanced at Straker and Fox; they were all carrying their G-36 carbines. His eyes were then averted to the truck behind which Hugo had disappeared.

"Keyes left a couple of his men behind to guard the vehicles," Straker deduced.

"What's the problem, Matheson?" Mervier asked.

"Why leave his steroid-enhanced brute behind too?" Matheson queried.

"Who cares?" she said, "He did take a good pasting at Ravenscliff,"

"We better catch up, sir," Straker advised.

"Okay, let's go," Matheson uttered, and they started to follow the rest of the team deeper into the valley.

CHAPTER 43

THE ANCIENT RUIN

Ophelia and Madison had stepped out into a rocky clearing that was surrounded by monolithic cliffs.

Vassilis joined them as Spears treaded backwards, keeping a watchful eye on the tree line and rocky passages behind them. Both men were carrying their M4 carbines.

Ophelia's group had entered the site of an ancient ruin.

The site was a small enclosure nestled in the valley, no bigger than the courtyard at Ravenscliff. There were broken stone pillars of what once used to be a small temple, and strut out from the ground.

Some of the half-pillars reached only twenty feet in the air, but most were in pieces and created a floor of stumps, amongst several other pieces of masonry that were scattered around.

Plant life, shrubbery and vines covered most of the stonework in the area. The place looked dead, and it wouldn't be much of an exciting attraction to most passers-by.

A few old stone statues still remained standing on their bases, and all of them were in a bad state of disrepair, having been neglected and exposed to the elements for hundreds or thousands of years.

The statues were sculptures of unidentifiable ancient Greek warriors from ages past. Some had arms missing, and others only had their legs that remained fixed to their bases. Their top halves had fallen centuries ago, and were now old pieces that were strewn around their plinths.

This, however, didn't make Ophelia and her companions any less cautious as they stealthily continued across the graveyard of stone statues, keeping a close eye on each one of them – she expected them to suddenly come to life.

But nothing stirred in the ruins, only the soft breeze that blew through the gorge and rustled the cypress trees around the perimeter of the dilapidated site.

"What was this place?" Ophelia spoke softly, just in case she awoke any of the decaying statues around her. She was taking no chances.

Madison peered down at some of the stone work and studied some barely legible inscriptions on a huge chunk of masonry. She believed that it was a part of the roof of the structure that once stood there.

"This must have been a Minoan temple," she said.

"And you wouldn't be wrong, Madison," Vassilis verified as he glanced around at the rubble.

"There's nothing here," Ophelia said.

Then, as if on prompt, Vassilis pointed in the direction at the foot of the limestone cliffs on the other side of the derelict site.

"Over there, look."

The group looked at where their guide was pointing to.

It was a cave.

The mouth of the cave was a result of natural corrosion over time, and was ten feet high and twenty feet wide. It also had broken slabs leading up to the jagged entrance.

Vassilis quickly made his way over to the cave, despite a warning from Spears. The women also followed him to the dark entrance.

Spears was about to turn to join them, but heard distinct noises emanating from the treeline a short distance away. Goats were seen racing away from the disturbances that were occurring beyond the thickets of trees. The sounds were of human origin, and the rustling got closer.

They had company.

Meanwhile, Ophelia and Madison exchanged looks of concern and then each took a step on one of the slabs below the entrance of the cave. Vassilis whistled to Spears, who had his eyes transfixed in the direction of where the noises were in the trees.

"We're out of time, they're here." Spears tried to throw his voice across at Vassilis without shouting.

Spears knew he wouldn't be able to hold off whatever force emerged from the clearing in a few moments. They had wasted so much time dawdling around the site as it was.

There were no areas of good cover as he was standing right in the middle of the ruins. The only protection offered were the damaged pillars and statues, and they wouldn't last long against the weapons Legionshield had, especially if there were more air reapers.

He would be overwhelmed in seconds, despite where his Black Knight comrades were. They would be hacked down to pieces the moment they would turn on Keyes' forces.

"Get back here, you fool!" Vassilis raised his voice.

Spears had no choice. He sprinted to the broken steps of the ominous cave, as Ophelia and Madison entered.

The men followed close behind.

The darkness swallowed them.

CHAPTER 44

REUNION

Ophelia had stepped into a huge ancient temple hall.

The cave had been converted into a large chamber which appeared abandoned and over a thousand years old, due to the cobwebs that were visible in every orifice. Vines snaked across the limestone walls.

Large decaying pillars supported the roof of the cave, and there were two rows of archaic statues that were lined from the entranceway to a flight of stone steps at the end of the hall. The steps ascended forty-five-degrees to a wide balcony that overlooked the chamber.

The balcony was perched fifteen-feet above the ground, and the only thing behind it was a flat stone wall. On one side of the balcony's platform was a single stone rod that was embedded into a small pedestal, and on the other side were a couple of chains hanging down from a crevasse in the ceiling.

Even though the temple cavern looked deteriorated and run down, Ophelia was still awe-inspired. She took note of the stone ground as she cautiously progressed down the hall, followed by the three others. They spread out.

The entire floor was chequered like a gigantic chess board. The squares were formed in an alternating pattern of jade-green and plain stone that matched the walls.

Each square slab was approximately three-meters square and was partially covered with limestone sand and dried foliage that had been blown in by the wind.

The group tested its foundations and the squares felt solid as they approached half-way across the hall. Ophelia's heart was pounding and Spears kept his rifle low, momentarily glancing behind his shoulder in case any intruders should enter.

"Astonishing," Ophelia whispered as she observed all around her.

"There are no exits or passageways, it's just a chamber," Vassilis commented.

"Oh, there are always secret passages, trust me," Madison quipped.

"She's here," Ophelia spoke, not really addressing anybody in particular. She had a strange sensation.

"Okay, look around, they're not far behind us," Spears advised, and the group split up, wandering around the spacious, converted temple.

Ophelia removed her Bergen and placed it on the ground. She was fumbling around looking for the small tranquiliser gun until, all of a sudden, the flame torches in the temple flickered to life – as if by magic.

Rumbling was heard from the top of the balcony which got everybody's attention. The group stood still, and glanced up at the flat wall that was behind the balcony.

The wall parted from the centre, and the two sections slowly retracted in opposite directions until they disappeared into slim cavities on either side – thus revealing a hidden tunnel.

Footsteps echoed from the other side of the wall's new opening, and Spears, along with Vassilis, raised their rifles in quick response.

Ophelia immediately raised her hand and signalled to them to lower their weapons. They obeyed.

From out of the darkness, Marzanna emerged, accompanied by Cora and four other maidens of the coven. Each maiden was carrying a traditional bow and a quiver of arrows that was slung over a shoulder. They filed gracefully onto the balcony.

The acolytes were wearing jade-green togas that were of a reptilian-scaled design. Their emerald green sashes were draped across their waists, and each had a dagger that was sheathed.

"So, you have returned," Marzanna addressed Ophelia softly, before the curator could find the tranquiliser gun.

Ophelia stopped rummaging and took a step forward. Her arms were outstretched passively.

Marzanna, despite her stern expression, looked resplendent.

The high priestess was wearing an elegant jade and emerald toga, very similar to her acolytes, but had gold-encrusted patterns flowing down her low-cut lapel. Her long, flowing dark hair cascaded down her back and bare shoulders.

On her head was a beautiful ornate gold tiara with an emerald stone in the centre glistening from the fire-torches that were mounted on the rows of pillars.

She was also carrying the sceptre.

Ophelia looked down at the green square she was standing on, and ironically thought – check-mate.

The others approached closer to the balcony until they were half-way down the hall, until Marzanna held up her hand, and with lightning reflexes, her maidens nocked their arrows onto their bow strings.

Spears and Vassilis raised their rifles and aimed them at the maidens. The acolytes in turn aligned their arrows at the two men.

"No wait!" Ophelia shouted.

She was re-living the same situation again as in the banquet room, only this time, it wasn't the detective she had to restrain. Ophelia trusted Spears not to escalate this, unless absolutely necessary.

Marzanna motioned to her five acolytes, and they remained in position, easing off the draw-pull of their bows.

Spears and Vassilis lowered their weapons slightly.

Ophelia exhaled a sigh of relief and pleaded to the high priestess standing regally on the balcony. She placed her hands on the intricate stone trellis in front of her and looked into Ophelia's desperate eyes.

"Marzanna, please, I have come here to warn you, you must believe me, you're in grave danger!" Ophelia said, in a heart-felt manner.

"How did you find me?" Marzanna enquired, puzzled.

"It doesn't matter now, our enemies have come for you, they are approaching now as we speak. I came here to save you!" Ophelia pleaded sincerely.

The curator was hoping that Marzanna could sense and feel her emotions. She deeply felt, that they still had a psychic connection – a spiritual bond, even.

There was a pause.

Marzanna turned to Cora.

"Dusk is almost upon us, it is time to awaken my mother," she gently said to her young acolyte. Cora bowed her head and disappeared into the open space in the wall behind her.

Ophelia's mouth dropped. Was she too late?

Marzanna turned her attention back to Ophelia and smiled, but not deviously.

"Ophelia, I admire your courage, but I must fulfil my destiny," Marzanna replied, her voice resonating throughout the whole chamber.

"No, please, come with us whilst you can, you must trust me," Ophelia tried again.

"It is time," Marzanna said.

Then another voice hollered across the chamber.

"You got that right!"

The group spun round and Keyes stepped inside the hall brandishing his bident, Vanessa stood next to him holding her pistol.

Ophelia looked shocked, as she saw the Greek soldiers led by Finellis spill into the room, followed by two of Keyes' operatives.

The dynamic had changed, and the maidens knew that they were hopelessly outnumbered. The intruders spilt up and scattered across the chamber, taking various positions – like chess pieces on a giant board.

Some of them had trained their weapons on Ophelia and her small group, others aligned their rifles at the balcony, causing Marzanna to step back a couple of paces.

She placed her hand on the stone stump which was protruding out from its plinth.

"It's game over, witch!" Keyes said, aiming his bident at her. Marzanna recognised the weapon.

Spears noticed Matheson at the entranceway, accompanied by Mervier and the two mercs. He was hoping they would do something, as he and Vassilis were surrounded by the soldiers.

"On the contrary, the game is just beginning," Marzanna replied calmly.

CHAPTER 45

THE LAIR OF THE GORGON

Cora pushed in a stone on the side of a wall, at the end of the secret tunnel. The passageway was lined with mounted flame-torches.

This triggered a mechanism that opened up a hidden wall which she was facing. A moment later, she entered a small dimly lit chamber.

The oval-shaped sanctuary had a low ceiling and was supported by four painted pillars. Each one had a flame torch attached, which illuminated the room, casting an ambient orange glow.

On the opposite side of the private chamber was an intricately carved stone altar with an assortment of ancient symbols and patterns etched into it. There was a circular space on top of the altar – large enough for a tablet.

The Gorgoneion talisman.

It was resting on a table at the side of the room.

Cora appeared nervous and heard the echoing and sinister sounds of hissing.

Snake hisses.

The young maiden glimpsed at the far wall. It had a dark crevice that led to another antechamber, but she knew that was a forbidden place.

A slender human-sized shape was seen approaching her from the darkness within the antechamber, and Cora averted her eyes to the ground. She slowly dropped to her knees and graciously bowed as the figure materialised from out of the shadows, and entered the sanctuary chamber.

The hooded woman slowly walked over to Cora. Her long cream silken toga flowed behind her with each step.

Cora continued to look down at the floor and all she could see was the woman's silhouette, and her bare, repulsive pale-green feet. Her toenails were decaying, gnarled and overgrown.

The woman's face was partially unseen due to the large emerald hood. Cora slowly raised her head, and got a glimpse of the woman's snake-scaled flesh on her bare arms. Her skin was in the same hideous condition as her feet, as well as the gruesome shade of a decomposed corpse.

Evidence of a divine punishment.

The hissing was louder, and as Cora lowered her head once more, she looked at the apparition's silhouette once again, and noticed the movement of small serpent heads that momentarily poked in and out from inside the top of her hood, as if they were tasting the air.

They were hissing, and forked tongues flickered in and out of their mouths.

"Forgive my intrusion, my deity, for it is your daughter's fiftieth divine day."

The hooded crone spoke with a raspy croak, but her words sounded soothing to Cora.

"I sense fear in you, my child."

She maternally placed her reptilian talon-like hand gently on the young acolyte's head.

"Armed marauders have arrived, they have come to destroy us all, and I fear we will not be able to defeat them this time," Cora said solemnly. A tear slowly trickled down her cheek.

A gnarled elongated finger tenderly touched Cora's cheek and the tear rolled onto the hooded woman's fingertip.

She collected it and rubbed the teardrop in-between her deformed thumb and forefinger.

"Have no fear, the ritual will have to wait a little longer."

The gorgon quietly moved past Cora, and swiftly disappeared out of the sanctuary chamber.

CHAPTER 46
THE TRAP

Suspense filled the air.

It was a standoff.

Marzanna viewed the chamber from her elevated position. There were nineteen people that were inside, aiming their modern weapons at others in their large group, as well as aligning their guns at the balcony.

Even the high priestess didn't know who was on whose side. But what she did know, was that Ophelia had spoken truthfully, and from the heart.

During the deadlock situation on the chequered floor, Marzanna looked deeply into Ophelia's eyes once she turned to face her. The curator was closest to the steps that led to the balcony, and she was adjacent to one of the stone statues which stood on its plinth, on one of the stone squares next to her.

Ophelia was standing on the edge of a jade square, and was inches away from a statue next to her.

Marzanna's voice echoed in Ophelia's mind.

"Step onto the statue, keep off the jade."

The high priestess' voice was soft and clear as Ophelia tuned into the psychic connection. She wasn't under any spell, though, she was highly receptive to the woman's thoughts.

Ophelia was aware of her plan, and looked over at Madison near her. Her associate was standing on one of the stone-coloured slabs, like Spears and Vassilis.

"Stay put, Maddy," she uttered quietly at Madison.

The curator had no time to turn back around to face the others, and had no idea where they were positioned. The mercs near the entrance had to take the risk, and hopefully had not fully entered the chamber.

Keyes stepped forward a few more steps with Vanessa, and aimed his bident at Ophelia thirty metres away. He didn't notice Matheson creeping behind him, slowly raising the muzzle of his G-36 to the CEO's back – Matheson stepped on the jade square which was previously occupied by Keyes and Vanessa.

Then, before anyone on the floor could take any further action, Ophelia leapt onto the statue next to her, just as Marzanna pulled the stone lever that her hand was resting on.

In a blink of an eye, the trap was activated.

Twenty-four jade square slabs suddenly, and simultaneously flipped down, like trap doors, plunging almost half of the intruders into deep twenty-foot pits.

It had all happened so fast.

The ones that fell into the dark chasms were three Greek soldiers, the two Legionshield operatives and Matheson, when the ground gave way beneath them.

Then the temple battle ensued.

The maidens released arrows from the balconies at the remaining assailants who were safely standing on the plain stone squares. Only now, were there twenty-four open spaces on the floor, which would make it even more difficult for the survivors to navigate across.

The four arrows whistled across the temple chamber. Two of them struck one of the soldiers directly in the chest, and he fell back, screaming into one of the pit spaces behind him.

Another arrow flew straight into Vanessa's thigh, and she shrieked in agony, dropping her handgun. The PA lost her balance and stumbled back, but was quickly caught by Keyes.

The only chivalrous thing he had ever done.

Keyes pulled her back into his space before she could plummet into the open one next to them and threw her behind one of the statues.

The fourth arrow sailed above the heads of the other two soldiers, and Finellis aimed his pistol at the maidens and fired. Bullets ricocheted off the stone trellis as the maidens re-nocked their bows.

The trap doors seemed to be on a mechanical timer, as the jade hatches started to slowly rise up – the overhanging chains on the balcony were moving, which indicated this.

Keyes re-aimed his bident and squeezed the modified trigger which was attached to the shaft, and a huge blast of blinding white plasma energy streaked across the hall and struck the top of the stone statue that Ophelia was clinging onto – barely missing her.

The statue was demolished immediately and chunks of rock crashed to the ground, sending Ophelia plummeting into the half-open pit next to her.

"No!" Marzanna screamed, as she saw Ophelia fall into the pit.

"Ophelia!" Spears shouted. He suddenly leapt into the air and nobly jumped through the small gap of the closing trap door, and into the pit. Vassilis had no time to follow as the hatch was now inches away from closing.

The moment they were swallowed up by the darkness, the hatch sealed closed again with a loud reverberating thud, exposing the jade square once more. They were trapped underneath the floor.

The entire ground in the chamber had returned to its former chess-board-look as all the trap door hatches sealed themselves at the same time.

Keyes observed this and aimed the bident at Marzanna before she could flip the switch again. The CEO released another lethal bolt of energy towards the balcony.

Marzanna reacted, and dove from the balcony onto the lower ground. Her maidens also saw the threat and vaulted over the trellis and landed on the floor, just as the bident's energy blast smashed into the balcony's wall, which sent massive pieces of limestone collapsing down covering the pedestal and lever which operated the trap doors. It was now buried underneath immoveable chunks of rubble.

Fortunately, the bident had claimed no victims yet.

Keyes snarled as he fired his powerful weapon for a third time. The maidens scattered once more and the energy blasts smashed into the rock wall behind them, creating a massive hole. Chunks flew off and rained down on the combatants that were trying to advance on the coven's acolytes.

Meanwhile, Fox and Straker had jumped back out of the chamber when the floor spaces were activated, and a second later the place had turned into a war zone.

Before they could return to the fray and pick a side, the two merc were distracted by a mechanical sound coming from the other side of the ruins outside the cave chamber.

It wasn't clunky or grinding, it was a smooth hydraulic range of sounds.

Encased in the ATTAC was Hugo, and he made his way at great speed across the compound.

Fox and Straker looked on in disbelief at the camouflaged, smooth and muscular-plated combat chassis. At first glance, it appeared like a futuristic, humanoid robot stomping towards them, until they focused in on the only visible evidence of there being a man inside; it was a curvy bucket-shaped helmet, which had a reinforced ballistic-proof, transparent full-facial visor, which revealed Hugo's determined face inside.

It was a terrifying and awesome sight.

"What the hell!" Straker said, and both mercenaries raised their weapons.

They knew it was Hugo, their supposed ally, and didn't engage. Behind him trying to keep up were the two other operatives carrying AR-15's.

Hugo viewed through his heads-up display on his visor the two mercs taking a step back each, but they had their rifles raised. Keyes had given him instructions that the moment the Black Knights showed any signs of threat or betrayal towards Legionshield, take the necessary measures.

Hugo didn't hesitate, and opened up rigorous high-velocity rapid fire from his wrist cannons.

Deadly rounds tore into the cliff and cave walls beside the mercs, and they immediately jumped down the make-shift steps of the cave's entrance and into the rocky compound. The thunderous barrage continued its onslaught as Hugo advanced.

Fox and Straker sourced out some cover behind half-fallen pillars and limestone rocks that jutted out from the ground, and returned fire from their G-36 carbines.

Their combined bursts bounced and ricocheted harmlessly off the heavily armoured ATTAC, including the headshots.

Hugo laughed, from within his indestructible shell.

Meanwhile, inside the temple chamber, the fight was intensifying.

Madison had taken cover from the crossfire between the coven's maidens and the remaining soldiers of the Greek squad. One of them aligned his H&K weapon on a maiden, and Madison was close enough to dive in-between them. The young kick-boxer kicked the H&K out of his hands, sending it spiralling into the distance.

The maiden noted this and saw Madison making good work of the soldier, pounding punch after kick into him with a flurry of fast combination techniques. Her foot showed no signs of hindrance due to her adrenalin.

Two maidens released their arrows again and hit the second soldier square in the chest, killing him instantly.

Colonel Finellis quickly jumped out from behind a pillar and fired his Browning Hi-Power at one of the maidens that had shot his squad member. The bullets pounded into her shoulder and she fell with a grunt, dropping her bow.

Her sister collected her from the ground, but Finellis had her in his sights.

Marzanna jumped, in covering an amazing distance and struck the crown of the sceptre on Finellis' head, cracking his skull. A flash of light occurred, followed by the power of the sceptre taking immediate effect.

Finellis turned to stone within seconds, and remained frozen in a mid-action pose of himself aiming the pistol – which remained in its steel form.

Madison executed a round-house kick that knocked the last soldier out cold, and he fell at her feet.

Mervier had been running around avoiding the bullets and plasma blasts throughout the skirmish, and was trying to close in on Marzanna. Their eyes locked, and Mervier paused.

Marzanna confronted the detective once again.

Mervier was lost for words. She knew she would sound ridiculous if she said, 'you're under arrest' after everything that was happening around her, but the detective remained steadfast and kept the gun trained on her. There were five metres between them.

Then, a huge explosion erupted in the space between them caused by the bident – Keyes' aim wasn't too great as he wielded the weapon from behind a nearby statue.

The damage was enough though, as the shockwave sent both Mervier and Marzanna flying in opposite directions, along with a hail of debris and rubble that had erupted from the stone square, as a result of the energy blast.

The detective was unconscious, and the high priestess was lying on the slabs bloodied and battered. Her prone, weakened state created a reaction from the four maidens who began rushing over to her.

Two of them nocked arrows, and aimed them at Keyes, who took cover behind the statue with the wounded Vanessa. He was pinned down.

At that point, Fox and Straker darted into the chamber, followed by intense barrages of fire from an unseen force. They turned and faced the entranceway and retreated back, returning suppressive fire at their foe.

Hugo, inside his ATTAC, dramatically entered the temple chamber, and received shocked looks from everybody except for Keyes and Vanessa, who grinned smugly.

Now the game had got interesting and took a turn in favour of Legionshield.

Marzanna and her maidens looked at the mechanical horror that stood menacingly at the entrance.

CHAPTER 47

THE LABYRINTH

Ophelia had landed safely with a great splash into murky waters.

Spears followed a couple of seconds later, and nearly crashed on top of her. The weight of his Bergen took him further into the depths of the square pool.

They had fallen only twenty metres and soon as both rose to the surface, they found that they were inside a pit with vertical unscalable walls around them. The stone hatch above them was sealed, encasing them in near-darkness.

The pit was dank and dark, and the only illumination came from a flame-torch that was at the end of a wide tunnel, which stretched out from the embankment of the pool.

It was the only way out of the pit, and the fifteen-metre-length tunnel led to a cross-junction which branched out to three passageways.

Ophelia took a breath as she treaded water.

"My backpack!" she shouted, as Spears climbed out of the pool and onto the rocky embankment, which faced the ominous tunnel.

Ophelia dove into the depths of the pool. She hated being underwater, but had seemed to overcome that phobia on her last adventure in the elixir lagoon.

The curator swum to the bottom and managed to find the Bergen that had dropped into the pit only moments ago. She retrieved the xiphos sword and a Glock 17 from the bag as she couldn't lift the weighed-down backpack, and she only had seconds of air in her lungs.

Ophelia emerged from the dirty surface and was helped out by Spears. Her top was torn and tattered from the sharp shards of stonework that exploded around her when Keyes had blasted away her cover in the chamber. Her face had fresh cuts and scrapes, but she looked more determined than ever to finish this.

Both of them were looking down the tunnel, trying to assess their dire situation.

She realised that each trap door above had sent anyone else that was unfortunate enough to be standing on the jade squares into individual pits that were honeycombed around the subterranean dungeon that they had found themselves in.

"Okay, where now?" Spears said. He looked up and deduced that the hatch above couldn't be blown out with rifle fire, or the walls, for that matter, couldn't be scaled either, even if he did have explosives to rig on the ceiling of the pit.

He was aware there was a full-scale battle taking place above ground, so even if they could breach the hatch, they'd most likely be picked off by Legionshield or the coven once they climbed out.

"We got no choice," Ophelia said as she looked down the passageway.

Spears got to his feet and led the way down the tunnel until they came to the cross-junction.

"Do you know anyone else that fell?" Ophelia asked as they looked down each of the three tunnels – they all looked identical and led to further cross-junctions.

It was a maze.

"I was too busy following you," Spears replied, as he switched on his light which was on his tactical vest.

Ophelia took a breath.

"Thanks for coming after me," she managed a smile.

"You know me."

"My hero," she said mockingly, although her tone was genuine.

"Well, now we have got a labyrinth to negotiate our way out of," Spears said, pessimistically.

Ophelia took a moment to analyse her surroundings.

"I hate mazes, we could be here forever," she tried to look at various carvings on the walls, like she was searching for any form of clue. She started brushing dust off each wall at eye-level, that led to each passageway – like an archaeologist.

"Why a labyrinth above a temple?" Spears asked.

"Maybe it's an ancient dungeon?" Ophelia suggested, as her hand wiped away some of the dust on the first craggy wall to her left – it revealed an old faded painting of a bull.

Her mouth dropped.

"We could be in deep shit, here," she uttered.

"You think?" Spears replied, as he shone his torch down the wide tunnels. The flame torches which were lined at various intervals across the walls didn't offer that much.

Then, a monstrous roar was heard in the distance, echoing through the eerie tunnels. They couldn't ascertain which direction it came from, but Ophelia knew that they had awoken someone – or something.

"We're in deeper shit!" she added.

Elsewhere in the labyrinth, the others that fell through the trap doors had landed safely in their respective pit-pools.

The two Legionshield operatives had fallen together and were gathering their senses in their pit. It looked exactly the same as the one which Ophelia and Spears plummeted into.

Located not far from them was a pit each for the three Greek soldiers, and they climbed out of their pool.

Meanwhile, Matheson wasted no time in clambering out of his pit. He was alone and heard the same growl that resounded through the twisting tunnels.

Each pit had a similar-looking tunnel that led to an option of passages.

The individuals that had fallen into the pits started to make their way through the network of ancient tunnels, making spot decisions at each junction. Every junction, every tunnel gave them more choices.

Ophelia brushed away more dust from the two other tunnels. The centre one had the image of a bull, the passageway to the left had a snake, and the one to the right was a winged horse.

"What was that?" Spears asked, referring to the hideous roar, which sent shivers down his spine.

Ophelia turned to him, and with a distressed expression, spoke.

"This is more than a dungeon," she said.

"Go on," Spears asked, not really wanting to know.

"This whole place is an ancient Minoan sacrificial temple," Ophelia revealed, gripping her xiphos sword until her knuckles turned white.

"A sacrificial temple?" he repeated.

"Thousands of years ago, King Minos sacrificed slaves and prisoners-of-war from their neighbouring enemies of Athens to appease Poseidon." The curator began her brief history lesson.

Spears looked down at his feet and saw the old bones of a goat.

"I know where you're going with this," Spears replied, knowing full well of the Greek legend.

"Well, that will save me some time, and it's time we haven't got. We got to get out of here," she urged.

"You got to be shitting me, how is that possible?"

Another roar echoed down the passageways – this time, closer.

"By that!" Her breathing became faster. Spears checked his G-36 and switched the safety off.

"No way, it can't be," Spears was still in denial, though he knew she was deadly serious.

"Nathan, we've witnessed flying gargoyles and the resurrection of a thousand-year-old sorcerer – anything is possible right now!"

"So how do we kill a mythical creature that has allegedly existed for thousands of years? For all we know, that thing could be just one pissed-off rabid dog!" Spears said, with a sense of anxiety in his voice.

"I don't know, but we can't stay here," she said.

"Okay, which way?"

"Follow the bull," Ophelia suggested.

"What?" Spears said, hesitantly, barely believing the words that came from her mouth.

"Maybe the signs were inscribed for people to avoid certain routes, as a ploy, they would be encouraged to take the alternative passageways, which would inevitably lure them to where the creature was hunting," Ophelia advised.

"Right, and you're basing this on…?" he paused, allowing her to finish his sentence.

"A hunch."

Spears rolled his eyes and exhaled sharply. Maybe this woman who he had loved and respected for years, had finally gone doolally.

"Well, the way in is no longer our way out, so a ball of thread will be useless," he said cynically.

"It's worth a try," Ophelia assured. At this point, she seemed calmer than Spears.

Nonetheless, the merc took the lead and both of them ventured off into the central tunnel.

Elsewhere in the darkened maze, one of the Greek soldiers wandered aimlessly down a tunnel that he had selected. He didn't spot the same three markings that were faintly shown on the walls.

Nor did he spot the huge creature that was stalking him from behind.

The terrified soldier heard deep snorts a few yards away, and he spun around to face an eight-foot monstrosity.

The creature appeared out of the darkness and was dimly lit by the two flame torches on either side of the wide tunnel – the soldier shit his pants.

It was a muscular hybrid monster with the head and tail of a bull, and the body of an immense man. He had a thick, shaggy coat of fur, large pointed horns, and muscles that bulged on every inch of his mutated form. A truly powerful physique.

Around the minotaur's neck was a large rusty chain, and dangling down from it was an octagonal bronze medallion with ancient markings etched onto it.

The solider was petrified and didn't have time to raise his rifle. Instead, he screamed as the minotaur charged towards him with full force.

He was ripped to pieces.

The minotaur had claimed his first victim.

A shuddering human scream was heard throughout the complex network of tunnels, followed by an unnerving silence.

Everyone else in their respective locations within the maze had stopped in their tracks.

The hunt was on.

CHAPTER 48

MARZANNA'S PLIGHT

Inside the temple chamber, the battle raged on.

The ATTAC fired its heavy machine guns and lasers at the retreating mercenaries who were trying to provide covering for the maidens. The superior firepower of the mechanical monster obliterated everything it hit – statues, pillars and stonework were blasted to pieces.

Straker was caught in the leg by another burst of intense fire and collapsed onto the ground, spilling blood across the chequered floor.

Fox raced over to him and dodged the incoming assault. He took cover and applied pressure on his associate's wounds. Straker was out of the fight.

The maidens released more arrows at the armoured behemoth that continued to stampede further into the temple.

The arrows bounced off like tooth-picks and clattered to the ground.

With each step that Hugo took, he unleashed more destructive hell from the ATTAC's attached weapons.

Keyes looked on with glee, as he shielded Vanessa from the debris being scattered in every direction.

Meanwhile, the maidens were shielding a dazed Marzanna, who was slowly shaking off the effects of the previous explosion.

Her loyal acolytes tried to advance towards the approaching ATTAC in a futile effort to stall it.

From inside the ATTAC, Hugo's digital visor-display zeroed in on the four women who tried firing at the facial visor on his helmet. The arrow harmlessly deflected off. Nothing could stop this marauding machine. He had target acquisition.

Hugo smirked again and aimed his right arm at the four maidens, who were conveniently clustered together. He then fired his rapid-fire wrist cannon.

A lethal spray of gunfire tore into the maidens.

Two of them were instantly killed, blood spattered everywhere as their bodies were blasted back. The other two had sustained bad wounds and fell to the ground, next to their dead sisters.

The two injured maidens desperately tried to crawl away as the ATTAC stomped closer to them.

Marzanna screamed like a banshee, and summoned the strength to get to her feet and sprint over to where her maidens heroically fell.

She launched into the air and executed a flying kick into the heavily armoured ATTAC's chest plate. The strike knocked him back a few yards, but the deadly machine did not topple.

Hugo laughed once again, and advanced towards his new target – he wanted revenge, and this was a re-match, which he had no intention of losing.

Marzanna came in again with her full super-human strength and struck the ATTAC with a powerful shoulder barge. Again, it barely budged him. Hugo counter-attacked by activating a close-quarters blade from his left wrist – the size of a broad sword.

She ducked underneath the first swing, and he tried to slash again, but this time it was parried by her sceptre. The force of the strike brought the high priestess down to her knees.

Marzanna managed to push the blade away from her with the last of her energy, and swung the crown of her sceptre down onto the helmet. She could see Hugo's leering and smug face inside – unaffected.

The sceptre couldn't get through the armour – nothing could penetrate.

She tried another part of his armour, but everywhere was encased, no human part of the body, or even a joint was visible or exposed.

Huge swatted her away like a fly with the ATTAC's bulky right arm, and Marzanna was catapulted back several feet, smashing into one of the last statues that had remained standing inside the wrecked chamber.

The sculpture collapsed to pieces, and Marzanna crumpled down to the ground with it, exhausted and badly wounded.

Vassilis dove out of cover and tried to protect the battle-damaged high priestess. He fired his M4 and shots struck the armour, having the same effect as everything else.

Hugo discharged two laser beams that hit the Cretan merc in the shoulder and leg. He dropped his weapon and fell back next to the almost incapacitated Marzanna.

He was unstoppable.

To make matters worse, the two Legionshield operatives entered the chamber and joined what was left of the fight to support the ATTAC – not that it needed support.

Madison was unarmed and couldn't do anything, so she tried to circle around the smashed pillars to close in on the unsuspecting Keyes. She had eyes on the bident – maybe that would work against this technological terror.

Hugo observed this and launched a mini-missile in her direction. It blasted some stonework close to her and the explosion caused debris to fall, crashing into the young woman. She lay there, knocked out.

Marzanna opened her weary eyes and the blurry image of the ATTAC approached. She was the primary target, and all her protectors had been effortlessly dealt with.

Almost all.

Appearing from a high ledge on the far wall, fifty-feet above the entrance way, a woman wearing a cream toga and green hood had emerged from a secret dark crevice, which had a high view of the temple chamber below.

She looked down at the carnage.

Anger consumed her, and she leapt from the ledge, and landed behind the ATTAC.

The battle was not over yet.

CHAPTER 49

THE FURY OF THE MINOTAUR

The labyrinth was filled with the sound of blood-curdling screams, which resonated throughout the twisting passageways.

The immensely-powerful minotaur ripped the head off one of the other soldiers who had the misfortune of encountering the horrific beast.

The creature was relentless and had already stalked, hunted down, and killed two other victims.

Matheson hurried his pace through the winding maze, and stumbled across two mutilated corpses of men wearing Legionshield uniforms. His choice of which tunnel to take was pure guesswork, and he had no idea of where he was heading.

He was posed with two options as he reached yet another junction. He thought he was going in circles – he probably was.

The two passages in front of him forked out very close together like the letter V.

He glanced up and saw two painted symbols etched into the stonework above each tunnel. One symbol represented a scorpion. The other was a bull.

This was the first time he saw these markings, and regretted not taking note earlier as he turned left and right until he eventually lost his bearings and sense of direction.

Matheson was about to venture into the one with the scorpion, until he heard gunfire and growling that were clearly coming from the other tunnel, further down.

Taking a breath, he decided to take the bull-marked passageway – there was someone alive down here, and he didn't care if the person was a friend or foe. Mathson pressed on.

Ophelia and Spears had heard the same shots fired, but couldn't ascertain where the gunfire originated, as they were faced with six exits – each wall had different symbols on it featuring animals. Luckily, she found the one that depicted a bull – if it was lucky at all.

"This way," she said, and both of them bolted down the stone corridor.

The last remaining soldier, however, was racing down an S-shaped tunnel as fast as his legs could carry him. At quick intervals, he turned and fired blindly behind him.

The savage minotaur was close behind, and thundered down the passageway, gaining ground on the fleeing man.

He didn't know where he was going as he was hopelessly lost, but he tried to increase his speed, as he heard the sounds of snorting and snarling from the monster getting closer.

At that moment, the soldier came to a dead-end.

He spun around and fear gripped him. He had no escape.

The minotaur had caught up and paused, breathing deeply. The soldier could taste the foul stench of the beast, looming closer and closer.

He raised his rifle and pressed the trigger at point-blank range.

'Click'.

His horrified face glanced down at the empty weapon, and then he looked up. The soldier swore he could see the minotaur look as though he was relishing the moment.

It was the last thing the soldier saw.

The minotaur lunged and claimed his fifth victim.

Ophelia and Spears heard another chilling scream, and then silence.

They had raced down tunnel after tunnel and were getting tired, until they saw another single exit that broke off the long tunnel they were in.

The pair could go straight ahead or right into the new area. Ophelia looked above the archway – it had a bull painting on it. Also, inside was a huge chamber that consisted of multi-levels of platforms, rooms, stone staircases, alleyways and more twisting passages.

It looked like a very small-scale village constructed of stone which had been excavated.

This was in fact the minotaur's personal domain.

"Jesus!" Ophelia looked through the archway and scanned her eyes across the gigantic chamber.

She then peered upwards at the highest platform. The stone flight of steps led to a massive closed metal door that looked like iron - strong and sturdy, to keep the beast in.

But a potential way out.

At that point, they both detected a silhouette that rose in size round the corner of the tunnel they were standing in.

Spears raised his M4 and waited, eager to unleash his whole magazine into what unholy abomination that would emerge.

Matheson appeared.

"Miles, thank God!" Ophelia smiled with relief, and Spears lowered his rifle.

"Helluva reunion, right?" Matheson stopped.

"Miles, we've found a large chamber, there looks to be a door. It could be our only exit!" she shouted.

Finally, good news.

Matheson smiled.

"Then, what are we waiting for. Let's get out of this hell-hole!"

Suddenly, two horns punched into Matheson from behind and tore through his chest. Ophelia screamed in horror, and Spears jumped back with her, raising his rifle.

"Miles!" she shrieked again.

The mercenary leader was hoisted up in the air, his upper torso still impaled on the minotaur's deadly horns. Blood spewed from his mouth and his legs dangled in front of the huge body of the creature, like a rag-doll.

Matheson's arms flailed at his sides as he dropped his weapon, and blood gushed from his mortal wound.

The monster shook his bull-head, throwing the mercenary off its horns, and Matheson landed in a bloodied heap on the ground.

Matheson was dead.

Spears wasted no time and opened fire on the creature.

Ophelia momentarily glanced at the creature's medallion, and then continuously fired her Glock 17.

Bullets pounded into the minotaur as he raced towards them in a wild frenzy. The creature reacted to each round, and small wounds were seen on its furry body, but they were more like pin-pricks to the raging monster.

The bullets that slammed into the minotaur only increased his anger, and they didn't alter the speed of the incoming charge.

Ophelia and Spears dove straight into the chamber as the minotaur stormed past them. His horns missed them by mere inches. The minotaur rammed into the wall instead, but this only stunned him for a few seconds.

"Head over to the staircase, hurry!" Spears shouted.

Ophelia sprinted into the massive chamber, and headed straight to the first steps that led to one of the multi-tiered platforms.

Meanwhile, Spears took a few steps back and unloaded his Bergen off his back, he rummaged inside a pulled out one of the fragmentation grenades from the two he had.

He threw one into the corridor outside, and turned around to catch up with Ophelia.

An explosion erupted from the other side of the archway, followed by a bellowing growl. Sections of the corridor outside collapsed and the archway shuddered.

Dust and debris spilt onto the archway.

"That should hold him for a while," Spears uttered to himself, although there was no guarantee that the grenade would have had any effect on the creature, which was probably half-buried underneath a load of rubble.

He didn't go back to check.

CHAPTER 50

THE VENGEANCE OF MEDUSA

Hugo was almost upon the sprawled-out Marzanna, as her two wounded maidens desperately tried to help their high priestess to her feet.

Inside Hugo's futuristic suit of armour, the ATTAC's motion detection system suddenly alerted him of a movement behind him. The visor's read-out display featured a new blip that had just appeared from nowhere.

With great mechanical reflexes, he spun around and looked directly at his new adversary, preparing to batter whoever it was that landed behind him.

The hooded apparition in the toga dress had landed on her feet, and was face-to-face with the transparent armoured visor of the mechanical brute; the hood dropped, revealing a truly horrifying sight.

From Keyes' and Vanessa's point of view, they observed the back of the slender woman's head.

With great astonishment, they saw a crown of a dozen writhing snakes on the woman's head, hissing and snapping at the air. Snakes that had once been beautiful, long-flowing hair.

The ATTAC raised its bulky arms and prepared to bring its huge gauntlet-blade down, but, as if it was stunned or malfunctioned – it suddenly froze in its place.

Vanessa hobbled out of her cover to have a closer look, just as the woman swivelled around and stared into Vanessa's eyes.

Medusa revealed her face to the gasping woman, and Vanessa didn't have time to scream or react.

Her terrified expression remained permanently fixed to her face, as she was immediately, and horrifically transformed to stone, except for the clothing she was wearing.

The gorgon's face was a grotesque pasty green tone and appeared reptilian-like. Sinister-looking bright green pupils were visibly distinct in the dark cavities that were her eye sockets. These chilling eyes would be the last thing any living thing would see before feeling the cold grip of being converted into a dead stone sculpture.

Keyes had quickly moved out of the way as the old monstrous hag gazed at Vanessa, luckily avoiding the deathly stare of the living legend.

He pressed himself hard against the pillar as this was the only source of barricade he had. The CEO grasped his bident tightly whilst panting hard. He looked around and saw his two surviving company operatives quickly split up. One was heading deeper into the hall, whilst the other made a break for it and darted for the exit.

"Get back here you coward!" he screamed, but the operative was having none of it after what he had just witnessed.

The gorgon leapt high above the operative as was dashing to escape the temple, and landed square on her feet in front of him. Medusa hissed as she gazed directly into his face, as he reactively looked at her.

Within a second, the man metamorphosed into a stone sculpture, just like Vanessa.

Keyes averted his eyes from the unbelievable sight, and raced to the far side of the chamber too, desperate to find his last henchman. As he sprinted past the static ATTAC, he managed to get a glimpse inside the helmet – Hugo's face was a look of startlement – but in stone form.

Even the mightiest and most hi-tech form of full body armour had no defence against the true dark magic powers of Medusa.

Keyes sensed someone behind him. His heart was pounding out of his chest and he closed his eyes and swung around, lashing out with his powerful bident. He swung blindly and prayed he struck someone – he didn't care who.

He heard a piercing scream that shrilled through the chamber, and a quick breeze of air, like if somebody had swiftly darted past him with haste.

Keyes opened his eyes and looked straight ahead, taking the risk. Medusa had disappeared, but the Legionshield CEO glanced down and saw fresh drops of deep red blood on the chequered floor.

"She can be killed," he uttered at himself. He then repeated the same swords, but shouting from the top of his lungs, hoping that any others who were still alive had heard.

As he whirled around, he looked at the twin blades of his bident – they were dripping with blood.

Keyes grinned, and felt a glimmer of hope. He had bled her and now had *her* blood that stained his bident, and had spilt onto the ground. He had no time to collect a sample just yet.

Everyone in the room now became the hunter and hunted.

"I want her head!" he bellowed.

CHAPTER 51

THE GATE OF THE HELL-MAZE

Ophelia dashed up three staircases of the minotaur's chamber and finally reached the highest-level platform.

She glanced over her shoulder thirty-feet below and noticed Spears not far behind. The mercenary had reached the foot of the last flight of steps that led to where she was.

Behind him, on the ground level of twisting corridors was a distinct form of the deadly monster. It had survived the grenade explosion in the tunnels, and continued to chase its last surviving prey.

"Hurry!" she shouted, as Spears took three long strides up the staircase to reach the top.

The minotaur had already cleared the first-floor steps with huge leaps, and was quickly ascending the next flight. The ferocious beast was closing in fast, and Ophelia with Spears had reached a dead end.

The only thing they faced was a huge wall with a massive flat iron gate in the centre. There were no handles, mechanisms, beams or panels on it. Only a small circular indentation in the centre. Their hearts dropped.

Trapped.

The only alternative escape was back down the steps and into the path of the minotaur, who was now on the second level platform. Spears hammered in his final magazine to his M4, and adopted a kneeling position – waiting for the mythical beast to reach the top of the staircase.

Ophelia examined the small cavity in the gate. It was octagonal, and it didn't take her long to realise the medallion that was worn around the minotaur's neck was probably the key.

"Oh, come on!" she cursed, as she assessed the predicament of their situation.

"What?" Spears shouted back, aligning his rifle, waiting for the horns of the beast to appear. The merc heard grunting and snorting beyond the edge of the platform.

It was approaching, and they had only seconds before becoming the minotaur's dessert.

"We have to steal the key to open the gate!" Ophelia said.

"Where is it?" Spears yelled.

"The minotaur's wearing it," Ophelia replied, gravely.

"Oh great! I'll just try and persuade him to give it to us, shall I?" Spears spat back. Even in desperate times, there was always room for sarcasm.

"It's the only way," Ophelia cried.

"We'll try my way," Spears said, and reached for his final grenade whilst training his rifle in front of him. He used his teeth and pulled the pin, backed up, and tossed the grenade at the gate. It rested at the foot of the gate. A perfect throw.

"Get over the edge!" Spears shouted, and they both rolled over the edge of the flat platform and clung onto it.

They desperately hung on with their hands, as they dangled precariously over the chamber below. If they fell from this height, there would be certain death.

The minotaur reached the top of the staircase, and extended his hands, which were claw-like.

As he surveyed his surroundings, he noticed that his two remaining victims-to-be had vanished. Their weapons and equipment were the only things on the platform.

The minotaur paused and grunted, confused, until he saw two exposed pairs of hands on the far edge.

The beast roared with glee, as he reacquired his prey.

At that moment, the grenade exploded, sending fragments of shrapnel in every direction. The shockwave blasted into the minotaur, knocking it down, scoring small wounds from the grenade's fragments. This had only temporarily stunned it, again, but remained laid out.

The grenade had no effect on the iron gate.

Spears and Ophelia could only hang on for so long, as they felt their upper body strength starting to ebb away, and their muscles burned. They both hauled themselves up onto the platform and collected their weapons. Ophelia scooped up her xiphos sword. She had discarded her pistol during her ascent, as it had been emptied earlier in the tunnel when Matheson was killed.

Spears, catching his breath, grabbed his rifle and approached the lifeless-looking creature. The medallion gleamed temptingly around the monster's neck.

"Is it dead?" Ophelia hoped the grenade would have finished it off.

Spears took no chances and emptied his entire clip into the dormant creature, for good measure. Rounds punched into the minotaur's hide, chest, head and back. Blood sprayed out from each wound, and the beast shuddered following each impact.

"Should be now," Spears replied, confidently.

Ophelia approached with trepidation behind Spears, as he dropped his M4, and pulled out his Glock. The mercenary kept his sidearm trained on the beast's head as he cautiously reached out with his other hand and grabbed the chain around the minotaur's neck.

It was a moment of suspense for them both, and Ophelia placed the tip of the blade at the creature's throat, preparing to run it through, if she saw the slightest stir from it.

Spears slowly guided the chain over the head and horns of the man-bull, ensuring it didn't brush against its face and avoiding rattling the chain too. It did require a good level of patience and dexterity.

The creature remained still, as Spears removed the chain fully and handed it over to Ophelia, who received it with the same care. The mercenary gestured to her without making a sound, and she crept over to the gate.

Spears retreated back, it appeared that the hideous hybrid wasn't breathing, and all he had left was twelve rounds in his pistol and a combat knife that was sheathed on his thigh.

Ophelia reached the gate and placed the weighty octagonal medallion, which was the size of a small saucer, into the cavity - It fit perfectly.

Nothing happened.

"What am I doing wrong?" she whispered, puzzled.

Spears turned his head towards her and frowned.

"Is there another space?" he asked.

She inspected the gate from top to bottom, looking for clues or markings. The massive iron barricade was flat and nondescript.

"Nothing."

"Try it the other way round," Spears suggested.

She pried out the medallion, then reversed it, and inserted it back into the hole.

Once again, there was no response from the gate. The curator didn't really know what to expect to happen, or if this was the true method of opening it.

"I don't get it," she said, frustratingly.

Spears then joined her to see if he could offer any ideas and looked at the medallion.

"Is it the right key?" Spears asked.

"It must be, we've come across nothing else around this hell-maze."

"Try turning it," Spears advised.

Ophelia pressed onto the medallion and grunted as she tried turning it clockwise, and then counter-clockwise. It didn't budge.

"Christ's sake!" she cursed.

"Let me try," Spears said, holstering his pistol. He exerted his strength and tried to press it in and turn it like a dial, but it remained stiff and immovable.

"This can't be it! Why give the key to get out of here, on that thing?" Spears said, as he tried again strenuously.

"Isn't it obvious? To survive and escape, you must defeat the minotaur, like a prize."

"And what's stopping it escaping itself. I mean it's got the key to get outta here?" Spears asked, switching the medallion and re-inserting it back into the cavity. He then tried rotating it again – but no joy.

"How the hell should I know? Maybe it's docile and doesn't know, or maybe it's aware of what's above ground and remains here, because it doesn't want to be a statue, maybe it's their damn pet!" Ophelia was getting increasingly agitated.

"It's not working," Spears said, defeatedly.

"Wait a sec," she intervened and pried it out again, "It's got eight sides, it could be a process of elimination!" The curator's voice sounded more excitable.

During all the puzzle-solving, they didn't notice the minotaur slowly rising from the floor of the platform.

One snort from its nostrils was enough for them to stop, exchange looks for a fleeting second, and turn around.

The creature salivated as he rose to its full height, and growled deeply. Drool dripped from his mouth, which was reddened with blood from the internal injuries he had sustained, but the powerful beast was alive and looked as fearsome as ever.

Ophelia brandished her sword, and Spears pulled out his Glock and knife.

"Can't this thing just die?" Spears groaned, exasperated.

The minotaur lunged and both leapt to either side, dodging the monstrous ramming attack. As Ophelia jumped aside, she swung her sword, grazing the creature's side. It roared and lashed its claw out, slashing her left shoulder, causing three bloody claw marks.

This knocked her to the edge of the platform, as blood oozed down her arm. Spears rolled out and came up on his knee, shooting the remaining twelve shots into the minotaur's chest.

This only stopped the beast for a few seconds, and he threw his pistol at it. The handgun bounced off its head, further aggravating the invincible creature.

Spears gripped his knife and faced the monster. His adversary closed in on him, which was enough time for Ophelia to pick herself up, scoop up her fallen sword and charge at the monster from behind.

She slashed a couple of times, scoring deep cuts across the minotaur's back, and then he spun around quickly, his muscular beastly arms flailing wildly. Ophelia ducked underneath one of the beast's swings and drove the sword upwards, stabbing him in the stomach.

Ophelia's sword penetrated his midriff, and she pushed hard, driving the short blade further through his tough sinew and muscles causing the minotaur to roar thunderously in agony.

As it staggered back, Spears launched onto the back of the beast and drove his combat knife multiple times into the creature's neck, trying to sever his carotid artery and slice his throat open. Blood spewed in every direction and gushed down his hideous hide.

The minotaur threw Spears off violently, and he landed hard on his side. He felt his ribs, shoulder and leg crunch. Ophelia took the opportunity and withdrew the blade with all her might out of the monster's body, and more blood spattered. The bloodied and badly wounded creature appeared weakened and staggered further back – he was retreating.

Ophelia advanced further courageously, preventing the minotaur from gathering any momentum to charge, but he growled more harshly. Blood continued to spurt out from his neck and stomach wounds and splattered all over the platform.

The minotaur's breathing became laboured, and he buckled onto one knee. As he peered up at his conqueror, she stared down into the beast's blood-shot eyes. They were human-like, they appeared defeated – even sad. Another victim of the Gods' divine punishment, or a hideous result of their lust for power, greed or revenge. A slave for eternity in this hellish existence.

She ended its eternal killing spree, as well as its own suffering, by cutting upwards and deeply slashing its throat.

The minotaur toppled off the edge of the platform and plummeted all the way down to the bottom of the chamber, crashing into the stone ground and landing in a contorted heap of fur and blood. There it remained – lifeless.

Ophelia stood above the edge holding the sword in her hand, peering down at the slain beast. She looked battered and bloodied herself, but stoic and victorious.

Spears struggled to get to his feet, and limped over to her, sheathing his knife. He acknowledged her proudly.

"Nice one, who needs Theseus?" he remarked, referring to the divine and legendary Greek hero, who, according to myth, slew the minotaur.

Ophelia turned to the wounded mercenary.

"Let's get out of here, before we end up finding out there're more of them," she warned. She had an image of hundreds of hybrid bulls filling the chamber.

Although Ophelia was confident that she had killed the one and only mighty minotaur, the curator didn't trust her luck. They dashed towards the iron gate and removed the medallion-key, turned it over, so the markings were facing her and made a note of the octagonal side that was originally in place.

They then turned the jagged disc a few degrees and placed it back into the slot in the gate.

"We've got eight chances, sixteen if we flip the key," she commented, as the first try didn't create a reaction from the gate. She repeated the action like before, and then re-inserting.

"And if they all fail?" Spears asked.

The gate shuddered and rumbling along with metallic grinding was heard from inside the old gate. Ophelia and Spears stepped back and looked down at the slabs beneath.

She had another image of the whole platform collapsing underneath them, and they had nowhere to jump or cling onto should that occur.

A nerve-racking pause, followed by more rumbling and the grinding of chains rubbing against metal. The two adventurers stepped back.

Then, the huge gate vibrated and slid open, revealing a domed room. As soon as the gate created a gap wide enough for a human, they shot through without hesitation, and jumped into the room.

They had escaped the labyrinth.

⟨◆⟩

CHAPTER 52

THE TREASURE VAULT

Ophelia and Spears found themselves in an ancient Greek version of Alladin's cave – a chamber full of beautiful objects and weaponry, which were stacked and placed around the circumference of the room.

Ophelia looked like a kid in a sweet shop. She didn't know where to put her eyes on, as the wide range of treasures took her attention from one item to the next.

Spears didn't identify any of them, and noticed the iron gate remaining open behind them. Opposite the gap was a large arched wooden door with a round metal ring which served as a handle. Hopefully they weren't locked in.

"What is this place?" he said.

"Some kind of treasure hoard, like a reward for the ones who manage to get out," Ophelia guessed.

Spears looked around at the cache of objects.

"Or a stockpile of spoils," he estimated.

Ophelia nodded in agreement, as her eyes scanned the room. Like she was a tour guide, she listed some of the legendary items from her knowledge, amongst normal treasures such as coins, shields, swords, trinkets and jewels - most likely recovered from ancient captured warriors and slaves.

"Look here: the Girdle of Hippolyta, the Staff of Tiresias, the Turtle-shell Lyre of Hermes, the poisoned arrows of the Hydra, and the string of Theseus." Ophelia walked past each wondrous item, gliding her hand over them.

Spears didn't have a clue as to what she was waffling about. He clicked his fingers as if to break her out of her captivated state. She spun towards him.

"No," he said bluntly.

The curator knew precisely what he meant.

"I know this is your forte, Ophelia, but look at all the drama your talisman brought with it, when you pillaged it from the people you came here to help," Spears reminded her.

"Fine," she relented, and turned to the gap that they had entered moments ago.

"Should we close it?" She asked.

"What if there are others still trapped down there?" Spears said. He had lost Matheson, but for all he knew, his friends could still be roaming the tunnels aimlessly.

Once again, Ophelia nodded. She was fully aware she had a task to complete, and she had wasted enough time in the labyrinth.

"We'll give them that chance, even if they're our enemies," she decided.

"Come on, it's not over yet." Spears went over to the wooden door, and rotated the metal ring. The door opened, which revealed an S-shaped stone corridor. They ventured through.

CHAPTER 53

CONFLICT

The temple chamber was relatively quiet, as the battle had faded due to the number of casualties that were strewn around the hall-cave.

Most of the surviving combatants were wounded by some form of injury.

One of the wounded was slowly getting to his feet. He was the last Greek soldier from the unit. He had been knocked unconscious by Madison, who, in turn, was laid out cold herself, half-buried underneath a small rubble of stone.

Medusa had vanished into the dark recesses of the chamber.

The CEO glanced around the aftermath of the skirmish.

Fox raced over to Madison and hurriedly started to remove piles of rocks from her prostrated body. He checked her pulse and she was alive.

Keyes spotted his last remaining operative emerge from the shadows, and exhaled a sigh of relief, knowing he had another ally who had survived.

"Over there," he pointed towards Fox's location, "Kill the traitors!"

The operative aimed his rifle, but suddenly an arrow came from the balcony and struck the operative straight in the back. The arrow was deeply embedded, and the tip pierced out of his chest. The last Legionshield henchman fell to his knees with a dumbfounded expression and crumpled to the ground – dead.

Keyes' relief was short-lived and he glanced over at the balcony.

Cora was standing there with her bow held out. The youngest acolyte had covered the weakened Marzanna and her two injured maidens, as they hobbled up the stone steps and onto the balcony.

"Go now, prepare the altar," Marzanna instructed her two ailing maidens.

As they disappeared into the space behind them, Cora nocked another arrow onto her bow string and aimed it at Keyes.

Keyes raised his bident and squeezed the firing mechanism of his bident – no plasma discharge was emitted.

The energy was drained, and he needed solar power to re-charge. The CEO knew he was inside a cave, and it had now turned to dusk, outside. This had to be hand-to-hand combat.

He looked over at the dazed soldier that was coming round.

Meanwhile, Detective Mervier opened her eyes and forced herself up, aching and dishevelled, close to the soldier and Keyes.

The Greek soldier, who was sporting a bruised eye socket from Madison earlier, pulled out his Browning Hi-Power 9mm from out of his holster and looked over at Keyes.

Keyes gestured to his last remaining ally, and the soldier rushed over to Mervier and grabbed her as a hostage, which completely startled the dazed detective.

Mervier assessed her predicament and raised her hands. She also looked ahead at the balcony and Cora aimed her bow at her. The soldier was using the detective as a human shield and pressed the muzzle of his 9mm onto her temple.

Keyes had leverage, even if he had to betray the detective.

He thought.

An arrow flew across the hall and thudded into the soldier's partially exposed head, a perfect shot. The arrow punched through his brain and he fell down. The pistol clattered to the ground.

Mervier gasped at the miraculous shot, as she had felt the wind of the arrow fly inches past her face, before it had claimed its true target, almost hidden behind her.

The CEO was out of allies.

"Get your people out of here," Marzanna shouted to Fox, who was getting a weary Madison to her feet.

Cora nocked another arrow to her string and aligned it at Keyes, who dove for cover behind a smashed pillar, knowing full well that she was an expert archer.

Vassilis got to his feet and assisted Straker. They both struggled and limped towards the exit. Fox held Madison, and she looked at the coven members, saving them.

Mervier observed the situation, and scooped up the fallen handgun.

Marzanna noted the detective's actions. They exchanged looks from across the hall. The high priestess slowly shook her head at her, as if to say 'no'.

They connected.

Mervier lowered the gun; She, knew her life had been saved.

There was silence.

"Kill her, and I'll split the profits, detective!" Keyes shouted as he cowered behind his cover. He dared not to even take a peep, as he knew the next arrow was for him.

The tide had changed.

"I'm not as corrupt as you, Keyes, my mission is over," she solemnly said and aimed the gun at him. Keyes' eyes widened.

"You stupid bitch, she's got you hypnotised as well!" Keyes yelled, as he glared at Mervier with contempt.

"He's mine." A gentle voice was heard in the detective's head.

At that moment, Mervier tucked the pistol in her belt and rushed over to Vassilis. She helped the Cretan merc carry the hobbling Straker out of the temple.

Fox supported Madison to her feet, but she could barely stand, so he lifted her up over his strong shoulder and staggered to the exit as well.

Marzanna turned to Cora, who eased off the pressure of the draw pull.

"Join the others, it is nearly time. I'll deal with this one."

Cora dashed down the tunnel and Marzanna slowly walked down the steps onto the chequered floor.

Keyes crept out from behind his cover and approached Marzanna, until they were only yards apart.

Both holding their special weapons.

"Noble, but foolish, witch," Keyes remarked. His eyes were full of hate.

It was another stand-off. Only this time, they were the only two remaining people left in the temple chamber. Ready for the final conflict.

The Legionshield boss had good knowledge of several martial arts disciplines in his time in the CIA, and he noticed the battered and ailing state of his adversary. This could be an even match.

"For centuries, malicious mankind like you have hunted us, and threatened our desire to live free. It ends today," Marzanna said.

"It certainly does, for you!"

Keyes summarised a strategy in his head. He had a six-foot bident which was now a powerful melee weapon. His opponent held a two-foot sceptre with a deadly crown which could transform him into stone the moment it touched him. The CEO had range, as long as he kept his distance. He remembered the training he had many years ago with a six-foot 'bo' staff, by a budo master.

Keyes adopted a defensive stance and stood back on his right leg, raising the spear into a lateral position close to his chest, the twin-pronged blades poised to taste blood once again.

Marzanna took a stance as well and waited for the longer weapon to come in.

Then the fight commenced.

Keyes wielded the spear expertly, and executed a diagonal strike down. Marzanna raised her sceptre and the two mighty weapons clashed.

CHAPTER 54

DUEL TO THE DEATH

Ophelia and Spears continued down the twisty passageway of the temple corridors until they reached a complete dead-end.

"Don't tell me we're still in the labyrinth?" Spears exhaled, limping more now and his breathing became laboured. He suspected that he had a couple of broken ribs.

Ophelia looked at the dark wall that blocked their progression. She inspected it closely, using only the flicker of light that emanated from the flame torch on the wall several yards away.

She found what she was looking for. A pale slab which was a slightly different shade to the rest of the dark limestone. It was situated in the centre of the far edge of the wall.

"I've seen this before," Ophelia revealed, as she took her mind briefly back to the spa chamber at the coven's Athenian temple a few weeks ago.

The curator firmly pressed the slab inwards, and the hidden wall slid open with a rumble, which revealed the temple hall chamber.

Spears smiled, but his relief lasted only a few seconds as they stepped into the remnants of the battle they had missed.

The place was a wreck. Statues that proudly stood an hour ago were smashed to smithereens along with other stone work and shattered pillars. Several dead bodies were laid across the floor except for a camouflaged robotic figure who was standing motionless in the middle off the chamber.

Luckily, Spears didn't recognise anyone he knew that were dead, that was good, but a heart-wrenching feeling surged through him. His comrades could be in the maze, or had fallen victim to the minotaur like Matheson.

Ophelia couldn't see Madison or Vassilis either, and thought the same as Spears.

Their concentration was then immediately interrupted as they caught a glimpse of two figures locked in a deadly duel in the far centre of the temple. They were Marzanna and Vincent Keyes.

They were fighting like gladiators in the large temple, with Ophelia and Spears as their only audience.

The high priestess was retreating back to the balcony area, and she was defending herself with the sceptre, as Keyes was relentlessly showering down repetitive strikes with the bident, trying to severe her fingers.

"Marzanna," Ophelia gasped, and tightened her grip on her sword. They both rushed over to the area of conflict. Spears tried to keep up.

Blow after blow by the bident knocked Marzanna back further towards the stone steps, and she realised this was an opponent that she had underestimated, and a weapon that didn't yield. Marzanna tried to counter-attack and thrust her sceptre. Keyes deflected it with the aft end of the bident and, in turn, countered by quickly cutting down, slicing Marzanna's forearm with one of the tips.

She shrieked, as blood poured from her arm, which caused her to drop the sceptre.

Keyes struck Marzanna's underneath the chin with his weapon's aft end, lifting her head up, and at that moment, plunged the bident's blades deep into the high priestess' midriff.

The woman screamed in agony as she felt the powerful metal of the twin spearheads inside her body, twisting and slicing her innards. Blood spewed onto the floor, and she coughed up red bubbles of blood too.

Marzanna doubled over and as Keyes victoriously withdrew the spear from her guts, she fell to one knee. Her sceptre was yards away and she couldn't reach it.

She knew that she was mortally wounded, she had failed, and feared she wouldn't be able to restore her mother.

The high priestess was aware that Medusa had been wounded whilst saving her, and was likely heading to her private sanctuary chamber to prepare for the ritual before sustaining any more injuries.

She wished Cora was here now to save her.

Keyes raised the bident for the final 'death-strike'. He wanted her head on a platter too. Marzanna looked up with anger.

"I'll wait for you in hell!" she croaked, coughing up more blood.

"It'll be my pleasure," Keyes replied, smugly.

The CEO swung the bident down diagonally in an effort to behead her, but at the last moment, the spear was blocked by a sword.

A Greek xiphos sword.

Ophelia Winters was brought down to her knees after parrying the deadly bident, as she shielded Marzanna.

Keyes growled angrily as he put more pressure down whilst the two weapons were locked together – it was a contest of strength and Ophelia felt the weight of her enemy's weapon as she resisted as hard as she could.

"Nathan, get Marzanna out of here!" she yelled.

Spears was approaching, and Keyes knew the odds were soon stacking up against him. Marzanna was using the remaining energy she had left of her super-natural endurance, to stay alive. She crawled back and tried to get to her feet.

Fortunately, from the entranceway of the cave, Fox and Mervier peered through, having reacted to Ophelia's shouting. The mercenary and the detective were administering medical aid to their wounded associates until they heard the curator.

Spears noted them both at the entrance, as he scampered towards Ophelia, holding her ground against Keyes.

"Fox!" he was glad to see him alive, though he had no time to find out what happened to Straker, Madison or Vassilis.

Fox bolted inside the chamber and aimed his G-36 at Keyes, but the man turned as Ophelia rolled to the side, ducking underneath the bident.

Now, Ophelia was in front of Fox's line of fire, but she managed to scoop up the sceptre with her other hand, during her escaping roll.

Spears tried to grab Keyes from behind and pulled him back, attempting to apply a choke hold, but Keyes re-angled the bident back, and sliced into Spears' arm before he could wrap his forearm around his throat. As the merc released the hold, he felt the aft end of the bident smash into his face from Keyes' reverse-thrust technique.

Spears fell to the ground next to Marzanna with a heavily cut eye. It was lucky he wasn't struck with the bladed end.

"Nathan, go!" Ophelia yelled again. It was the protected that became the protector, and Spears aided Marzanna to her feet.

"Through there," she said, weakly, motioning to the stone steps that led to the secret exit behind the balcony.

Spears helped her ascend, and they made their way into the tunnel.

Meanwhile, Fox and Mervier gained closer to the warring duo, and tried to get a good position to fire, but Ophelia was locked in a close-quarters battle with Keyes, and both were constantly moving, ducking, and weaving in their intimate fighting space.

"Ophelia, get out of way!" Fox shouted, but his voice fell on deaf ears.

The mercenary and the detective would have to engage point-blank.

Keyes noticed the other merc and the cop gaining ground. He had to end this quickly. The curator wasn't skilled at swordplay but was holding her own, and, for an amateur, was defending well, but she was tiring. He slashed her leg, and she dropped to one knee, screaming in pain.

Keyes locked eyes with her and swung the bident down to cut her in half, and as Ophelia raised her old sword to parry, the short blade was smashed to pieces, leaving her holding the hilt.

The bident was swung again to deliver the fatal blow, as Keyes stepped closer her, but Ophelia ducked once more, and she repeated the same kind of tactic she used against the minotaur.

But, instead of the sword, it was the sceptre.

Ophelia thrust the ancient magical weapon straight ahead, and Keyes was horrified to see that it hit him straight in the stomach. He felt the blow, and had the wind out knocked of him.

Keyes grasped the bident tightly, but then suddenly, experienced a new cold sensation. Within seconds, his body stiffened, and he froze in place. His expression of fear and surprise remained on his face as it was converted into pure stone.

The rest of his body transformed into a sculpture as well, until it remained standing, still holding the bident aloft.

Ophelia took a big breath, and slumped to the ground exhausted. She had defeated him.

Fox and Mervier rushed over to her, as she put pressure on the bloodied gash on her thigh.

"Are you okay?" Mervier asked. The detective felt guilty about everything, but knew she couldn't turn the clock back.

Ophelia nodded, trying to catch her breath.

"I'm so sorry," Mervier added.

Fox helped the curator up on her feet. She staggered, like a newborn fowl.

"Why don't you do as you're asked next time?" he smirked.

"Was kinda busy," she managed.

"Matheson?"

She shook her head sadly. He understood and looked to the ground in remorse.

They stood there looking at the stone statue that was now Vincent Keyes.

"Just in case." Fox aimed his G-36 and fired the rest of his clip into the sculpture, blasting it to pieces. The rest of the stone collapsed on itself from top to bottom, until the only thing that remained were two stumps, which were Keyes' feet and ankles.

The bident fell from the smashed stone hand as the statue fell, and clattered on the floor.

Ophelia turned around and glanced at the space in the wall behind the balcony.

She picked up the sceptre from the floor, before Mervier could even contemplate acquiring possession, and slowly limped to the steps.

"Where are you going?" Fox asked.

"Stay here, I'll be back."

CHAPTER 55

THE RITUAL OF RESTORATION

"Thank you, but you must leave us now," Marzanna whispered to Spears, as he guided the weak and frail high priestess to the antechamber.

Spears nodded and smiled sympathetically at the dying demi-goddess.

As the mercenary turned around and disappeared into the tunnel, the two maidens came through the open door and collected their pale high priestess.

Inside the sanctuary chamber, Cora had placed the sacred talisman into the niche in the centre of the altar.

The two battle-weary maidens assisted the critically-wounded woman inside and guided her to the altar. The high priestess stumbled and fell to a knee.

"Marzanna." Another soft voice spoke from behind the altar.

Medusa stepped over to her daughter, and helped her to her feet. The gorgon was hooded and had her face obscured from her worshippers, but they knew to keep their eyes down at all times, throughout the impending ritual.

Medusa also had a red slash mark on the side of her toga. She had been cut lightly near her ribs, by the tip of one of the bident's blades. It was a glancing strike and posed no critical damage – unlike what her daughter had sustained.

Blood still oozed out from her two punctured stab wounds, and Marzanna pressed onto them with her blood-drenched hand to ease the flow. Every second mattered for her to fulfil her final act on this earth.

"Mother, I have failed you." Marzanna managed to speak. She felt her life ebbing away.

"Come my daughter, you can live," Medusa replied. Then she looked at the wound.

"I've lived long enough, mother, I'm ready to embrace the peaceful sanctuary of death, and restore you to living the life that you have been deprived of, for as long as we have existed," Marzanna found the strength to utter the words, but she could feel the coldness of death at her feet.

Medusa, Cora and the maidens helped her to the altar, and they all assembled around it. Marzanna was the only one who could perform the magical mantra.

In her weakened state, the high priestess recited the ancient text which was inscribed on the tablet-talisman, she placed her two blood-stained fingers gently into the eye indentations that were carved on the talisman, and finished her incantation.

Meanwhile, Ophelia met up with Spears in the long tunnel. Both were terribly wounded, clothing torn and sporting numerous cuts and bruises.

"Ophelia, I knew you'd make it, where's Keyes?" the merc said, ensuring she lowered the sceptre.

"He's resting in pieces."

She tried to push past him, and he placed his hands on her shoulders. She winced as he touched her wounds. He also noticed the slash mark on her leg.

"Whoa, where are you going?"

Ophelia didn't have the answer, but she felt compelled to go and see the outcome of all of this.

"Ophelia, leave them be, it's over, they're safe."

"Go back to the others, I need to return this," she replied, insistently.

Spears shook his head with disapproval, but he knew he couldn't stop her.

"Where is she?"

"Straight ahead, no turnings."

"Go back." She gave him a reassuring smile, and looked beyond him at the dark tunnel.

Spears had no time to respond, as Ophelia brushed past him, and headed straight on.

The ritual was complete, and Cora with the two maidens stepped away from the altar, keeping their heads down.

Marzanna's eyelids were half-closed, and as she lowered her head, Medusa removed her hood.

The gorgon, even in her grotesque form, sorrowfully looked at her daughter, and a tear trickled down her pasty green cheek – there was indeed a human being behind the hideous façade, even her hair of snakes looked subdued and silent.

A soothing soft white hue irradiated over Medusa, as if it was summoned by Marzanna, and sent by the gods.

Then, the miraculous transformation occurred.

The light enveloped her, and her reptilian-like skin slowly disappeared, revealing the natural skin of a human. Her arms were tanned and toned. The same magical conversion affected every inch of her slender and curvaceous figure.

Medusa's demonic serpentine eyes were changed to a warm, beautiful colour of emerald-green, and her abhorrent face dematerialised and de-aged. Her haggard and repulsive looks were rejuvenated by the face of a ravishing young Greek woman in her mid-thirties. The rosy colours in her shapely cheeks showed signs of health and life.

She appeared like the younger version of her daughter – the face and body of who Medusa truly was, before her cursed transformation thousands of years ago.

She looked resplendent.

Finally, her snake-hair started to fade, and reshape into long silky black hair that draped down her rounded shoulders and smooth lean back.

Marzanna managed a loving smile as she saw her mother complete her metamorphosis, and return to her true form. A beautiful priestess. A mortal woman.

She had fulfilled her destiny.

"Mother," Marzanna uttered softly, and she slowly succumbed to her mortal wounds.

Ophelia Winters staggered into the sanctuary chamber, and saw the two maidens carrying the lifeless body of Marzanna into the antechamber next to the altar.

The procession was followed by Cora and a woman who was a little older than the other acolytes.

The curator's face was a look of sadness and grief.

Her eyes were drawn to the taller and more mature woman of the group, and she turned around with Cora to face their visitor.

Medusa looked at Ophelia, and there was a momentary pause.

Cora placed her hand on Medusa's arm.

"She tried to save her, she is of no threat to us," Cora declared.

"I know," Medusa replied, with a fresh, young and friendly voice.

"Medusa," Ophelia spoke, as her lips parted. She stared at the graceful woman in disbelief.

Medusa acknowledged with a polite bow of her head.

Ophelia glanced over at Marzanna, being carried off out of sight by the surviving maidens. Cora followed them out, and they vanished into the darkness.

"My divine daughter has passed on, and now sits with the gods. She gave her long life to restore mine."

"Marzanna was a remarkable woman," Ophelia commented. She couldn't believe that this moment was happening, talking to the real-life myth, which was Medusa - in flesh and blood.

"She spoke of you with great affection. You are welcome to join us, Ophelia."

Ophelia smiled at Medusa, and held out the sceptre.

"My world is out there."

"Which is the world I have desired to live in for many millennia, as a normal mortal woman, my daughter has gifted me that honour," Medusa said, with a kind, genuine smile.

"The Sceptre of Hephaestus, it will be safer with you." Ophelia offered her mystical weapon.

"We are no longer hunted, nor do we have the intention of ever attracting it. Those days are over now. We have no need for it any more. It is a gift from the gods. The honour is now yours to preserve and protect. I declare that you are now the new guardian of the sceptre, guard it well, Ophelia," Medusa announced.

Ophelia looked down at her prize with adoration and respect.

"Will I see you again?" Ophelia asked.

"There's a wonderful new world for me out there. Who knows? Keep well and take care, Ophelia."

Medusa bowed one more time to the curator, and left the sanctuary chamber elegantly and vanished into the temple, leaving Ophelia holding the sceptre.

The battered and fatigued adventurer studied the ancient relic in her hands, and nodded her head, satisfied that she had safely recovered another opulent treasure, but was saddened by the loss of the woman that gave her life for the love and life of her mother.

At least Medusa could live out the rest of her natural days as a normal woman, a life, as Marzanna once said, that she was deprived of, many lifetimes ago.

Ophelia had to return to her friends, and started to turn towards the exit, when she stopped.

She glimpsed back where the coven had departed, and she vaguely heard the echoing hiss of snakes in the darkened corridors – or maybe it was her imagination?

Ophelia shook her head, shaking out what she thought she heard, with a smirk as if to say, 'don't be silly.'

Medusa had been saved, and Marzanna achieved her destiny with her noble sacrifice. Ophelia's task was complete.

The legacy of the gorgon was now in her hands.

It was silent once again, and Ophelia Winters vacated the Minoan temple.

CHAPTER 56

A CHRISTMAS RE-OPENING

7 months later
St George's Museum
York

5.00pm

It was Christmas Eve.

Snow fell gently from the evening skies and settled across the rural landscape which surrounded the newly-built Museum.

Inside the exquisite refurbished main concourse of St George's Museum, a Christmas party was in full swing.

A huge decorated pine Christmas tree was standing in the centre, which overlooked the large crowd who had gathered around the brand-new ground-floor galleries, and continued to circulate amongst the other guests.

It was the grand re-opening of the museum, and Ophelia, dressed in a stunning cocktail dress was meandering through the mass of immaculately dressed people that had come to support the prestigious event.

Waiters and waitresses floated around with trays of champagne, and there wasn't one guest who didn't have a champagne flute in their hand, as everyone was socialising and enjoying themselves.

Ophelia wandered from one group to the next, being congratulated and receiving handshakes and warm hugs from them. It was a great bustling atmosphere.

As the champagne flowed, she made her way over to the top of the stairwell and joined Madison and Professor Reginald Shaw, who couldn't wait to be there, to celebrate the re-opening party. Madison now sported a short new trendy hairstyle, and was wearing a red off-the-shoulder dress that elegantly flowed to the ankle, and Shaw was in a black dinner suit. A far cry from the usual tweed coat and trilby hat which he usually wore.

"They're waiting for you," Madison said into Ophelia's ear. The curator glanced upwards at the high balcony where a huge ribbon was stretched across the entire length of the concourse. The Mayor of York was the dignitary guest and waited at the top, sipping a glass of champagne.

Ophelia made her way up the polished new staircase to the balcony and joined him. Shaw and Madison followed.

She looked over at the hundreds of guests that had attended. It was an open event, and everyone was formally dressed for the occasion. She felt emotional at the strong support.

"Ladies and gentlemen, sponsors, and honoured guests, I can't thank you enough for supporting and attending this event to celebrate our long-awaited re-opening," she said, addressing the crowd.

"I know it was a perfect excuse to get out of the house, and for some of you, to escape some excitable kids, but I truly appreciate that you are all spending Christmas Eve with us at your new St George's Museum," she continued.

The crowd chuckled, as Ophelia held a pair of huge red scissors with the mayor.

"I won't keep you from your champagne, my friends, so, it gives me great profound pleasure to officially declare – St George's is now open."

Together, Ophelia and the Mayor cut the ribbon in the centre, and both ends parted gracefully, and glided away. This was received by a thunderous round of applause and cheering from the crowd. Everybody raised their glasses.

"And Merry Christmas!" Ophelia shouted. Madison and Shaw embraced her, and they both walked down the staircase to mingle with the crowd.

"Congratulations Dr Winters, it is marvellous to see our beloved Museum back." The mayor shook her hand, followed by his wife.

As the dignitaries descended the steps, Ophelia was left on the balcony, fondly observing her party guests.

Most were still clapping.

Ophelia's eyes wandered across to certain guests in turn.

Nathan Spears, Ashley Fox and Mohammed Straker were there together, proudly looking up and applauding her. They were joined by Vassilis, who was wearing his signature Hawaiian shirt underneath his dinner jacket.

They supervised the chain of events after the temple adventure in Crete. The Black Knights had re-formed under the leadership of Spears, and had blasted the entrance to the cave, sealing it forever. Prior to that, they checked the treasure vault, and it had been completely cleared out. Undoubtedly by the coven, shortly after the events.

But the coven had long gone, before the mercenaries returned to the temple.

Standing next to the men was Nicole Mervier, in a black gown and heels. She had reported back to very dissatisfied superiors, and informed the constabulary that the 'suspect' was dead, and the artefact was destroyed. She also mentioned Legionshield's involvement, and a major inquiry was launched.

Mervier said to Ophelia that the organisation was under heavy scrutiny, and a Dr. Delanski had taken the position of CEO. All industrial business projects were still deemed classified, but under strict joint control of the British and US governments.

Shortly after, Mervier left the force, and joined Interpol.

Ophelia also read that a new owner had inherited Ravenscliff Castle. Her name was Cora-Medea Dumas. She was allegedly an adopted daughter of the countess, who had since disappeared into obscurity, and Cora was the beneficiary of her entire estate.

The sceptre and the bident were safely secured and stored in an undisclosed location that only Ophelia, Madison and Shaw were aware of.

Ophelia's eyes then peered over at the far end of the concourse, and she noticed a beautiful woman dressed in an elegant modern turquoise dress.

She looked exactly like Marzanna, but a younger version.

Ophelia recognised her as Medusa, in her true glamorous form.

Medusa was also clapping, and gave Ophelia an acknowledging nod of her head. She was happy, and smiled at the curator with heart-felt pride.

Next to her was Cora, equally dressed in a similar-coloured luxurious gown, and also smiling at Ophelia.

A group of guests then wandered in front of the two women, obscuring Ophelia's view, and when the group had passed, Medusa and Cora were gone.

Ophelia's eyes darted around the concourse, trying to reacquire sight of them, but they had vanished.

The curator blinked a few times, and wondered if she had just imagined it. It had been a long night, accompanied by a few sips of expensive champagne.

Either way, they were nowhere in sight.

If it was her, then she had finally found peace amongst the world she was living in, and Ophelia felt touched that she was there to support and join her in the re-launch of her unique Museum.

If she was actually there a moment ago?

Ophelia took a glass from a tray as Madison came up the staircase again and joined her.

"Aren't you joining the party?"

"Yeah," Ophelia was still mystified.

"Are you okay?"

"Yeah, I just thought I had seen someone," Ophelia uttered, scanning the bustle of the crowd below her.

Madison raised her brow, expecting Ophelia to add to her sentence.

"Never mind," she exhaled, and took another sip of bubbling champagne.

"It's been a long few months, so what's next, finding out if Santa Claus exists, the search for a magical flying sleigh and reindeer?" Madison sniggered.

"Okay, there's no need to take the piss. Besides, if he did exist, I got a bone to pick with him, when I was seven, I never did get that new doll which could eat, drink, sleep and the other stuff," she said, chuckling to herself.

"What did you get, instead?" Madison asked.

"My father was always getting practical stuff, and reached out to our interests which we shared together. That year, it was a pair of hiking boots, and a compass, oh, and a junior archaeologist kit."

"Oh my god, really?"

"Thing is, I loved them," Ophelia said, fondly.

"Cool," Madison smiled.

"But I was still pissed off that I didn't get that damn doll."

Both women laughed.

"Anyway, you better skedaddle back to the party. I think your group of eager Scandinavians want a quick tour of the vault," Ophelia mentioned. She was referring to a party of six men and women from the Nordic Museum of Antiquites.

"I'm on it," Madison said, finishing her flute of champagne, "Oh, I forgot to mention, there is a present for you, in your office."

"Thanks," Ophelia responded, quite surprised.

"Who knows, maybe it's the doll?" Madison said, laughing.

"Have a good one," Ophelia winked, and Madison glided down the steps to join the excited group, as she returned to her enthusiastic tour guide mode.

Ophelia smiled, turned around and entered her office.

EPILOGUE

Ophelia closed the door to her office behind her. It was clean and tidy, which was a stark contrast to how it was seven months ago.

She had a stack of envelopes on her table, which she hadn't opened yet – most likely Christmas cards from friends and family.

In the centre of her office desk was a single square brown parcel with Christmas ribbons tied across it, like it had been specially gift-wrapped, with her name on the front. This must have been delivered earlier and placed on her desk by security, as she had been busy all day, preparing for the party.

As everyone knew, she rarely frequented her own office.

Ophelia made herself comfortable in her swivel chair, and looked at the parcel curiously.

It was no more than twelve inches wide, with a depth of ten inches.

Maybe it was the doll, she thought for a fleeting second.

She looked at the special delivery postage stamp, to see where the package had been dispatched from. It read 'Kyoto, Japan', amongst the Japanese kanji text.

The curator untied the ribbon and removed the wrapping. Inside was a box with a small seasonal greetings card. She unfolded the card, and read it to herself, aloud.

"The path of the Samurai lies *within his soul*," Ophelia whispered, emphasising the last three words, which were written in a handwritten italic font.

Ophelia opened up the box, and gently pulled out a light porcelain statue of a samurai warrior, in full traditional armour and brandishing a katana sword. The figurine was approximately eight-inches tall, and looked quite old – albeit very light, as if it was hollow inside.

She frowned, a little baffled. There was no other message or a card, to determine who had sent it.

Ophelia inspected it, examining his armour plating, his weapons, his face concealed behind the demonic-looking half-mask, but there was no clue. She weighed it in her hands, and it couldn't have weighed more than a small old vase that she used to dig up in her excavations. It had the density of a cheap ornament one would find at a street market.

"The path of the samurai lies within his soul," she repeated to herself.

She shook the figurine lightly, and nothing was heard bouncing off the insides.

"I'm sorry, fella," she spoke to the cheap ornament, and smashed it on the table.

The statue broke apart easily, and amongst the shattered shards and fragments of the samurai statue, was a small rolled-up scroll.

Ophelia's lips parted, and her expression changed to a look of awe.

She opened up the scroll, which had been secretly concealed in the statue. It was handwritten in English.

Ophelia read the message. She imagined the Japanese woman's voice in her head.

"My dearest Ophelia, I am sorry to send you this, but I have nowhere else to turn to in my most desperate hour. It is Akiko Masaki, the sister of your former lover, Riki."

Ophelia cast her mind back ten years ago, shortly before the death of her father, and the man who she was deeply romantically involved with at the time. He was of mixed race of Japanese-English descent. She never talked about her past relationships with anyone, and kept her private life to herself – even her uncle and Madison weren't aware of Riki.

She was very fond of Akiko, a young twenty-year-old adventurer back then, and a part of her father's expeditionary team in the far east on the odd occasion. Over time, they had all sadly drifted apart, due to career commitments, and especially during her own father's illness.

She continued reading the letter.

"Your brother and I discovered the secret location of the sacred katana, the *Oni no Tamashii*, 'Soul of the Demon'. It possesses dark mystical powers, unlike any other."

Ophelia had heard of many legendary and magical swords from Japan, and many were stored and secured in their museums and shrines, but this one, which many considered, was the most mythical and supernatural of all. Legend has it, that the sword was forged by demons.

"During the recovery of the katana, we were attacked by a clan known as the 'Shadows of Tengu', a guild of protectors, which we were once affiliated with, until they were corrupted by evil. A treacherous sect took possession of the blade, which in turn possessed them. A small splinter group of us had to free the katana, and we managed to escape with it. But at a cost. I was severely wounded and was the only survivor. I had to hide the cursed sword before it could consume me too, and went into hiding. I fear for my life. I am sorry to inform you that Riki died during the escape. The sect believe I have it, and are still hunting me. I need you to retrieve the Oni no Tamashii, and take it to a place of safety before they find me or the katana. News of the theft has circulated, and I cannot risk dispatching it out to you by any other means. You have the connections and the resources. Nobody knows of this message. I have left clues inside the warrior of where it is hidden, just in case the guild or the sect find me first. I cannot be contactable. You can seek me out, should you feel compelled to, within the samurai, but the recovery of the katana is the priority. I entrust you to complete the quest which my brother gave his life for. It will only be a matter of time before they reach me - Akiko."

Ophelia took a moment to digest the words. She felt surreal, and the noise of the party below had faded, as she studied the letter again, and then the jagged pieces of the samurai.

On the inside of four of the fragments were Japanese markings and letters, and, like a mini-jig-saw, she placed the pieces together.

They formed another cryptic message. The location of Akiko's hidden whereabouts, and the secret place where Akiko hid the mystical Oni no Tamashii katana – deep within the Valley of Demons.

Ophelia looked ahead at the door with a serious look of determination.

"I'm coming for you, Akiko."

THE END

Ophelia will return in Book 3
The Chronicles of Ophelia Winters:
The Blade of Dark Souls.

www.ingramcontent.com/pod-product-compliance
Lightning Source LLC
Chambersburg PA
CBHW071120180726
48291CB00007B/2095